Privileged to Kill

Property of Ávila
Retirement Community

His Bibliography

Westerns:
The Killer
The Worst Enemy
Leadfire
Timber Blood

The Bill Gastner Series:
Heartshot
Bitter Recoil
Twice Buried
Before She Dies
Privileged to Kill
Prolonged Exposure
Out of Season

Privileged to Kill

Steven F. Havill

Poisoned Pen Press

Copyright © 1997 by Steven F. Havill.

First Trade Paperback Edition 2001

10 9 8 7 6 5 4 3 2 1

Library of Congress Catalog Card Number: 2001087785

ISBN: 1-890208-65-5

All rights reserved. No part of this publication may be reproduced, stored in, or introduced into a retrieval system, or transmitted in any form, or by any means (electronic, mechanical, photocopying, recording, or otherwise) without the prior written permission of both the copyright owner and the publisher of this book.

Poisoned Pen Press
6962 E. First Ave. Ste 103
Scottsdale, AZ 85251
www.poisonedpenpress.com
info@poisonedpenpress.com

Printed in the United States of America

For Kathleen

Acknowledgments

I'd like to thank Regina Bassett, David Martinez, and H. L. McArthur for information generously shared.

1

I saw Wesley Crocker for the first time on a cold Thursday afternoon in October, three weeks before Election Day. He was pushing his bicycle eastward along the shoulder of State Road 17, an asphalt-patched remnant of highway that the interstate had made obsolete.

When I saw Crocker, I was sitting warm and comfortable in the Posadas County patrol car, cruising west, looking for no one or no thing in particular. Lenticular clouds formed, spread, and shredded over the San Cristobal mountains that separated Posadas County from Mexico, and rain had been predicted by morning.

The wind was driving out of the northeast, gusting strong enough to rock the car. Moisture might have been in the offing, but at that moment the only thing in the air was the New Mexico prairie. Fine, stinging sand scudded across the macadam like tawny snow, the larger pieces rattling against the white paint of the Ford. Occasionally a *kochia*, its brittle stem snapped off at the ground, would perform a clumsy imitation of a tumbleweed, jouncing across the road to pack against the barbed-wire fencing.

Crocker was walking toward Posadas, head pulled into his heavy coat, chin against his chest. His methodical pace planted one foot in front of the other in a rhythm that said he was no stranger to the asphalt.

His bicycle was an old, heavy thing with balloon tires, the sort of bike that paperboys with calf muscles like steel springs peddled around their paper routes in the 1950s. The top frame between seat and handlebars was bloated with stamped steel into a fake gas tank. My oldest son had once had a bike like that. He'd regularly stolen his mother's clothespins so he could clip playing cards to the front forks. When the wheels spun, the cards barked against the spokes—an impressive motorcycle for sure.

But Wesley Crocker was long past the playing-cards-on-spokes stage and the bike was a handful to push, even if there had been no quartering wind gusting in his face.

I slowed to thirty-five as I drove past and saw two enormous saddlepacks that bulged with Crocker's belongings. Another duffel bag was lashed to the front basket.

It wasn't just the wind that was giving the man trouble. The back tire of the bike was flat, the weight of the saddlepacks digging the rim into the asphalt. The three miles into Posadas was going to be a lifetime.

He didn't lift his head as I drove past. Maybe he didn't see me. Maybe he didn't care. Maybe he knew how far the next village was and all his determination was focused on the ten thousand steps it would take to get there.

I glanced at my watch. At his pace, by the time he reached Posadas the sidewalks would be rolled up and stowed. He wouldn't find a store open that carried a tire or tube or patch kit. If he could manage to fix the tire himself, one or two places could supply the air.

For a quarter mile after I had driven by, I watched him in the rearview mirror, wondering who he was, where he was from, where he was going. With a shrug I slowed the county car, swung wide, and made a U-turn.

I idled up behind the man and his bicycle and when I was within a dozen feet, he stopped, looked over his right shoulder at me, and then with great patience lowered the kickstand and balanced the overloaded bike against it, making sure that the stand wasn't going to sink in the loose gravel of the highway shoulder and capsize the whole mess.

He ambled back toward the patrol car, and I buzzed down the window.

He bent down and placed his hands on his knees. "And a good afternoon to you, sir," he said. Older than I had first thought, he was ruddy faced with a tangled thatch of salt-and-pepper hair held in place by a black knit cap. His smile didn't show many teeth.

I hesitated, loath to encroach on his world, and I suppose he mistook my hesitation for the arrogance of disapproval.

"Wasn't speeding, was I?" he said, and grinned even wider.

"No, sir," I said. "Do you want a lift into town?"

One of his eyebrows shot up. "Say, that would be welcome, kind sir, but I tell you what. I sure do hate to leave my rig unattended along the highway."

I looked at the mammoth bike and tried to calculate how it would fit.

"It'll go in the trunk," I said.

He straightened up and surveyed my county car. "That would be a mite tight."

I popped the electric trunk lock and then opened the door and heaved my two hundred and ten pounds out of the car. At five feet ten inches, I stood nearly a head taller than the traveler, but when the two of us grunted to pick up the bicycle, his proved to be the stronger back.

After he unstrapped the various packs, we pushed, heaved, and shoved until the bike's back tire was planted in one corner of the trunk and the front forks were cranked around so that the front wheel stood vertically.

He then nestled the packs on top of the bike.

"She'll stay," I said. "We'll go slow."

"What about the trunk lid, sir? You want to tie it so it doesn't flop up and down?"

He produced a piece of brown twine from one coat pocket, and in another minute the trunk lid was secured, lashed down through the bike's chain crank to the lower trunk latch.

I started around to the driver's door, and he hesitated. "Come on," I said, not the least bit eager to stand out in the chill wind a moment longer than necessary. "Climb in." I saw him glance toward the backseat and added, "Up front."

We settled into the car and both of us sighed with relief to have the wind and cold locked outside. My passenger thrust out a hand. "Wesley Crocker," he said.

His grip was firm, his hand callused and rough. "Bill Gastner," I replied.

"My pleasure," Crocker said. His gaze wandered around the inside of the county car, taking in all the expensive junk that goes with the profession.

He reached out and ran a finger along the top of one of the radios as if he were checking for dust. "Things have sure changed, haven't they?" he said as I pulled 310 into gear.

"Changed?"

"The law used to be just a man on horseback, wearing a badge and a gun," Crocker said. He indicated the radio and computer stack that sat astride the transmission hump, then patted the fore-end of the shotgun that rested in the electric lock. "Now look at all this."

I shrugged. "Times change. I'd hate to be sitting on a horse in this weather."

"You don't happen to have a cigarette, do you?"

I grinned at the sudden change of subject. "Sorry. I don't smoke, Mr. Crocker."

"You used to, though, didn't you?"

I looked over at him with amusement. His eyebrows were enormous, tipped with the same gray that was creeping into his hair and week-old beard.

"Yes, I used to."

"Quit, huh?" I nodded and Wesley Crocker continued, "I should, too. I could make better headway against this wind if *I* had more wind."

"And some air in your tires," I added. "How far did you come today?"

"From just outside Playa. You know where that is?" I nodded. I almost said that my twenty-four years with the Posadas County Sheriff's Department probably had been enough time to learn the names of all seven villages in the county, but I spared Wesley Crocker the sarcasm. His seventeen miles of travel wasn't much to show for a day's work, but it was a hell of a lot more than I'd accomplished.

"Tire went flat about five miles back. 'Course, I don't hurry, you know. I just kind of mosey along. There's a lot to see in this big country."

"The middle of nowhere is what most tourists say," I chuckled.

"But see, I just bet that they aren't really looking when they say that. If they *looked*, they wouldn't say that. Do you know what I saw back up the road a ways? Just the other side of the Guijarro wash?"

"What?" I was doubly surprised that he knew both the name of the dry little arroyo bed and how to pronounce it.

His voice became animated and he half turned in the seat. He needed a bath as much as he needed air for his tire. "The light was just right, kind of comin' through the clouds and all, and just before I started down that long, kinda easy slope to the bridge, I looked off to the north." He stretched out his hand and spread his fingers. "And I could see the faint cuts in the prairie where Bennett's Road used to run."

I grinned. If I had been the frontier lawman on the horse with badge and gun, Crocker would have been the man in the black frock coat, driving the little buckboard, Bible tucked under his arm. "You sound like you've spent some time around here."

"Well, no. But I read a lot, see. It mentions the road in one of those government pamphlets I read over in Arizona. Talks about it just kind of in passing, don't you know. But I could see those tracks plain as day."

"That's the only place in the county you can see them. Right from this road."

Wesley Crocker leaned toward me as if he hadn't heard right. "You don't say so? The only place?"

I nodded. "You've got sharp eyes. The old cattle trail—what you call Bennett's Road—jogs around that low mesa to the north of the highway. The rancher who owns the property happens to be something of a history buff. He fenced off that section of the trail so the livestock wouldn't obliterate it."

Crocker patted his right knee with satisfaction. "Well, I'll be. I'll be." He looked out the window as we approached the outskirts of Posadas. It wasn't much of a sight, but it had to be a relief from blow-sand between the teeth. As we passed the first buildings, a series of low rental storage sheds, he mused, "You gotta wonder what folks like Josiah Bennett would have thought of 1996."

"Not much, I expect."

With another knee pat, Crocker said, "Still, there was a time when old Mr. Bennett would have been just as happy to see you come along."

I didn't know much about Josiah Bennett, but I did know the story about him trying to push two thousand head of cattle north out of Mexico, headed for his ranch up in the Magdelenas. Some of the cattle had made the trip, but he hadn't. His brains had been mixed with the prairie dirt thirty miles northeast of Posadas.

His family had tried to blame Apaches, but that didn't work. When the story finally leaked out, it was Bennett's own son-in-law who was hanged for the murder. Old Josiah Bennett would have been teary eyed with pride to know a dirt road had been named after him a century later.

"Do you have a way to fix that tire?"

Crocker nodded. "Got me a patch kit, but my hand pump broke." He shook his head. "Isn't that just the way of things, though. The tire's no good, so I just elected to walk it on in. You think there's someplace in town where I can get me a tire?"

I glanced at my watch again. "Not until tomorrow."

"Well, then, you can just drop me anywhere along here, and that will be dandy." As we neared the intersection with Twelfth Street, Crocker saw the Don Juan de Oñate restaurant on the left. "Now say, this is fine right here," he said, and I pulled over onto the shoulder of the highway.

We unloaded the cumbersome bicycle, and I slammed the trunk lid. Crocker straightened the saddlepacks and took a deep breath.

"Say," he said, and I knew what was coming before he said it. "You don't suppose you could spare a dollar for a pack of smokes, do you?"

I laughed. "Where do you buy smokes for a dollar in this day and age, Mr. Crocker?" I fished in my shirt pocket, pulled out one of my business cards, and jotted a note on the back of it. "Give this to a gal named Shari in the restaurant. She'll fix you up." Crocker's face brightened.

"Well, bless you, sir." He held the card out at arm's length. "Undersheriff William K. Gastner," he read and his grin spread even wider. "I thought at first that maybe you were the state police, but then I remembered their cars are black in these parts."

I nodded. "You take care." I walked back toward the car door. "And by the way," I added. "Just down this street a ways is a little village park, over on the north side. You can't miss it. There's a World War I tank sitting in it. Just past that park is Guilfoil's Auto Parts, right on the main drag. They'll take care of your bike for you in the morning. If you have any problems, give us a call."

He held up the card in salute. "Couldn't ask for more, sir. Thank you." I got in the car, and he appeared at the window. "May I ask you one thing before you go?"

"What's that?"

"You haven't asked me where I'm going, or where I come from." He grinned again and looked east, down the street. "If I was you, I don't think I could drive away without knowing. Just natural curiosity, you know."

I looked at his gentle face, at the crow's feet around his eyes that cracked his weather-beaten, sun- and wind-burned skin. "I don't think that it's any of my business, Mr. Crocker. You're free to come and go as you please."

He straightened up. "Isn't that something." He turned the card over and over in his hand. "Isn't that something."

"You have a good evening."

As I drove off, I could see him pushing that monstrosity of a bicycle across the highway toward the restaurant. It wasn't any of my business, but he was right. I did wonder. And he hadn't offered.

2

"Are you going to work late tonight?"

I looked up to see Posadas County Sheriff Martin Holman standing in the doorway of my office. The little digital clock on my desk said 5:53 P.M. and that didn't seem particularly late to me. It was certainly too early for the sheriff to feel solicitous, unless he figured it might earn him another vote.

And as usual, no matter what the hour, Holman's clothes looked as if they were fresh from the dry cleaner's. I wouldn't have been surprised to see the barber and manicurist following at his heels like trained spaniels.

"Why?"

Holman smiled and held up a hand. "I just wondered if you wanted to go get some dinner."

I pushed the deposition I'd been working on into the pile of papers on the right side of my desk and dropped the pen on the desk pad. "Are you a bachelor tonight?"

Holman grimaced and nodded. He stepped over to the left side of my desk and picked up a magazine that lay on top of the detritus. "She has a Republican Women's dinner of some sort. 'Meet the candidate's wife night' or some such. I wasn't invited." He thumbed through the magazine and I saw his left eyebrow lift. He glanced up at me and held the magazine so I could see the cover.

"You into canoeing now?"

I pushed away from the desk and stood, hitching up my trousers. "Used to do some with the kids years ago. When I was stationed in North Carolina."

"Not too many rivers around here."

"No, there aren't. The thought had crossed my mind to travel some." I shrugged.

Holman dropped the magazine on the desk. "Somehow I can't picture you in a canoe." Neither could I, but then again, maybe my belly would keep the center of gravity low. "If you're looking for a hobby, why don't you come play a round of golf with me sometime?" He held up an index finger. "Now there's a hell of a game."

"It would be, the way I'd play it."

"Good exercise, no matter what."

"So is eating. I was planning on going to the Don Juan after a bit. That suit you?"

Holman made a face. "Do you have to eat that stuff morning, noon, and night?"

"Yes," I said. "I do." I headed for the door, picking up my Stetson on the way. "Without green chili, there is no point in hobbies of any kind. Life stops."

Holman followed me with a sigh.

The Don Juan de Oñate restaurant, one of the few truly memorable things about Posadas, New Mexico, was nine blocks west of the sheriff's department…or, as Sheriff Marty Holman was fond of calling our office when he wanted the county legislators to fork over more money, the "Public Safety Building."

As I idled the county car down Bustos Avenue, Holman drummed his perfectly trimmed fingernails on the passenger window sill. "Did you see the *Register* today?"

"Yes. In fact, it's in my briefcase here." I lifted my elbow so he could reach the paper if he wanted it.

He shook his head and said, "Did you read the editorial?"

"I read the whole paper. Right down to the last want ad."

"That's right. I forgot that you do that. So what did you think?"

"Politics is not a hobby I'm considering, Martin. But most of the newspaper's endorsements made sense."

"Ah, *most*, you say," and he grinned as if he'd sprung a clever trap. "I was half expecting them to come out in favor of Estelle."

I shook my head. "Not likely."

"Why not?"

"Not in this century, Martin. She's a woman, she's under thirty, she's college educated, she's a Mexican...how many more reasons do they need?"

"And you're not going to publicly endorse, are you?"

"No. And not privately either, for that matter."

Holman chuckled and then frowned. "If I win, do you think she'll quit the department?"

"I would hope not. But that would probably depend more on you than on her." I turned at the intersection of Twelfth Street and Bustos, then bumped the patrol car up into the restaurant's parking lot. Half a dozen cars were parked helter-skelter. Leaning against the building near the west entrance was Wesley Crocker's overloaded bicycle.

Holman saw it as well. "Jesus," he said. "Now there's hobby for you, Bill. Pedal one of those things from Alaska to Argentina. Or L.A. to New York."

I parked the patrol car with its nose facing Bustos Avenue and got out. Holman walked across to the bicycle and scrutinized it. "Look at all this stuff," he said, pointing at the side packs and front duffel bag. Crocker's heavy navy surplus coat was folded over the seat. "Probably everything he owns." He knelt down and looked at the back tire. "Only flat on the bottom," he said. "I sure as hell would hate to have to push that thing." He grinned at me. "I haven't seen a bike like that since the Norman Rockwell covers on the *Saturday Evening Post.*"

"Looks like something out of about 1950," I said.

"Columbia Roadmaster," Holman said with authority. "That's what they called 'em. It's probably worth some money to a collector."

We went inside and Holman wrinkled his nose. "What's that smell?"

"They're burning piñon in the fireplace, Martin. It lends ambiance. They probably prefer to call it 'aroma.'"

"Shit, smells like they should clean their chimney."

Shari Chino saw us standing in the foyer under the ugly velvet painting of Don Juan de Oñate, his helmet shimmering against a background of gaudy purple and black. If the don had known that he was going to be remembered that way, he might have drowned himself in the El Morro pool up north, instead of carving his *paso por aqui* on Inscription Rock.

Shari hustled over. "Two for dinner?"

I nodded, but Holman saw an opportunity. He painted on his best public relations smile and handed Shari one of his campaign cards.

"Appreciate your vote," he said.

"Do you want your usual table, sir?" Shari asked me, deftly sliding the campaign card into her apron pocket without a glance. That was one vote for Estelle Reyes-Guzman. Holman kept smiling. She led us back to an isolated alcove whose tinted window faced Twelfth Street.

"I've lived in Posadas for thirty years," Holman said as we settled into the fake-leather-upholstered booth. "Don't ask me why, but I have. How come I don't have a 'usual table' anywhere, except home?"

"One of the very few advantages of living alone," I said.

Holman leaned forward quickly and dropped his voice to a husky whisper. "And that's another hobby you should take up, Bill. Chasing women. Think of what that could do to spice up your life."

"Make it very short, probably," I said. I was about to add something else when Shari Chino arrived laden with chips, salsa, water…and Wesley Crocker walking escort at her elbow.

She set things down and sidestepped Crocker with a nervous glance. Maybe in the short time he'd been in the restaurant, she'd seen all of him that she wanted to see.

Crocker beamed at her and reached out to touch her on the elbow as she disappeared around the partition. He turned the smile on us and surprised me by revealing a well-kept set of false teeth. Earlier on Highway 17, the teeth must have been riding in his coat pocket. Then he extended his hand to me. His grip was hearty but no knuckle duster, and his hand was a hell of a lot warmer than it had been a couple of hours before.

"Gentlemen," Crocker said. "Good to see you again, sir." Holman was looking askance, his eyes taking in Crocker's road-worn coveralls, scuffed boots, and knit scarf. Crocker held his cap in both hands, and I saw that his hair was cut about an inch long uniformly around his skull, like the burdock cut I used to inflict on my two sons when they were little squirts.

"Your choice of restaurants was superb, sir. Just superb. And such a nice young lady running the place, too."

"I'm glad you enjoyed it. The cigarette machine is by the cash register."

He grinned and I knew he'd found it long before he'd sampled the food. "Thank you, sir."

"By the way, this is Sheriff Martin Holman." The good sheriff did his best not to look stricken, and Wesley Crocker shot his hand across the table to pump Holman's.

"Wesley Crocker," the traveler said. "I saw one of your campaign signs west of town. Yes, I did. Best of luck to you."

"Thanks," Holman said lamely. He didn't dig for a business card.

Crocker held up a hand. "I'll leave you two to enjoy your dinner. I just wanted to say thank you again."

I nodded and Crocker disappeared around the partition.

"Who the hell was that?" Holman asked.

"He belongs to the bike outside," I said. "I picked him up earlier this afternoon a few miles west of town. We put the bike in the trunk and I gave him a lift. It's tough pushing a flat tire."

"You didn't tell me that."

"I just did."

"I mean outside," Holman said impatiently. "You didn't say anything about that." When I didn't respond, Holman added, "So where's he headed? Who the hell is he, anyway?"

"I don't know."

"You didn't ask him?"

"No."

Holman looked puzzled, then irritated. "You are so damn close-mouthed sometimes, Bill. It drives me nuts."

I leaned back and wiped my lips, savoring the heat of the salsa. "I suppose he's just passing through. When I offered him a lift, I didn't see that it was any of my business where he was going. He wasn't breaking the law, except maybe by walking on the wrong side of the highway."

"Watch. He's probably got eighty pounds of uncut heroin in those saddlebags of his." Holman snatched a chip and started to scoop it into the salsa, then thought better of it. He crunched it dry.

I chuckled. "Wouldn't that be something."

"Where's he spending the night?"

"Martin, get a grip. I don't know. I didn't interrogate him." Shari returned and we ordered, Martin Holman predictable as always by ordering fried chicken so he didn't have to face green chili. I held up a hand as Shari was turning to go. "Did the gentleman who was just here leave his ticket?"

"Yes, sir. Do you want me to just add it to your total here?"

"That's fine."

"He bought some cigarettes, too."

"That's fine. Just total the whole thing."

She left and Holman leaned forward, his voice a hoarse whisper. "You bought that guy dinner?"

"Yes," I whispered back.

"Jesus Christ. Saint Gastner to the rescue. And cigarettes, too?"

"Yes."

"I'll bet you ten bucks that's the last you'll ever see of that money."

"It wasn't a loan, Marty."

Holman shook his head and looked out the window. Crocker's bike was on the opposite side of the building, or the sheriff would have been watching his every move.

"I wonder where a guy like that goes. I mean, where he's going. And why. Why the hell doesn't he just get a job somewhere? He reminds me of all those bums you see on the street corners in the city—like up in Albuquerque. 'Will work for food.' And you know they probably never intend to do an honest day's work in their lives."

"Probably not."

"And you're not curious about where he's headed? Who he is? Why he's just tramping around?"

"No. It's his life. There's no law that says he has to stay in one spot and build a nest."

"Build a nest, shit." Holman looked across what little we could see of the dining room from the alcove. "Maybe I should just go out and ask him."

"Spare the man, Martin. He can't vote in this county anyway."

Holman knew I was joking but he still managed to look hurt.

"You'll probably never hear from him again," he said. "And you'll never know. I still say he's probably pushing around eighty pounds of heroin."

I saw Shari Chino come around the corner. "No doubt he sells a little now and then to finance new bicycle tires. Hell, why not." I grinned as Shari set a platter down in front of me. "As long as the chili is hot, that's all that matters. Thanks, sweetheart."

As the aroma rose to clear out my sinuses, all thoughts of Wesley Crocker vanished from my mind. Martin Holman poked tentatively at his dark, generic fried chicken, then looked wistfully across the table at my masterpiece. "Maybe I should have had that," he said, always willing to admit his shortcomings.

"Yes, you should have," I said around a mouthful of green chili enchilada.

"The heartburn would keep me awake all night," the sheriff said, and he started to pick some of the hard, grease-embalmed skin from a chicken wing.

"It's worth it." I knew insomnia would keep me awake most of the night anyway. And that was why, eight hours later when the telephone rang at two in the morning, I was sitting at the kitchen table of my old adobe house on the south side of Posadas, burping the aftertaste of my rich chili dinner and drinking coffee. I picked up the receiver, expecting to hear the voice of the sheriff's department night dispatcher.

"Sheriff, now I hope you believe me when I tell you I wouldn't be calling at an hour like this if it wasn't important."

I recognized Wesley Crocker's quiet, polite voice.

3

I glanced at the clock over the stove and jotted down the time on the telephone pad just as he added, "This here is Wesley Crocker. You might remember that you gave me a lift into town earlier."

At that hour, there was no point in chitchat. He wasn't calling to thank me again for dinner.

"What can I do for you, Mr. Crocker?"

"I hope I didn't wake you."

I briefly wondered why people who called in the middle of the night bothered to say that. "What can I do for you?"

"Well..." And he stopped talking. I could hear a voice in the background, and then Crocker said, "Yes, sir," obviously not to me. I waited. The unmistakable crackle of a two-way radio came next, and I knew where Crocker was before he spoke.

"Sir," he said, "I'm in kind of some trouble here. I didn't know who else to call." He murmured something apologetic that I didn't catch, then added, "I still have your card, thank the Lord."

"Where are you, Mr. Crocker?"

"I'm...I'm down at the village lockup." Again I heard a voice in the background and Crocker said to someone else, "Yes, sir. Here."

"Bill?"

"Yes." I would have recognized Sheriff Martin Holman's voice in the middle of a deep sleep. "What's going on, Marty?"

"I didn't know he was going to call you right off the bat or I would have beaten him to it," Holman said. "We've got a real mess down here at the village P.D. I already called Estelle Reyes-

Guzman and some of the others. But it sure would help if you'd come on over."

I took a deep breath, knowing it did no good to get testy with Holman's oblique nature.

"Sheriff," I said, measuring my words as if I were talking to a four-year-old instead of a reasonably intelligent former used-car salesman, "what happened?"

"Well, the village got a report of a possible person down. Over under the high school bleachers. Looks like it's a twelve- or thirteen-year-old kid."

"Dead?"

"Yes. Tom Pasquale's first guess is that it was assault."

I managed not to groan. Tom Pasquale had worked his way up from hopeful volunteer to paid part-timer for the village department, adding his overly enthusiastic weight to the village's two-man squad.

The young officer's application for employment with the county had taken up residency in my filing cabinet more than a year before. I was sure there was a carbon copy at the state police personnel office as well.

Pasquale spent a good deal of his time trying to impress whoever would pay attention. He would have been better served by going to the police academy in his spare time...but he wasn't going to attend on our buck.

"And he arrested Wesley Crocker?"

"Well, it seems logical to me," Holman said. "Officer Pasquale said the man was camping near the bleachers, apparently. Are you coming down?"

"I'll be right there. Who is the victim, do we know?"

"Not yet. They haven't moved the body yet. They're waiting on Estelle. She was going to pick up Francis at the hospital and head over."

"All right. I'll see you in a few minutes. Who's standing by at the scene? Is someone protecting that?" I had visions of huge Pasquale boot prints squashing evidence into unrecognizable pancakes.

"Bob Torrez said he'd take care of it until you or Estelle got there. Chief Martinez is there with him."

"Good. I'll be right there." I hung up, closed my eyes, and took a deep breath. Before the night was over, we'd know who the victim was, if Estelle Reyes-Guzman and the deputies had to knock on every door in town. That would be half of the puzzle.

I left the quiet darkness of my old adobe wondering how long it would take to find out who Wesley Crocker really was.

I drove 310 out of Escondido Lane and turned onto South Grande Avenue. Grande split the village in half from north to south. The only thing grand about it was its name.

The streets of Posadas were deserted. Even traffic on the interstate was sparse with winter still too far away for the snowbirds to be heading for Arizona or Mexico and too late in the fall for family vacations...just the consistent, dull flow of trucks.

I turned on the radio and was greeted with silence. Holding the coffee cup and steering wheel in one hand and keying the mike with the other, I said, "Three-oh-eight, three-ten."

The response from Sergeant Robert Torrez was immediate. "Three-oh-eight."

"Three-oh-eight, I'll be there in a few minutes."

"Ten-four." Torrez sounded half asleep, but he would sound that way in the middle of a train wreck. "You might want to park in front of the school, in the bus loop."

I acknowledged with two clicks of the transmit button and then slowed down as I continued north through the intersection with MacArthur. The high school was the dark hulk off to the left, on its own island, surrounded on all sides by the families who supported the place.

As I turned onto Piñon, I buzzed down the window, listening to the night sounds of the village. Piñon jogged to Sylvester and then I turned the patrol car onto Olympic, the narrow macadam service road that skirted the football field and track. Someone shot a flashlight beam at me, but I didn't stop the car. Instead, I continued on, circling the grounds by turning left on Pershing and away from the field.

The semicircular driveway in front of the high school was aglare with three sodium vapor lights, and I idled the patrol car into the driveway, aiming to park behind Torrez's unit and the chief's blue Pontiac.

I pulled to a halt beside a SCHOOL BUSES ONLY sign. The night air was cool, but the wind had finally given up. I heard another car before I saw it, heard it accelerating hard, its oversized engine howling. Headlights flashed on Pershing and the tires of the village police car chirped as the vehicle swung into the driveway and pulled up beside me, driven like something out of Hollywood.

Patrolman Tom Pasquale looked across at me and raised an eyebrow in what he no doubt hoped was an imitation of his favorite movie star. He opened his window but didn't get out.

I half wished that Pasquale had been asleep somewhere, skull propped against the seat's headrest, mouth open and blissfully ignorant of the world around him.

I stepped out of the county car and hitched up my trousers. "Thomas, who's at the police station?"

"The sheriff's still there, sir. And Deputy Mitchell. And Cindy."

The village department's girl Friday, Cindy Aragon, worked very hard to keep Pasquale out of trouble. "So tell me what happened."

"Sir, someone called the P.D. to report a possible downer. I took the call. I happened to be the only one in the office at the time other than Cindy. So I drove right over to check it out."

"And then?"

"I hopped the fence by the track, over there on Olympic. I crossed directly to the bleachers and saw the body by the foundation of the press box. I determined that the subject was deceased. On the way back to my unit I saw another subject over near the east end of the football field. In that small grove of trees by the pump house."

"You were able to see him in the dark?"

"The field night lights are bright, sir."

"And that person turned out to be Mr. Crocker?"

"Yes, sir."

"And you took him into custody."

"Yes, sir."

"Did he resist in any way?"

"No, sir." After the briefest of pauses, Pasquale added, "I almost wish he had, sir."

"No...you don't." I started to walk off and then stopped. "On what grounds did you make the arrest, by the way? Did Mr. Crocker admit that he had anything to do with the incident?"

Pasquale's head jerked forward as if he'd just been startled in the dark. "No, sir, he didn't say much of anything at all."

"You read him his rights?"

"Yes, sir. That's when he said he needed to make a call. That there was someone here in town that would vouch for him."

"Yeah, well..." I motioned at the walkway between the main building and the gymnasium. "Let's cut through there." We left the cars and walked through the inky black passageway between the buildings, Pasquale's flashlight stabbing into each dark crevice.

A yellow crime scene ribbon stretched across the parking lot, effectively blocking off the rear of the bleachers.

Sergeant Robert Torrez and Chief Martinez appeared out of the shadows, looking like Mutt and Jeff. Torrez, six-four and walking like a hunting cat, led the chubby chief of police.

"Estelle coming?" Martinez asked, sounding altogether too cheerful for the time and the circumstances. I liked Eduardo Martinez as a human being and thought he was ridiculous as a law officer. But Posadas was an incorporated village that budgeted its own law—the chief and two part-time patrolmen.

Most of the village night calls were handled routinely by the sheriff's department, logical since the P.D. had no dispatcher of its own and not enough manpower to cover twenty-four hours. Martinez was a parade cop...polish the car and turn on the lights for the Fourth of July.

"Yes. Estelle's on the way. You gentlemen stay here for a minute." Pasquale wanted to go with me, but I waved him back. I knew perfectly well that he liked to spend time in Sergeant Torrez's company, but this wasn't the time for impressions. The chief understood the same thing and put a chubby hand on the kid's arm to hold him still.

I ducked under the channel-iron braces and worked my way carefully along under the bleachers, keeping my footprints immediately beside the row of concrete pillars. In the center of the structure, a cinder-block foundation arose like a huge chimney, providing support for the press box and announcer's station above.

The circle of light from my flashlight played around the blocks, and sure enough there was a bundle pressed over in the corner. A casual glance could have mistaken it for a garbage bag left behind by the custodians after the last home football game. Pasquale had good eyes, at least.

I approached to within a dozen feet and stopped, playing the light slowly this way and that, surveying the area. The footing was crushed stone, broken glass, torn Styrofoam, a sock or two—a delightful place. I stepped forward carefully.

The corpse lay like a broken rag doll, flat on its back. A brightly colored coat was bunched around the upper body, concealing the face. I grimaced at the bare knees that looked absurdly small and fragile in the harsh beam of my flashlight.

One arm was twisted under the body, the other was caught up in the loose fabric of the coat, as if the garment had been hastily wrapped around the child.

I turned the light and looked at the only patch of skin I could see besides the two spindly legs—the back of the child's left hand, fingers dug into the fabric of the coat, dirt caked with blood on the smooth brown skin.

With a grunt, I shifted balance and pulled the coat far enough down that I could see a tangle of long, black hair. Maybe a girl, maybe not. The hand was cool to my touch. I slipped my hand inside the coat and pressed two fingers to the side of the kid's neck and waited...waited longer than I needed to.

4

Deputy Eddie Mitchell transferred Wesley Crocker out of the small, leak-stained plasterboard and industrial yellow police department office to the county Public Safety Building—more grand in name, but not much more—three blocks down the street.

Dr. Francis Guzman, Estelle's husband and the county coroner, had ordered the victim's body removed to the morgue at Posadas General. We still didn't know who she was, or how she'd died. I sent Deputy Mitchell to shag the high school principal, Glen Archer, out of bed. If anyone knew the girl, he would.

Sheriff Martin Holman met me with a thinly veiled "I told you so" look when I walked into the sheriff's office at 3:35 that morning. "Is Estelle on the way?" he asked. I nodded and headed for the coffeepot.

"Has Crocker said anything?" I watched the creamer dissolve into the oily surface of the coffee, the brew turning about the color of Portland cement.

Holman snorted derisively. "He's just sitting there, hoping he can use his 'get out of jail free' card. I haven't let anyone upstairs other than Howard Bishop. Howard's keeping the suicide watch."

I sighed and dropped the plastic spoon on the pad of paper towels.

"You ready to go on up?" Holman asked.

"I want to wait for Estelle."

"Is Chief Martinez still out at the school?"

I nodded. I didn't add what we both knew...that at the first opportunity, Chief Martinez would turn to Sergeant Torrez and say, "Well, you've got this pretty well nailed down," and than

Eduardo would nudge his big, comfortable Pontiac toward home, where he'd have the good sense to jump back in bed with his big, comfortable wife, Essie. Eduardo Martinez was chief because the Posadas council paid him $11,600 a year—three thousand less than a first-day rookie with the sheriff's department. The village got what it paid for.

"What's the matter?" Holman asked, and I realized with a start that I was staring vacantly at a spot about three feet under the floor tile. "What are you thinking?"

I shrugged. "Nothing, I guess," and I started toward the stairs that led up to the three cells and the two small conference rooms on the second floor. With my hand on the bottom of the banister, I stopped and frowned. "Marty, what time did you get to the P.D.?"

"Tonight, you mean?"

"Yes."

"I would guess maybe ten minutes before two. Something like that."

"And someone called the police department's number to report the body, not 911?"

"I assume so. Otherwise the call would have been routed through here."

I glanced down the hall and could see our night dispatcher, Ernie Wheeler, sitting at the console, patiently waiting for something to happen.

"And the caller was anonymous."

Holman nodded. He rubbed a hand on the side of his jaw, checking for the single, odd whisker that might have avoided his electric razor and that might end up in a photograph should the press corps be awakened. We heard the back door of the sheriff's office open. "That should be her now," he said, and in a moment Estelle Reyes-Guzman appeared in the dispatch hallway.

Her clothes were as plain as could be, a blouse and skirt of tan cotton that she laughingly called her "Taiwan suit" and a dark blue poplin windbreaker. Her long black hair was tousled and ignored. She still managed to look lovely. A month before she had stopped wearing the tailored pantsuits that had been her trademark. With her impeccable timing, the election would be history before she really started to show that her two-year-old son didn't have much longer to enjoy his status as an only child.

A deep frown darkened her features. "Sir, I talked with Tom Pasquale over at the school. He said that the man in custody is an itinerant—that you gave him a lift into town yesterday?"

"Yes."

"And that then the both of you"—she nodded at the sheriff as well—"saw him at the Don Juan after you bought him dinner?"

"Also true," I said, and Holman's head bobbed a little. I could see a flush crawl up from his collar. It wasn't hard to figure out where Pasquale had heard the story.

Her frown deepened. "Maybe Pasquale knows something we don't," she said, half to herself.

"The man's name is Wesley Crocker. He's upstairs when you're ready."

"I'm ready," she said.

"You want a cup of coffee or anything?"

She almost smiled at me. "No, sir." She patted her stomach. "A green chili breakfast would taste good after a while though."

I followed her up the stairs, with Sheriff Holman bringing up the rear.

Deputy Howard Bishop had moved Wesley Crocker to the smaller conference room, a twelve-by-fourteen affair with no windows. As we entered the room, Crocker was seated, his hands clasped in front of him on the table, handcuffed at the wrists.

"Take those off," I said, and Bishop did so. Crocker just sat quietly, eyes fastened on the grain of the old oak table. When the notebooks and pencils and tape recorder and cassettes and manila folders were in order, I took a deep breath and said, "Mr. Crocker, I am aware that Posadas Patrolman Thomas Pasquale has informed you of your rights, but I want to go over this document with you." I turned a printed copy of the Miranda warning and slid it until it touched his knuckles. He didn't move.

I threaded my way, one sentence at a time, through the legalese. When I finished, Wesley Crocker nodded mutely.

"Mr. Crocker, do you understand your rights as you have read them, and as they have been explained to you?"

"Yes, sir." His voice was husky, and his hand was already rising to take the pen I held out.

"If you have no questions, you need to sign and date the document." He did so.

I sat down directly across the table from him. Sheriff Holman remained standing near the door, beside the hulking, red-haired Deputy Bishop. "Mr. Crocker, I think you know everyone in the room except Detective Reyes-Guzman." Estelle sat to my right, at the end of the table. She regarded Crocker without expression.

"Yes, sir." He turned his head and nodded at Estelle. "Good evening, ma'am." He might as well have been talking to stone.

"Mr. Crocker, do you know why you're here?"

"Yes, sir, I do."

"Are you willing to talk to us without counsel?" He nodded. "I need an audible answer for the tape recorder, Mr. Crocker."

He looked up quickly, as if he were alarmed at committing such an indiscretion. "Of course I'll talk with you, sir. Whatever you need to know."

"Would you state your full name?"

"Wesley Albert Crocker, Junior."

I fingered the worn Social Security card and the faded military identification card that Pasquale had taken from Crocker's wallet when he'd arrested him.

"How old are you, Mr. Crocker?"

"I'm fifty-one."

"Do you have a permanent address?"

"No, sir, I don't. I kind of use a sister's address when there's a need, but otherwise, no."

"Where's your sister live now?"

"Anaheim, California."

"Yesterday afternoon, I picked you up on State 17 just west of town and then dropped you off in the vicinity of the Don Juan de Oñate restaurant." Crocker nodded. "What did you do then?"

"I went and had me something to eat, is what I did."

"You just ate and that's all?"

He hesitated. "Well, no. It was early yet, and the young lady..."

"The hostess?"

"Yes. She said I was free to take up a booth just as long as I wanted. So seeing as it was early yet, I just sat right there and watched the weather go by."

"You remained in the restaurant for some two or three hours?" Holman asked. "Just staring out the window?"

"Well, sir," Wesley Crocker said, "I got to admit that I imposed a little on this good man's generosity. I had me another plateful, not too long before you two gentlemen arrived at the restaurant."

"So you left the restaurant shortly after six?"

"Yes, sir."

"Where did you go?"

Crocker frowned at the table. I watched his hands, watched as his right index finger traced and retraced an imperfection in the oak grain. "I walked up the main street, there. I forget the name. The waitress had said that I might try the park as a place to camp out, that probably nobody would bother me there. That's the park you mentioned, good sir," he said, glancing up at me. "So I did just that. I walked until I saw the old tank, just like you said, and the two cannons."

"And you were going to camp there?"

"Well, I thought I might give it a look. I found me a spot to sit for a bit, so I could look at that old tank and wonder about how old Black Jack Pershing ever thought he was going to catch Pancho Villa using something that slow and noisy." He grinned. "I wished the village had put one of those airplanes he used. I would have liked to have seen that. But I guess they wouldn't weather so well, the canvas covering and all."

"How long did you stay there?"

He turned his head slightly, apologetic. "It was pretty much after dark, but I don't tend to keep track of such things, you know." He shrugged. "I got my health still, and the good Lord has seen fit to let me go my own way, so I don't bother much with keeping up with the time. It just passes as it passes."

Estelle hadn't moved a muscle during the conversation. She still regarded Crocker expressionlessly, her deep, black eyes studying his whiskered, ruddy face. I would have liked to have known what she was thinking, but I would find out in due time.

"You decided not to spend the night in the park?"

He nodded. "It just seemed kind of open, you know. Like bedding down on somebody's front step, with those busy streets on each side."

I hadn't thought of the streets of Posadas as busy.

Crocker continued, "So I was just ambling along, thinking I'd go over to that convenience store that's just a bit south. Maybe see if they had any newspapers or magazines. There was about half a dozen youngsters there, and that's the first time I saw the village police."

"What do you mean?" I asked.

"Well, I was just leaning my bike up against the side of the store, kind of around the side there, behind the telephone booth, when the black-and-white drives up. The officer gets out and he starts talking to the youngsters kind of mean-like."

"Mean-like?"

"Well, his tone of voice was hard, if you know what I mean. I couldn't hear just what the argument was, but after just a little bit the officer grabs one of the kids by the arm and swings him around so he thumps up against the car. He sure had a swagger to him, that young fellow did."

"The youngster, or the police officer?"

"The policeman. Anyway, I just tried to mind my own business. I went inside the store and got talking to the clerk—young fella there surprised me by knowing something about the area. We shot the breeze for maybe ten minutes, and he told me of this old mining town east and south of here that I should visit. I said I would, and he gave me a copy of one of his *Mining West* magazines. I sure did appreciate that. He's the one who suggested I might camp out over in that grove of trees at the end of the athletic field."

"And did you?"

"Yes, sir, I did." He grinned. "I leaned my bike against the fence at the end of the football field and found me a nice spot in the middle of them trees. Had it all arranged just fine. And then seeing as how I didn't have enough light to read by, and it was early yet, I hopped over that low fence there and plunked myself down right under the goalposts. Had me a night sky view all the way to Peru, I guess."

"And that's where you stayed?"

He nodded vehemently.

I looked down at the folder. There had been no time for Thomas Pasquale to fill out the reams of paperwork still facing him.

"When did you see the police officer again?"

Crocker pursed his lips. "Well, like I say, I don't carry a watch. But it was after the kids left from across the way."

"What do you mean by that? Across the way where, and what kids?"

"Sure enough, over behind the school. There was a couple cars full of them. Kind of sidled around behind the gymnasium, there. One of the cars left after a bit, but the other stayed on. Now and then I'd hear voices coming' across. They were just doing what kids do, I guess." He squirmed uncomfortably.

"Did they ever see you?"

"I don't think so. If they did, they never let on. And then the other car, it left, too."

"And you have no idea what time that was?"

"No, sir, I don't." His face brightened. "I was sure enjoying my grandstand view of Orion, though."

"Orion?"

"The constellation. I was staring at it, letting my mind wander here and there, way up there where those stars were."

"And after the kids left, things were quiet?"

"Yes, sir."

"Then what happened?"

His forehead creased. "Sometime later, this young police officer arrived. I'd gone back in the trees, and I guess I'd drifted off. I woke up when I heard the car pull in on the other side of the field, right across from where the big bleachers and speaker's building are. He got out, jumped that little fence there, and darned if he didn't jog right across the field to the bleachers. That's when I got up and walked on over to the fence."

"But by this time the two other vehicles that you saw earlier had gone?"

He nodded. "That's why I was curious, I guess. I saw his light over under the bleachers for a bit, and then he come out like his tail was afire."

"When did he see you?"

"I don't know, sir. I truly don't. But it could have been at just about any time. I was just standing there, leanin' on the fence. He got to his car and sat in it for a minute or two with the door open. I could hear some bits and snatches of radio talk. And then he got out and walked right down the sidelines fence and cut across to where I was camped."

"And what happened?"

"I saw it was a young fella, the same one from the convenience store earlier. He was breathin' hard and edgy and had his hand right on the handle of his gun. So I thought to myself, Wesley Crocker, if he says stand on your head, you just say 'yes, sir' and do it."

"What did he say to you?"

"He asked me to stand up, and I did. He asked me how long I'd been there, and I told him. He asked for identification, and I gave him all I had, those two cards right there." He reached out and pointed at the folder. "And then he told me I was under arrest."

Crocker looked up at me, his light gray eyes puzzled. "I didn't know what for, except maybe trespass, and I surely would have left if he'd just said so."

"When did you find out what the arrest charge was, Mr. Crocker?"

"When I heard everyone talking down at the police station." He turned to Martin Holman. "I believe when you came in, sir," and he turned back to me. "The good sheriff here and the officer were talking about a body found under the bleachers. Terrible thing." He shook his head. "It's the times, it truly is."

I leaned back and took a deep breath, gazing at Wesley Crocker, trying to assess what might be going on in his mind.

"Mr. Crocker, why did you call me?"

He gazed at me for a long minute, his face composed. The crow's feet at the corners of his eyes crinkled. "I called you because I knew something about you, and right then I needed somebody who didn't have no axes to grind, who could see things in a fair light."

"All that because I spotted you a meal and some cigarettes?"

"Well, there's that," Wesley Crocker said. "But mostly because you never asked me where I was going or where I'd been." Out of the corner of my eye I saw Estelle's left eyebrow lift. It was the first expression I'd seen on her face since we entered the room.

I looked down at the folder and its meager contents, then snapped it shut. "What a goddamn mess," I said.

5

"You're going to turn him loose."

I didn't respond to Sheriff Martin Holman. His remark wasn't a question. I knew perfectly well that he meant it as one, but I didn't have an answer for him. I sat down heavily in my ancient leather-padded swivel chair and tipped back into that comfortable lounging posture in which my brain had always worked its best. It wasn't doing so well just then.

Holman moved away from my office door as Estelle entered, a steaming cup of herbal tea in her hand. She toed the door closed and the three of us looked at each other.

"What do *you* know?" I said to Estelle, and the instant the words were out of my mouth, I realized how petulant they sounded.

"The victim is an unidentified female, somewhere between eleven and fifteen years of age."

"That's it?" Holman asked.

"That's it."

"You think she was a Mexican national?"

Estelle frowned and sat down in the straight-backed chair by the small east window. She blew over the top of the tea and then said, "I don't know, sir. I would guess that she's Mexican. Beyond that, I don't know. Bob Torrez and I went through her clothing. We found a single dollar bill. Other than that, nothing."

"No label in the coat?"

She shook her head. "No. No identification, no candy wrappers, no nothing. We don't know who she is, or where she came from."

"Mitchell went to roust Glen Archer. If the kid went to Posadas schools, he'll know her. Did someone talk to people who live around the school? Neighbors?"

"Deputy Mears is doing that, sir."

"And no one has called to report a child missing?"

"No, sir."

"That's goddamn wonderful." I looked over at the wall clock. "Two minutes to four in the morning, and we've got a kid dead and nobody is asking about her."

"Maybe she was dumped by someone," Holman said.

I glared at him and then relaxed, knowing he wasn't as stupid as the remark made him sound. He'd had eight years as sheriff, and if the upcoming election went true to prediction, he'd have four more. After thirty or forty years, maybe he'd learn enough to take charge of his own cases. At least he had the good sense not to pretend he was a cop. "Of course she was dumped, Sheriff," I said patiently. "I don't think she just crawled under there and died on a whim."

I leaned forward and rested my head in my hands.

"Maybe the crime lab will turn up something when it processes her clothes. Some fibers that shouldn't be there, something like that," Holman said, trying again.

Estelle Reyes-Guzman set the foam tea cup down on the floor beside her chair. "And there were no unusual marks at the scene. She wasn't dragged through the dirt. She didn't leave a trail of blood. At the moment, there's no way for us to be sure about *where* she died."

"Maybe she died right there. Maybe that's where the assault took place...if there was one," I said, and Estelle nodded. "Did Francis say how she died?"

"He's not sure."

I looked at Estelle with interest. "Oh?" Usually, very little escaped her talented husband's attention.

"There were no obvious wounds, other than a torn left index fingernail. That's where the blood on her hand came from. He thinks that possibly she was choked."

"Huh," I murmured. "Was she molested?"

"Maybe."

Holman cleared his throat. "I think that all we need is one little piece, and he'll talk. One little piece of hard evidence that ties him to the scene."

"Who?" I asked. "Crocker?"

Holman nodded. "I think he's just trying to test the waters. See how much we know."

"We don't need anything to tie him to the scene, Marty. He was there."

"That's what I mean." Holman walked over to my desk and plopped down on the corner. Frustrated, he let his fingers mess with my papers. "He can't be sure just what we know. One little connection is all we need, and that's it."

I looked across at Estelle. "Did you get a chance to talk with Pasquale at any length?"

"No, sir. Just a preliminary."

"Did he say why he arrested Crocker?"

"Apparently because he was there, sir."

"And that's it?"

"I don't see what other reason he needs, Bill," Holman said. "Even if he didn't commit the murder, Crocker knows more than he's telling us."

"You think so?" I said.

"How could someone be camped on the playing field and not see what was going on just a hundred yards away? I can't imagine that girl sitting around quietly and letting herself be murdered. There'd be all kinds of ruckus. He'd be bound to hear."

"If that's the way it happened, Martin. She may have been killed before Crocker even got there. Let's get Pasquale in here for a few minutes," I said. "Let's see what was going through the young man's mind, if anything."

Holman grunted. "You sound like you're more concerned with protecting this bum of yours than finding out who butchered a little girl."

I turned my head slowly and regarded Holman. "That was a stupid thing to say." Silence hung heavily. The sheriff's hands twitched nervously in his lap, and then he busied himself picking tiny pieces of imaginary lint off his knee.

"I'll call in Pasquale," Estelle said after a moment, and I nodded.

"Thank you."

"Well, you know what I mean," Holman continued lamely as Estelle opened the office door. "We've got a killing here. Or at least, an unattended death. An innocent little kid."

"I'm painfully aware of that," I said.

"It's just that if this is a murder, with every hour that passes, the odds of solving the case don't improve. What's the statistic? In instances where the crime isn't witnessed, at least sixty percent of capital cases go unsolved? Something like that?"

I grimaced. "And other fascinating election eve trivia, Martin."

"Now listen...You didn't even ask Crocker if he did it."

"That's because I don't think he did."

"On what evidence?"

I leaned back farther and hooked my hands behind my head, regarding Martin Holman through my bifocals. The lower lenses made him nice and blurry, as if he were standing in a fog at a great distance.

"I think the evidence is supposed to go the other way," I said.

"If you don't think that he had anything to do with it, why don't you let him go, then?"

"Because."

This time, Holman actually grinned. "Yes?"

"Because...I'm as confused right now as you are. I don't want to rush into some stupid mistake. It won't hurt Wesley Crocker much more to spend a couple of hours as a guest of the county."

"What do you mean, 'much more'? It won't hurt him at all," Holman snapped. "And the sad thing is that nothing we do will bring that girl back either."

"That's the way it is," I said and let my chair rock forward with a bang. Holman was about to say something else when he saw Officer Tom Pasquale standing in the doorway of my office.

The kid's face was pale, and he nervously twisted the handle of his nightstick.

Sergeant Robert Torrez appeared in the hallway behind Pasquale. He caught my eye and asked, "Do you need me for anything?"

"Not for a few minutes."

He held up a black-and-white photograph. "Mears is with Glen Archer over at the school. They're doing a preliminary autopsy at the hospital, and Doctor Guzman wouldn't let them in yet. I'm going to take one of the morgue photos and see if Archer can give us an I.D."

"Good idea." Principal Archer called us often enough in the middle of the night when some vandal popped a window or beat the crap out of a soda pop machine. Like it or not, trying to identify dead students was as much a part of his job as pinning ribbons on spelling bee winners. "You might get lucky."

He nodded and left, and I beckoned Tom Pasquale toward a chair.

"Do you want me to stay?" Estelle asked.

"Yes, I do."

Martin Holman paced his corner of the room, too nervous to sit. I fixed Pasquale with a steady stare and let the silence build for a few seconds.

"Officer Pasquale, we want to run through what we've got so far," I said. "Before we make any other moves." I picked up a pencil and drew a small circle on the notepad that lay in the middle of my desk calendar. "Who called the P.D. about the possible victim?"

"I have no idea, sir."

"You took the call?"

"Yes, sir."

"On the regular business line, not 911?" He nodded and I added, "And the caller wouldn't give a name?"

He shook his head.

"Did you ask?"

"Yes, sir."

"Was it a man or woman?"

"A male voice, sir. If I had to guess, I'd say teenager. Late teens, maybe."

"But you didn't recognize the voice, then. Exactly what did the person say?"

"He said that there was a child's body under the bleachers by the football field. He said the body was right beside the center foundation."

"That's the term he used? A child's body?"

"Yes, sir."

"He didn't say, 'a hurt child' or anything like that? He actually said those three words…'a child's body'?"

"Yes, sir."

"Why didn't you tell me that in the first place?"

"Sir?"

"When I saw you over at the school earlier, you said that someone called you," and I used the eraser of my pencil to push the small pages of my notebook until I found the spot. "Someone called you to report a 'possible downer.' That's what you called it. A 'possible downer.'

Pasquale looked confused. "It's just a slang expression, sir."

I looked at the young officer and counted mentally to ten. When I had my temper under control, I said, "Let's have an understanding, Officer Pasquale. We are in the middle of a homicide investigation. The apparent victim is a child, and we have a man in custody. This might be a nice time to dispense with slang and stick to facts and correct terminology. Does that sound reasonable to you?"

Pasquale flushed. Out of the corner of my eye I saw Holman finally sit down, backward, buckaroo-style, on one of the straight-backed chairs. He was probably happy as a clam to have me angry with someone besides himself.

"Yes, sir," Pasquale said, and I silently commended him on his self-control. He could have said, "Look, I don't work for you, you fat old son-of-a-bitch. Get off my back." And there wouldn't have been much I could have done, except bluster.

I softened my tone one click and asked, "So when you responded, you did not assume that the call was a crank call…a joke. You felt there was some chance that you were responding to a possible death, even though the caller did not use the emergency number?"

"Yes, sir. That's the way the boy's tone of voice impressed me."

"You thought he was serious," I said, and Pasquale nodded. "But you didn't think it was necessary to call for any backup? You knew that Sergeant Torrez was working the county, did you not?"

"Yes, sir."

"Was he busy?"

"Yes, sir. He had just responded to a domestic dispute call north of the village. I didn't think it would hurt to make a preliminary check and then call for backup if necessary."

"And so you arrived at the school. Where did you park?"

"Along Olympic, right next to the visitors' side of the field. I jumped the fence and ran across the field."

"Did you have your handheld radio with you?"

"Sir?"

"Your handheld. You left your patrol car, so I presume you had your portable radio with you in case you did need backup."

Pasquale took a deep breath, and the flush rose again. "No, sir."

"What did you do then?"

"I ran across the field, ducked under the bleachers, and saw the body. There was no response to my verbal orders, so I checked to see if the victim was alive."

"How?"

"I felt the neck for a pulse. There wasn't one. The skin was cool to the touch. There was no sign of respiration." He sounded as if he were reading from a freshman criminology textbook.

I leaned back and tossed my pencil on the blotter. Before I could form the question, Martin Holman said, "And when did you first see the suspect?"

Pasquale's head snapped around and he looked first at Holman and then at Estelle Reyes-Guzman. Estelle's expression was politely expectant.

"I saw him as I ran back toward the patrol car. He was standing by the fence, over at the east end of the field. Outside the fence. I remember seeing his bicycle. It was leaning against the fence."

"The arc lights are pretty bright there, aren't they," Holman said helpfully.

"Yes, sir. There are two right at the end of the field."

"You had satisfied yourself that the victim was dead, and then you approached the suspect," I said.

"Yes, sir."

"You didn't think that with a homicide on your hands, it might be a good idea to call for backup from an experienced, certified officer?" I asked.

Pasquale looked at the floor and took a deep breath, almost a sigh. "I suppose so, sir. I did go back to the car first, though. I heard Sergeant Torrez tell dispatch that he'd be ten-ten for a little while. I was going to call in, but then I didn't want there to be any chance of the suspect slipping away. I didn't see any reason that I couldn't handle it alone. And I had seen him earlier, over at the convenience store. I knew he was an older guy. I knew he was a vagrant."

I reached out and took the pencil again, toying with it. "A vagrant? You mean if I decided to ride a bicycle across the country, that makes me a vagrant?" With my girth, it would have made me dead, but no one in the room smirked.

"No. That's not what I mean. I mean, he had everything he owned on that bike of his. So, a homeless guy. Not necessarily vagrant. Homeless."

"Why did you arrest him, Officer Pasquale?"

"Sir?"

"Why did you take him into custody? On what evidence?"

"I asked him how long he'd been camping near the field. He couldn't tell me, other than that maybe it had been since just after dark. Since it was nearly two by then, I figured the chances were excellent that the victim had been killed, or dumped, since Mr. Crocker had arrived at the field. He had to know something about it. But he said he didn't. So I informed him of his rights and took him into custody."

"I asked you this once before, but I'll ask again. Did he resist in any way?"

"No, sir, he did not. In fact he was unusually cooperative."

"Do you know why he was cooperative?" I asked.

Pasquale's forehead wrinkled and he shook his head. "No, sir, I don't suppose I do. Except he must have known that there was nowhere he was going to go."

"How true. And then you took him to the village lockup?"

"Yes, sir. I was about to call the sheriff's office when Deputy Eddie Mitchell arrived."

"One more general thing, Officer Pasquale, and then we'll want to go over this again. When you saw Mr. Crocker at the convenience store, what time was that?"

"I'd have to look at my patrol log, sir. But I would guess it was about eight-thirty or so."

"Were you responding to a call when you saw him?"

"A call at the store? No, sir. I stopped to talk to a group of middle-school youngsters who were in the parking lot."

"What were they doing?"

"I saw two of them making obscene gestures at a passing motorist, sir."

"Ah. So you were busy with them and chose to ignore Mr. Crocker."

"Yes, sir. And I can see that was a mistake, sir. If I'd stopped to talk to him then, maybe that little girl would still be alive."

I decided to let Officer Thomas Pasquale agonize over that judgment call without assistance for a while. It would be cause for some long, sleepless nights. And maybe that was just what he needed.

6

By half past four, we'd pounded Officer Thomas Pasquale long enough. We'd had no word from Dr. Guzman, and Sergeant Torrez hadn't returned from working the identification of the dead child.

Sheriff Martin Holman gave up trying to keep his eyes open and headed home to bed, optimistic that when a new day dawned in a couple of hours, all his problems would have resolved themselves. We assigned Thomas Pasquale the task of locating Crocker's alleged sister in Anaheim. I fervently hoped that the young officer couldn't get in trouble on the telephone.

I trudged upstairs to check on Wesley Crocker and found him sleeping soundly.

After reminding the dispatch deputy to check on the prisoner every ten minutes, I headed for the door, ready to idle around the county for a while to give my mind a chance to sift and ponder.

I pushed open the side door that led to the parking lot and damn near tripped over Estelle Reyes-Guzman. She was sitting on the top step like a little kid, arms circling her drawn-up knees.

"I thought you were going home," I said.

"Not yet. I was just sitting here stargazing."

"A new hobby," I chuckled. "Crocker could give us lessons."

The detective looked up at me and then unfolded and pushed herself to her feet. "Do you have fifteen minutes, sir?"

"That's all I have, is time," I answered and glanced at my watch. "Give it another two hours and it'll be time for breakfast." We walked across the parking lot to my patrol car. "Does Irma ever squawk?"

"About the hours, you mean? No. She's used to it." Francis and Estelle had hired Irma Sedillos as a full-time housekeeper/nanny, and the girl was earning her keep. Since her older sister, Gayle Sedillos, was our office manager and chief dispatcher, Irma must have had some inkling of what she was in for when she signed on with that frenetic household.

I opened the door of 310 and grunted my way inside. Estelle was already settled, brooding, by the looks of her forehead, by the time I closed my door.

"I'd like to visit the football field again," Estelle said, and I nodded and started the car. At that hour in the morning, Bustos Avenue looked like an extension of the parking lot, empty and bleak. Even during the middle of a July 4 parade, Posadas was a quiet place. At 5 A.M. in mid-October, it was comatose.

We drove the few blocks in silence, and I pulled the car to a halt on Olympic, approximating the spot chosen by Officer Pasquale.

Estelle got out and I followed her toward the east end of the field, staying on the outside of the fence. When she reached a spot opposite the goalpost, she stopped and switched her flashlight back and forth. "Bicycle tire marks," she said. "This is where he leaned the bike up against the fence." She pointed off into the grove of trees on our left. "And then he camped over there, in the trees."

"That's what he told us," I said, and zipped my jacket. Along the fence were two utility poles whose sodium vapor lights flooded the area. Her flashlight beam was nearly lost in the flood of the two lamps as she walked into the grove of trees.

"And this is where he said he was when Pasquale arrived," she said, pointing her light down at a scuffed, matted spot on the ground.

"Probably."

"So when he saw the police car, and realized something was going on, he got up and walked out of this grove, over to the fence." She walked to the four-foot-high chain-link as she narrated.

"That's how Pasquale could see him. The lights would have made that easy enough," I said. Estelle squinted up toward the lights, forehead furrowed.

She leaned against the chain-link and observed the out-of-bounds and the end zone ahead of her. "Is that gate back there open?" And before I could answer, she walked quickly back along the boundary fence until she reached one of the small gates that opened to the field. I followed, my hands thrust deep into the pockets of my jacket.

Once through the gate, the sod underfoot was soft and quiet—the rich, thoroughly watered relative of the dry prairie grass that died brittle and tawny that time of year.

We walked to the goalposts and I didn't bother to ask Estelle what was on her mind. I knew from long experience that it was useless to rush her. I fished a toothpick out of my shirt pocket. It was one of the mint-flavored ones from the Don Juan de Oñate restaurant and reminded me that it'd been too long since dinner.

Between wind gusts, it was almost warm...perfect weather to sit in the bleachers and watch the Posadas Jaguars rack up yardage against some unhappy rival. Estelle walked over to one side of the goalpost and slid down to sit at its base.

"If I do that, I'll never get up," I said.

She leaned back against the red and white steel of the post, eyes searching the sky. "Shouldn't Orion be right about there, sir?" She pointed toward the western horizon.

"I beg your pardon?"

"Where is Orion this time of year?" She swept a hand overhead. "The constellation Orion. Where in the night sky?"

"I don't have the faintest idea." I spent very little time looking heavenward, and my ignorance of the heavenly bodies and where they should or should not be at any given time was close to total.

"If it's just rising in the late evening, then by this time it should be well past the zenith, and headed for the hills." She swept her arm in an arc, finally pointing toward the bleachers and the high school beyond. "Maybe it's already set," she said. "I'm not sure."

I craned my neck and looked overhead, squinting against the sodium vapor lights. And just as suddenly, I knew what was bothering Estelle.

"How can you see any stars at all with these lights?" I asked, and Estelle stood up.

"I've been thinking that same thing," she said. "Wesley Crocker said he had a view 'all the way to Peru.' Do you remember him saying that?"

"Something to that effect."

"And then he said he was looking at Orion when the kids arrived."

"And you're wondering how he could have been seeing any stars at all with all this light."

"Yes, sir."

I looked up again, frowning at those two sodium vapors. Their hum was steady, like a distant truck that never made progress. They were spaced ten or twenty yards on each side of the goalposts, far enough back so that someone booting a field goal wouldn't be kicking right into the glare.

Estelle turned and looked off toward the east and the wash of light that rose from downtown Posadas—about the same amount of light as would be cast by a poorly decorated Christmas tree. The eastern horizon was just beginning to show signs of life behind the grove of bare trees.

"This field lies east to west," she said and thrust her hands in the pockets of her skirt. "If Wesley Crocker arrived here some time around nine P.M., which fits with Pasquale's version of things, then Orion would be low in the eastern horizon—depending on what time he got here, it might not even have risen above the lights of downtown."

We both stood in silence, staring off into space.

"So Wesley Crocker is lying," I said finally. "Or mistaken."

Estelle didn't answer, but out of the corner of my eye I caught the slightest of shrugs.

"What do you think?" I asked.

She folded her arms and leaned against the goalpost, gazing off toward the bleachers. "I think it's almost certain that he knows more than he's telling us. And I think it's almost certain he wasn't counting stars through the glare of two sodium vapor lights."

"Do you want to talk with him again?"

"Yes, sir. I do. Before he eats. Before he gets too comfortable."

Her pace back to the car was brisk—almost predatory. If Wesley Crocker was in the middle of an entertaining dream, he had about five minutes to wrap it up.

7

Sergeant Robert Torrez pulled his patrol car in beside mine just as I shoved the gear lever into "park." His face didn't show any excitement, and he methodically gathered his paperwork before uncoiling his large frame from the front seat.

The air was the crisp of predawn with the sun just beginning to highlight the tops of the San Cristobal mountains to the west. If Orion had ever been in the sky, it was long gone then. It would have been a nice morning to sit on the back steps, enjoying a cup of fresh brewed coffee and a cigarette. Out of habit, my fingers began to grope in my shirt pocket and settled for a perfunctory pat of the pocket flap.

Torrez held up a manila folder.

"Archer let me borrow his guidance department's file on the girl."

I stopped short and frowned. "She's local then. How come none of us knew her? And who are her parents? Has someone contacted them yet?"

Torrez held open the back door of the old red adobe building that had housed the sheriff's department since the structure was built in 1934, and then followed Estelle and me inside. "You'll get a pretty good idea about that when you look at the file, sir."

"Who's talking with her parents?" I repeated. "Did you assign someone to that?"

Torrez took a deep breath. "Eddie Mitchell said he'd work on it."

"Work on it?" I frowned again. "Let's see this thing."

And at 5:15 A.M., the paperwork that had accumulated to mark a brief life was spread out on my desk.

I tipped my head back so I could see the small typing. "Maria Ibarra," I read. "Doesn't ring a bell."

"She was fifteen," Estelle murmured, reading over my shoulder.

"And looked twelve," I said, reading the short biographical information form quickly. "Did Eddie find this guy?" I tapped the space for "parent/guardian" that listed the name Miguel Orosco. "I know a *Manny* Orosco, but he sure as hell doesn't have a Las Cruces address...or a kid."

"We haven't found him yet," Torrez said.

I frowned. "Did he check this?" Orosco had listed a Las Cruces address for residence, but it was a post office box number—no street address.

"He's working on it, sir," Torrez said.

"There's not much here," I said. "The school just lets them walk through the front door like that? Where was she living? In a culvert somewhere?"

Estelle Reyes-Guzman took a deep breath. "A public school isn't a high security place, sir." She indicated the handwritten addendum for "shot records" at the bottom of the form where someone had printed "REF/Paddock." "Dawn Paddock might know about her."

"She might." Dawn Paddock had been the school nurse for eighteen years. When my youngest son had busted his ankle playing basketball in gym class, she'd told him to lie down on a cot outside her office for half an hour to see if the ankle felt any better. My hopes for information from her didn't soar. But it was something.

The rest of the information added very little to the picture. A copy of her schedule showed that Maria Ibarra had been taking all the standard eighth-grade academic courses, along with art and Spanish II as electives. "Do eighth-graders take second-year language courses?" I asked, and Estelle shrugged.

"If she didn't speak much English, they might have put her in a second-year Spanish class as a way of helping her. Especially if she was an accelerated student. Glen Archer would know."

I picked up a form labeled *Parent/School Cooperative Checklist*. The lines for student and parent signatures were blank, as were the twelve items.

"'I expect my child to act respectfully and be treated with respect,'" I read, and tossed the paper back on the desk. "Cute." The home language survey form was also blank. "And this is all that Archer had?"

Torrez nodded. "Apparently the girl was new in the district."

"Apparently very new," Estelle said with considerable acid.

"Well, she had to have been living with somebody," I said. I gathered the papers and handed the file to Torrez. "Keep after it, Robert. Talk with the nurse, the counselor, whoever. Get 'em out of bed."

Estelle was already moving toward the door, and I followed her out into the hall and up the stairs toward Wesley Crocker's cell.

Crocker wasn't asleep. I'm sure his interior clock had told him half an hour before that it was time to be up and pushing that bicycle into another bright New Mexico day.

The jail cell was far from bright. Crocker lay on his back, contemplating the ceiling, one arm hooked behind his head.

When he saw us, he sat up quickly and swung his feet to the floor.

"Well, good morning to you, sir...and to you, miss." He turned slightly and patted the heavy brown blanket just above the hem where the legend POSADAS COUNTY CORRECTIONS had been stenciled in black ink. "I've certainly slept on worse."

I unlocked the cell and motioned him out. "We'd like to talk with you again, Mr. Crocker." He rose to his feet and I indicated the conference room down the hallway. I didn't bother with the handcuffs and Wesley Crocker didn't offer his wrists.

He took the same chair he'd used before and folded his hands on the oak table, expectant.

"Mr. Crocker, you understand that you haven't been formally charged with any crime?" He nodded and I flipped through the pages of my small pocket notebook. "When we last talked, you said a couple things that puzzled me."

His eyebrows met over his nose but he didn't say anything.

I gazed at him for a long moment until one of his hands fidgeted on the tabletop. "Mr. Crocker, why did you lie to us about what you did last night?"

His eyebrows knit even further, and his head tilted a fraction. "Sir?"

"You told us that yesterday evening you were out there on the football field by the goalposts, enjoying the stars. Under the glare of two sodium vapor lights. That's hard to do." He started to say something, and I interrupted. "And you mentioned the constellation Orion—how you had a grandstand view of it. At this time of year, it isn't visible in the western sky until just before dawn." I sounded as if I knew exactly what I was talking about. Wesley Crocker looked down at the table.

Estelle and I waited while Crocker mulled things over. Finally he held up his hands and said, "It was a stupid thing to say, sir."

I waited.

"Did you ever get caught doing something when you were a kid and you were so eager to get off the hook that you said too much?" The crow's feet at the corners of his eyes crinkled, but I wasn't in the mood to share childhood humor. "Well, that's about what happened, and it wasn't just the smartest thing I ever did, I can see that."

"Explain."

He shrugged. "There ain't nothing much more to it. I was campin' right where I said I was, trying' to decide if I was going to be able to get any sleep with all the glare from the field lights. That's all. When you folks talked to me, I just padded the story a little. Kind of…you know, to make it sound maybe a little better. I shouldn't have done that."

I sat back in the chair and folded my arms across my chest. "Did you know what the officer was looking for when he arrived?"

"No, sir."

"You had no idea that there was someone under the bleachers?"

"No, sir. I sure didn't."

"When you heard the kids in the cars earlier, did you see any of them get out of the cars? Anything like that?"

"No, sir. It was too dark, too far away. My eyes aren't just what they should be anymore."

"Did you hear anything else?"

"No, sir. Well, now, wait a minute. One of the cars was quiet, and one was a little louder, if you know what I mean. It might have been a diesel, maybe."

"Car or truck? Pickup?"

He shrugged helplessly. "I couldn't say. It was just dark forms and taillights."

"They didn't have their headlights turned on?" Wesley Crocker shook his head. "And how long was it from the time the two vehicles drove away to the time the police officer arrived?"

Crocker frowned. "Well, like I say, one of 'em left first, then the other after a few minutes. And I'd say that it was fifteen minutes after that when the police car showed up. Maybe twenty at the most."

"And that's it."

"Yes, sir." Crocker didn't bother tacking on the *I'm telling the truth...why don't you believe me?* that kids do when they're lying through their teeth.

Estelle Reyes-Guzman tapped the eraser of her pencil on the table thoughtfully.

"Mr. Crocker, who are you?"

"Ma'am?" Crocker said uneasily.

"Who are you?" Her black eyes held Crocker without blinking. "An officer is working up a background check, but save us some time."

"Well, I...I been around a bit. Like I said, the good Lord has seen to bless me with my health, and there's a lot of this country I still want to see."

"Do you work?"

He shook his head. "No, ma'am. I mean, not at any one thing for any length of time."

"Why not?"

He frowned at that, and spent a handful of minutes sifting possible answers. He settled for a shrug. "It's not my way, I guess. Now and then, maybe, for a little while. And then it always seems more important to me to be movin' on."

"When was the last time you worked for someone?"

"For pay?"

"For whatever."

Crocker glanced at me as if maybe I was going to help and then turned back to Estelle. He leaned forward so that he rested his chest on his hands. "I stopped for a few days...it was three days...at Thomas Lawton's place east of Button, Utah. Lawton's Wagon Works, is what he calls it. He makes all kinds of wagons. Repairs old ones. That sort of thing."

"What did you do for him?"

"He was building a new corral. He said his tractor was broke down and so he couldn't use the posthole digger. I dug holes." Crocker smiled and held up his right hand, pointing to the remains of what might have been a blister under his ring finger joint.

"For three days?"

"Well, we did a lot of talking, ma'am. He knows about all there is to know about old wagons, and I had lots of questions. It's fascinating."

"When was the last time you talked with your sister?"

A flicker of regret stabbed across his rough features. "I told you about her? I know I gave her name to that young officer."

"You told us you had a sister in Anaheim."

He nodded. "I don't call her much. Me and her don't see eye to eye on most things. I tell her that yes, maybe someday I'd like to settle in one spot, maybe have my own post office box number." He grinned. "That always makes her mad. You talk to her and you'll see what I mean." He traced the grain of the table with a stubby fingernail. "I like to keep a journal of things. Places I've been, folks I've met. I write down just about everything and then I send it all to her. I've asked her to keep my records for me. Someday, maybe, I'd kind of like to see them all together." He smiled again. "See what all those years and all those miles look like in one place."

"So she has this diary of yours?" I asked.

"Yes, sir. At least I asked her to keep it. She said she would. You can read that and see just exactly where I've been, and who I've seen over the years." The silence returned, and after a moment Crocker added, "And that's why it's so stupid, that fib I told you. You want to know about me, you just read that journal."

"We'll do that."

"I gave that young police officer my sister's name and address."

I nodded.

"Do you have any police record, Mr. Crocker?" Estelle asked. It wouldn't take long for the National Crime Information Center to spit out whatever it had on Wesley Crocker, but it was always interesting to hear a person's own version of scrapes with the law.

"No, ma'am. Never."

"If we ask you to stay available for a few days, do you have somewhere to stay? Other than the park or the football field?"

"No, ma'am."

"Mr. Crocker," I said, "you understand that you may be an important witness to events that happened last night?" He nodded. "The county will pay for a room at the MotorCourt Inn over by the interstate interchange. We'd like you to stay there."

Crocker waved a hand. "No need to spend that kind of money. My little room down the hall here is just fine." He grinned. "You might leave the door ajar. That would make it a bit more homey."

"We really can't do that," I started to say, thinking of the myriad reasons why the sheriff's department couldn't become a civilian R. V. park. Estelle stood up.

"Call it protective custody," she said. "It might be better if he stays here. We don't know who else saw him at the football field."

Wesley Crocker looked skeptical. "Oh, now, there isn't anyone who'd care much about me," he said.

"You have too much faith in your fellow man," I muttered.

"Yes, sir. But I don't mean to be any trouble."

"I'm sure," I said.

"You're thinking of assigning Pasquale to him?" Estelle said, but it was one of those rare occasions when she hadn't read my mind correctly.

"No," I said. "I've got other plans for Officer Pasquale."

8

Button, Utah, was a tiny place along the banks of the Dirty Devil River. I had never been there and didn't plan to go, but I pictured half a dozen buildings languishing in the weakening October sunshine. I'd never met Thomas Lawton, but I could imagine him grimacing with annoyance when he heard the telephone.

"Yep," the voice said after the ninth ring.

"Mr. Lawton?"

"Yep."

I glanced at the wall clock again and then jotted down 7:35 A.M. in my notebook. Detective Estelle Reyes-Guzman had gone to the high school to assist Sergeant Torrez, and I planned to join the party myself. Principal Glen Archer was going to have a wonderful Friday. It would have been simpler for him to just close the school for the day, but not for us. There were too many people we needed to talk to.

"Sorry to bother you so early," I said. "This is Undersheriff William Gastner, down in Posadas, New Mexico. I am looking for some information on a man you may have met a while ago."

There was a moment of silence, and Lawton said, "Who did you say you was?"

"I'm with the Posadas County Sheriff's Department down in Posadas, New Mexico."

"Where the hell is that?"

I smiled. "Posadas is over in the southwestern corner of the state. About twenty miles from the Mexican border."

"Huh," Lawton said.

"I'd be happy to leave my telephone number and you can call me back collect, if you like. Ask the dispatcher to transfer you to Undersheriff Gastner."

"No, no. That ain't necessary. I'll take your word you're who you say you are. What can I do for you?"

"Do you know a gentleman named Wesley Crocker?"

"Crocker..."

"Short, stocky, late middle age. Rides a bicycle."

"Oh...well, son of a gun. Sure. He spent some time here. Helped me out of a real jam. Say, I hope he's all right."

"He's fine. And he speaks highly of you."

Lawton chuckled. "Well, I tell you what. I ain't never talked so much in three days as I did when he was here. He had more questions about this country than any ten historians. Seemed to know quite a bit, too. He even knew about Denning's Pass, west of here, and I bet there aren't ten men outside of the locals who know about that spot."

"When was he there? At your place, I mean?"

"Let me think, now. Back in July, I think. What's your interest in him?"

"We believe he may have been a witness to an incident here in Posadas. This call is just a routine background check to confirm some of the things he mentioned to us. He told us about your place."

"Well, he was here. And he's a good man. Can't sit still in one spot, but he's a good, God-fearing man."

"Did he ever talk to you about a sister in California?"

Lawton hesitated. "Yep, he mentioned her a time or two."

The door to my office opened and Ernie Wheeler stuck his head in. I held up a hand, but he just held up two fingers and mouthed, "It's important."

I nodded and said, "Mr. Lawton, hold on a moment, would you?"

As soon as he saw my hand slide over the receiver, Wheeler said, "There's a Mrs. Elna Tyler long distance for you on line two."

"Who the hell is Elna Tyler?"

"She says she's Wesley Crocker's sister, sir."

"Christ." I punched down the line one and hold buttons together, and then hit line two.

"Mrs. Tyler? This is Undersheriff Gastner."

"I asked to speak with the sheriff," a woman's crisp voice said.

"Sheriff Holman isn't in the office at the moment. I understand that you're Wesley Crocker's sister?"

"Yes, and I'd like to know what's going on."

"I'm glad you called, ma'am. I'm handling that case, and I'll be with you just as soon as I wrap up another call. If you like, leave your number, and I'll call you back in five minutes."

She did so, and I switched back to Thomas Lawton. "Sir, did Mr. Crocker say anything about sending notes or a journal...diary pages, maybe...to his sister? That sort of thing?"

This time the hesitation was considerable, and I prompted "Mr. Lawton?" thinking that perhaps he'd hung up.

His voice was quiet and gravelly. "Seems to me that a man's diary is kind of personal property. If he keeps one."

"Yes, it is, sir. And I'm not asking to read it, although Mr. Crocker offered it to us. I'm just trying to confirm his statement that he kept a journal of his travels."

"Well, I believe he did."

"And he was with you for three days?"

"Just about that."

I thanked Lawton and hung up, my mind now on Elna Tyler. I wondered what Officer Thomas Pasquale had told her. I took a deep breath and punched out her number. The phone rang once before she picked it up.

"Mrs. Tyler, this is Bill Gastner." I tried to keep my tone conversational and pleasant.

"Is my brother all right, Mr. Gastner?"

"Yes, ma'am, he's fine. As Officer Pasquale may have told you, your brother could be an important witness to an incident we're investigating."

"Your officer told me no such thing. He said that Wesley was being held *in connection* with an investigation. He made it sound like Wesley had done something terrible."

"No, ma'am. That's not the case at all. And the reason we called was simply to verify some of your brother's statements to us. He doesn't carry much paperwork with him, as you probably well know."

This time Elna Tyler managed a laugh. "Oh, Wesley, Wesley."

"How long has he been on the road, ma'am?"

"He didn't tell you?"

"I haven't asked him yet."

"I see. Well, Officer, I would guess he's headed for some kind of world record. He's been pedaling that bicycle, or one like it, for the better part of thirty years."

"And he just roams?"

"That's a good way to put it. He loves history. If you've talked with him at all, you already know that. But he doesn't focus on anything in particular." She laughed. "He just absorbs it all like a big sponge. And I don't think he ever forgets a thing."

"He sends you his diaries?"

"He told you about those? Well, he sends them faithfully. I don't know where he gets the money for the postage, but he always manages. I wish he'd say a little more about his experiences, but he doesn't. He just talks about the history of wherever he happens to be, or whatever he's seen. I've got cartons and cartons of his papers."

"When did you last hear from him, Mrs. Tyler?"

"Let me go look." The receiver thudded and in the background I heard unintelligible voices. In a moment the woman picked up the phone again. "The last thing I have from Wesley was mailed at the Forest Service ranger station in Springerville, Arizona. The postmark says October seventh. I was happy that he was heading south with late fall coming on. You know, once he spent the winter in the Dakotas."

"That must have been an experience," I said, mentally picturing Wesley Crocker pushing a bicycle through five feet of snow.

"Not one I'd cherish, I'm sure," Elna Tyler said. "Now, are you sure there's nothing I can do? Wesley's all right?"

"He's fine. As I said, we called as part of a routine background check."

"Well, now, I'm relieved. Talking to that other officer made it sound like Wesley had tried to steal the atomic bomb or something."

I didn't comment on Thomas Pasquale's phone technique, but I said, "I'll tell Wesley to drop you a line, ma'am."

She laughed. "That'll be the day. He'll send me another page of historic trivia, but nothing about himself. I've learned not to worry about him anymore, I guess. He'll go his own way. The rest of us should have such a full life."

With a promise that I'd keep her posted about any new developments and that I'd let her know when her brother hit the road again, I hung up and glanced at the clock. In another five minutes, the buses would start to roll into the Posadas school parking lot. The patrol cars and the yellow crime scene ribbon would fuel plenty of talk. Among those three or four hundred teenagers, there would be some who knew a little about fifteen-year-old Maria Ibarra.

Maybe one or two would know quite a bit.

9

I entered Principal Glen Archer's office with relief. The halls behind me were filling rapidly with noisy kids, a vast sea of people-to-be, and Archer's office was a quiet island. I had met Sergeant Robert Torrez in the lobby and reminded him that I didn't want Officer Thomas Pasquale out of his sight for ten seconds. I had no illusions that they would find anything under the bleachers beyond what we already had. But daylight was always a different story. We could always hope.

By the time Torrez and Deputy Eddie Mitchell finished combing the bleachers and the rubble under them, we'd be sure.

Archer closed the door and indicated a couple of chairs. "Sit, sit," he said to Estelle and me. His forehead was furrowed with worry and fatigue. "This has really thrown us for a loop. I just can't believe it. This is the sort of thing that happens in big cities." He shook his head. "It still might have been better if we'd just closed for the day." He glanced at me and didn't receive any support. "Do you want the counselor in on this?"

"Not just yet," I said.

"Coffee?"

"No, thanks. Glen, what can you tell us about Maria Ibarra?"

He sat down heavily and rubbed his face. His complexion was pasty from lack of sleep and marbles could have tracked in the dark gutters under his eyes. "Before we get into that, let me ask you something. None of the deputies I spoke with earlier this morning would say whether this is a murder we're working with, or what. I mean, what exactly happened to this girl, do we know?"

"Not yet. Dr. Guzman is working up a preliminary autopsy. Until he gives us something..." I shrugged. "Right now we're treating it as a homicide. That's all that makes sense."

Glen Archer sighed and shook his head. "I knew who Maria Ibarra was. That's about it. And that's a hell of a thing for the principal of a small school to have to say. But that's the size of it. I understand from Sergeant Torrez that you're looking for the parents." He shrugged. "I don't know how much help we'll be. I don't think her situation was too...too..." He waved his hands, groping for the right words. Finally he settled for, "I'm not sure who she was living with. I was going to do some digging, but the sergeant told me to hold off."

"How many kids do you have attending school now?"

"In this building? About three hundred and eighty, grades seven through twelve. Across the parking lot, K through six is about two seventy. Give or take."

"What grade was Maria in?"

"We placed her in eighth grade. Being fifteen, maybe she should have gone into ninth, but she was small for her age. And Pat—Patricia Hyde—thought that she wasn't ready for high school yet. She was very bright, apparently, but she spoke very little English."

"When did she check in?"

"Late September. Maybe the first week in October. So she's only been here a week or two, maybe a little longer."

"And you never met her parents? Or guardians?"

Archer shook his head slowly. "I didn't see her that day at all. Pat processed her enrollment. Let me call her in here."

"Just a minute," I said. "Before you do that, let me ask you a couple other things. We have reason to believe that close to the time that the girl's body was discovered, two vehicles were parked behind the school. We don't know yet if there is a connection."

"There are lots of dark corners on this campus, Sheriff."

"Yes, there are. How many kids drive their own vehicles to school?"

"You think a student was involved in this?" His forehead furrows deepened. "I guess it makes sense that there would be."

"I don't know." My response was bald and unsympathetic, but it was the truth. "If there was a student involved in the death, and if that student was in one of those two vehicles, then the odds are good that one or both of the vehicles that were parked behind the school last night are out in your parking lot right now."

Archer looked at me hard for a minute, then turned and pulled a black ring binder off the shelf behind his desk. "God, I hate this," he said, and took a deep breath. "Here's a list of parking permits." He spread the binder open on his desk. "We don't have a closed campus, as you are well aware. And the school board is as opposed as they can be to barbed wire and tall fences. But any student who drives to school has to have a window sticker."

He ran his finger down the column of numbers. "Right now, we have two hundred and nineteen students who have been assigned stickers." He looked up. "Do you want a copy of this?"

"Yes."

"But you don't have a description of the vehicles that you think may be involved?"

"Not yet. And as I said, we don't know for sure."

"What else can I do to help?"

Estelle shifted in her seat. "We'd like an absentee list for yesterday, and today as well."

Archer grimaced. "This is Friday, and we've got an away game tonight against Sierra Linda. The list is going to be longer than usual, but I'll be happy to get it for you."

The football game schedule for the Posadas Jaguars was taped to my refrigerator door. We'd beaten Sierra Linda once in our season opener at home, and I'd shouted myself hoarse from the top of the bleachers. Earlier in the week, during a moment of boredom, I had considered driving the ninety miles to watch the rematch.

"Did you have occasion to see Maria Ibarra while she was here at school?" Estelle asked.

"Sure. Of course."

"Was there a particular group of kids that she hung around with? Did she have any friends in particular?"

"Now that I couldn't tell you. Maybe Pat can, or one of Maria's teachers. I tend to see kids either in here, or in clots out in the hall. Bunches of them together. It takes a while to really get to know one out of many. Some I never get to know beyond recognizing a face in a crowd. You really need to talk to Pat, though." I nodded and he held up the book of parking patrons. "Let me make a copy of this for you, and I'll call her in."

Patricia Hyde must have been hovering near the office, because Glen Archer had only to open his door and beckon. At the same time I saw him hand the parking data book to a handsome kid who had been talking to one of the office secretaries. Archer spoke to the boy for a minute, giving him instructions, and I glanced at Estelle. She raised an eyebrow but said nothing.

Glen Archer started to close the door and hesitated.

"Do you folks want privacy? You want me to take a hike?"

I shook my head and he closed the door, ushering Patricia Hyde to one of the overstuffed chairs beside his bookcase.

Ms. Hyde's eyes were red-rimmed and she sat on the edge of her chair with her hands clasped together on her knees. She was a stylish dresser, pushing forty, and tending to fat. She managed a tight smile and nodded at Estelle.

"Ms. Hyde, I'm sure you know why we're here," I said. "To tell you the truth, we're looking for a starting point. If there's anything you can tell us about Maria Ibarra, anything at all, we'd appreciate it. For starters, we're having trouble finding out who she lived with."

"I think she lived with an uncle."

"An uncle? Is that this Miguel Orosco who's listed on the student enrollment form?" I opened Maria Ibarra's folder and held out the short form.

"I believe so, yes."

"Did you have the opportunity to meet Mr. Orosco?" Estelle asked.

Patricia Hyde closed her eyes and shook her head. "She—Maria, that is—had the paperwork with her the first time I saw her." She shrugged. "There was no reason to see the uncle, as long as the signatures were in order."

"Where would Maria get these forms, Ms. Hyde?"

"Sir?"

"Where would she get the forms? Here in the office?"

"Of course."

"Anywhere else?"

Patricia Hyde looked perplexed. "No. I mean, they're not confidential or anything until they're completed and become part of the student's file."

"So she could have just walked in and requested a set of paperwork?"

"I suppose. That's not normally the way it's done. Usually the parents come by and request all the information."

Estelle Reyes-Guzman reached for the folder and gently leafed through the papers until she extracted one that listed the girl's schedule. "Maria was taking regular eighth-grade courses, plus art and Spanish II?" she asked.

"That's right."

"Did she speak English, Ms. Hyde?"

The counselor shook her head. "Very little."

"But she wasn't enrolled in the bilingual program?"

Hyde shook her head. "She wanted to take Spanish instead."

"Is that usual?"

"No, it's not. But she seemed very bright. She was also very outspoken...and that's unusual for Mexican children in our schools. Usually they're quite shy at the beginning."

"And she told you that she had attended school previously in Las Cruces?"

"Yes." Patricia Hyde leaned forward and tapped a blue form. "We haven't sent the r-f-r form yet."

"Request for records," Estelle prompted.

"Right. Normally we have everything sorted out by about Christmas." Ms. Hyde's smile was tight and humorless.

"Ms. Hyde, did Maria ride a bus to school?"

"No. She told me that her uncle brought her and picked her up."

Estelle frowned. "And the uncle lists a post office box in Las Cruces as an address. Had he moved here, do you know?"

"I don't know that. I guess that I just assumed that he had."

The counselor's voice had taken on an edge and Estelle held up a hand. "Please, I'm not being critical of your procedures, Ms. Hyde. I understand that this is a public institution." She smiled that wonderful, warm, electric smile that lit up her otherwise dark features. "What was it that Mr. Gordon used to say to all the kids who tried to ditch his American History class…'If you don't walk through the door, I won't have to try to teach you.'"

Ms. Hyde almost smiled, and so did I. Every one of my own four children had suffered through Wyatt Gordon's classes. If they ever ditched, they had the sense not to tell me.

"The only paperwork that a student absolutely has to have before they're allowed to continue coming to school is their immunization record. That's state law."

"Maria had hers?"

Ms. Hyde shook her head. "She said that her other school had the copy and would be sending it."

"Is that something that you check up on fairly quickly?" I asked.

"Dawn Paddock would."

"We'll check with her," I said, then added, "in the few days that you've had the opportunity to work with her, did Maria seem to have any particular circle of friends? Anyone she talked to?"

"No, and that's something we work on. The person who could tell you more is Maria's Spanish teacher, Roland Marquez."

"Do you want me to call him in here?" Archer said, rising from his chair. A knock interrupted us, and Archer crossed to the door and opened it. "Ah, good. Thanks, Denny," he said, accepting the parking book and copies from the office aide. He closed the door and handed the copies to me.

"Yes," I said. "We'd like to meet with Mr. Marquez briefly. But before we do, I have a request."

"Sure."

"I don't mean to be unreasonable, but when we request information, would it be possible for it to go directly from you to us, rather than by way of the students?"

Archer frowned and looked perplexed. "I don't follow."

I held up the copies. "The young man who made these. I assume he's a student?"

Archer opened his mouth to say something, and before any sound came out, the light came on in his head. "And I'm sorry. I just now realized. The contents of the book aren't confidential, but there's certainly no need for anyone to know that you requested those contents."

"Exactly," I said. "He talks, and then and then and then. And pretty soon, if we're not careful, the killer knows what move we're making before we make it. I'd rather that didn't happen."

Archer took another deep breath and I felt a twinge of sympathy for him. He glanced at his watch. "I really need to say something this morning on the announcements. Any suggestions?"

I glanced at Estelle and then at the poster on the wall behind her. The bold red letters announced 101 WAYS TO PRAISE A CHILD. "Glen, that's your department. I'm not much into warm fuzzies or sugar-coating explanations." I heaved myself to my feet. "You might tell 'em that if anyone goes behind the school and crosses the crime scene ribbon, they'll be arrested. Other than that, I can't think of a thing. Unless you think it would work to say, 'Will the useless son of a bitch who killed Maria Ibarra come to the office immediately.'"

Glen Archer winced and looked at Patricia Hyde. "I wish it would be that easy."

"So do we, Glen. Just keep your eyes and ears open. Let us know if you hear anything."

10

We didn't spend long with Dawn Paddock. I got the impression that her reaction to our presence was to protect her turf. It was neat turf, with precisely lettered labels and color-keyed folders, filled with whatever information school nurses collect in their off moments between patching up the losers of hallway brawls. But she had never met Maria Ibarra. She had no records, immunization or otherwise, for the girl.

"You know," Ms. Paddock said, and stuck a pencil into her hair bun as if that ended that, "we can't force them to bring in their records."

"I understand that," Estelle Reyes-Guzman said quietly. "How long does the school generally give them? Before they're no longer admitted."

"To get their shots, you mean? Well, the state says that if they don't have up-to-date immunization records, they can't be allowed in school, period. Not one day. But..." And she hesitated and shrugged.

"But obviously they are," I said.

"If nothing is forthcoming in a week or two at most, then we call the parents and have them come in and pick up their child. We tell the parents face-to-face that the child may not return until we have a note from the physician stating that their immunizations are current."

"And that wasn't done with Maria Ibarra?" I asked.

"Not yet." She turned and scanned the files again in the open top drawer of the cabinet, her fingers pausing in the I-J-K section.

"As you can see, I haven't even received the registration papers on the young lady. I don't have a folder for her. When I do, then the process starts."

Estelle was frowning, maybe at Paddock's cheerful implication that someday she would receive a file folder on Maria Ibarra. "It seems like it should be a straightforward process," she said.

"It would be very simple if all children had responsible parents," Ms. Paddock said. "But they don't."

"Or parents at all," Estelle muttered, and she turned quickly toward the door. I thanked Nurse Paddock and followed Estelle out into the hallway. She leaned against the wall, her shoulder against one of the lockers. Down the hallway a solitary student disappeared into one of the classrooms and then the place was quiet. Estelle squinted at the floor as if she were counting the polished tiles.

"What's the matter?" I asked.

She blinked a couple of times and then shut her eyes. "I can't believe this," she said finally. "A child is murdered sometime early in the evening, but no one calls to report her missing." She tipped her head back and stared at the white acoustical ceiling tiles. "And then we come here and find that their records of this girl are all but nonexistent. They don't know who she was living with, or where, or anything else." She turned to glare at me. "Do you think that they would have bothered to put her on the absentee list today if her body hadn't been found?"

"I'm not sure that's fair, Estelle."

Her laugh was bark short. "Neither is being murdered."

The door behind me opened and interrupted my reply. The nurse beckoned. "There's a call for you on line one, sir. You can take it in my office if you like."

Estelle Reyes-Guzman hadn't moved a step when I rejoined her.

With a hand on her elbow, I started down the hallway. "They think they found Miguel Orosco," I said. "I know who they found, and I hope to hell they're wrong." Estelle looked puzzled, but fell in step.

We drove into the gravel driveway of the Ranchero mobile home park. As the crow flew, the place was less than a quarter mile from my own home on Guadalupe Terrace. But that quarter mile was a world away. The manager of the park, if he was home, didn't come out to greet us.

At the far end of the park, beyond the last trailer, I saw Sergeant Torrez's patrol car. As we idled to a stop, Torrez got out and pointed toward the interstate embankment behind the hedgerow. That wasn't what he meant, though.

"Somebody lives back there?" Estelle asked as we got out of the car.

"The wrong Orosco," I said wearily.

Three enormous cottonwoods shaded the postage stamp of land where Manny Orosco lived behind the Ranchero mobile home park, separated from the park's patrons by a thick, unkempt hedge of scrub elm, locust, and cactus.

Over the years, Manny had squatted here and there around Posadas, living with his bottle in complete, alcoholic contentment until someone became irritated enough at his presence to evict him. I never thought much about him, guessing that most villages had their own version of Manny Orosco's adventures.

The Ranchero manager had started to erect a tall board fence across the back of his property to close out both the eyesore of Manny's camp and to help cut down on the continuous drone of the interstate. He had three posts in the ground for starters. The fence was a long-term project, so Manny must have been keeping to himself, not bothering the park patrons.

I could see why the Ranchero manager had started the fencing project. Those cottonwoods were the only touch of grace for the spot that Manny Orosco called home. Behind those trees was a ditch that, before the interstate had been bladed through, had been part of the Arroyo Escondido. On the far side of the junk-filled ditch was the upsweep to the interstate right-of-way. Orosco had found himself a tiny sliver of land on which to squat. A week's research in the county courthouse might have turned up the original owner of the land, but I wasn't willing to place bets.

Orosco's home was a delivery truck, the tall boxy kind with slab windshield halves favored by tool vendors and package delivery firms. Its driver's-side glass had been replaced with cardboard, but that didn't matter. Its driving days were over.

"You're kidding," Estelle Reyes-Guzman said. Torrez wasn't, of course, even if he knew how.

"I think you've got the wrong Orosco, Bobby," I said.

"You know who lives here?" Estelle asked.

"Sure," I said. A narrow path led through the tangle of underbrush. I stepped into the clearing by the truck and stopped. The old vehicle sat nearly level, a stack of boards supporting each corner of the suspension. Its broad, windowless flanks had faded to a blotchy pattern of muted camouflage.

"He's home?" I asked, and Torrez nodded.

"Eddie Mitchell found him, sir," he said.

"That wouldn't take much looking," I snorted. "And Eddie thinks this is where the girl was living?" I didn't wait for an answer, but circled around to the rear double doors. One of them was ajar and I pushed it open.

Manny Orosco was either dead or sleeping through the first half of another day. He lay on what had once been an army cot, a blanket wadded up under his head. The cot was jammed against one wall. Above his head was a row of metal bins welded to the bulkhead, low enough to knock him senseless if he arose suddenly. But he wasn't apt to do that. A rap or two wouldn't have hurt his pickled brain anyway.

I stepped into the truck, surprised that the place didn't smell worse than it did. His mouth open and a wet spot on the rough blanket under his head, Manny Orosco lay on his left side, curled up tightly. If he'd had his thumb stuck in his mouth, he'd have looked like a fifty-year-old infant.

"Mr. Orosco?" I said loudly. I might as well have been talking to the truck. I touched his neck and felt a ragged but strong pulse. His breathing was even and gentle.

"A late riser," Estelle said from the doorway.

I nudged the bottle of cheap sherry that stood corked near the cot. There were a couple of ounces left. "And then he can have breakfast," I said.

I stood up, holding one of the wall bins to steady myself. The truck was stuffy and dark. "No running water, no electricity, no nothing," I said as I surveyed the interior of the truck. I made my way forward, toward the cab. In one corner just inside the sliding front door was a dark mound, maybe Manny's laundry for the year.

The front door was closed. I tried the latch and the door slid back easily, letting in a flood of light. I stood for a moment, one hand on the bulkhead just behind the driver's seat, trying to make sense out of what I saw.

It wasn't laundry that was in the corner. The neatly folded blanket rested on top of a pad made from an old, quilted bedspread. It would have made a nice bed for a pet spaniel.

I bent down with a grunt and picked up a spiral notebook and what looked like a math textbook.

"Son of a bitch," I murmured. "Accommodations for one more." I flipped open the notebook and even my tired old eyes had no trouble reading the neat, angular script.

"Maria Elena Ibarra, period six. Mr. Wilkie." I looked up at Estelle and added, "Problem set 5." I extended the notebook toward her.

"I thought you said..."

I dropped the notebook and math book back on the blanket. I felt like I had to vomit, and I stepped quickly out of the old truck, nearly losing my balance. I steadied myself against the warm metal.

"Are you all right, sir?"

"Yeah, fine," I lied. "And I was wrong about Manny Orosco, too. Or Miguel, or whatever his name really is."

"What was the girl doing here?" Estelle stood by the back door, refusing to enter. Manny Orosco slept on.

"I don't know," I said. "Maybe Manny bought himself a young wife."

"That's not funny, sir."

"Indeed it's not. Neither are any of the other possibilities." I motioned to Sergeant Torrez. "Call an ambulance to pick up Mr. Orosco. As soon as the docs say he's detoxed enough to understand you, take him into custody. Charge him with felony child abuse for starters. If the hospital doesn't think it's wise to have him go cold turkey in a cell, make arrangements for a secure room at the hospital. I don't want him crapping out on us."

I took a deep breath and pushed myself away from the truck. "As soon as he's coherent, let me know."

"Will you help me here, sir?" Estelle asked. "I'd like to take this place apart one small piece at a time. There have to be some answers in there."

I nodded. Some answers would be a welcome change.

11

Maria Elena Ibarra had lived inside the old truck for an indeterminate period of time. That's what an hour of meticulous searching told us. We didn't know exactly when she'd last been there, or for how long she'd been a full-time resident of one of the village's more dismal corners.

After Estelle took hair samples from the bedding, she bagged the quilt and blanket. The material wasn't fresh from the cleaners, but it was tolerable.

"She'd have to curl up like a cocker spaniel to fit on that bedding," I muttered, but Estelle looked almost relieved.

"At least she wasn't sharing the cot with the drunk," she said. "Better to curl up in any corner than to put up with that."

"Let's hope so," I said, realizing as I said it that Maria was long past caring.

Where the girl had attended to the other of life's functions that most of us performed with some privacy was another question to which there were no obvious answers.

Hung from the aluminum frame of the driver's-side window were changes of clothing, kid-sized. The two wire clothes hangers seemed like an unexpected luxury. None of the clothing was freshly laundered, but it would pass casual inspection. "She favored blue," I said and unhooked the hangers and handed two blouses to Estelle. "What's the label say?"

Estelle ruffled the collar and cocked her head. "One is from Price World, and that could be anywhere in the Southwest." She opened the other collar. "This one was made in Mexico. What about the slacks?" I unhooked the single pair of dark blue slacks from the window track and handed them to Estelle. "Mexican," she said after a glance.

"And that's it," I said. Estelle handed the sacked collection to me to hold and then bent over and retrieved a small plastic bag that had been shoved down beside the driver's seat. She opened it and scanned the contents.

"Not quite all. There are maybe three pairs of socks and a change or two of underwear here."

I added that to the collection while Estelle contorted herself downward in the door well so she could see under the driver's seat. "Here we are," she said with interest, and then added, "huh."

"Do you want another evidence bag?"

"Yes." After a minute she turned slightly to one side so she could swing her arm free. I held out the clean evidence bag and into it she dropped a chunk of fried cherry pie, the kind sold in any convenience store anywhere in the country. The wrapper was neatly folded over the open end.

"I don't know of a teenager alive who only eats half of something like that and stashes the rest for later," I said.

"Maybe she didn't know for sure when her next meal was coming," Estelle said quietly. "And maybe no one told her she could get a free lunch at school."

"The only food Orosco believed in was alcohol," I said.

She nodded and pointed at the piece of pie with her lips, like an Indian. "The date on the wrapper is current. Maybe somebody will remember her buying it." She shifted position and grunted. "This was her private spot." She handed me a twenty-four-count bottle of aspirin with less than a dozen tablets remaining.

"Pie and aspirin?" I said.

"Ah, there's some more stuff here." And one by one, the contents of Maria Ibarra's stash went into the evidence bag. One nail file, nearly new. Half a card of bobby pins. One small tube of toothpaste, hardly squeezed. That made sense, since we didn't find a toothbrush. A plastic cup showed traces in the bottom of what might have been cola. The price bar-code label was still on the underside.

"I think that's it, sir," Estelle said, and she took another minute to probe under the broken seat's springs with her flashlight. I leaned back against the bulkhead and shook my head.

"A talented little girl," I said.

"Sir?"

"To survive like this, even for a couple weeks. What kept her from just running?"

"Nowhere to run to." Estelle pushed herself upright and looked askance at me. I made no effort to move, and she held out a hand for the bag. "Are you all right, sir?"

"Yes," I said. I stepped past her, down to the sliding door. "Just disgusted. Hell, this is not much more than a good shout from my place across the way." I waved a hand toward the south. "I've got more room in my smallest closet than there was in this kid's master bedroom."

She reached out a hand and touched me on the arm, one of those feather-light grace notes that Estelle used instead of speech. "I'll get my camera," she said, and she walked back toward the patrol car. I grunted and followed, head down.

"I'll sit in the car and try to get my thoughts together while you finish up," I said. But, by the time Estelle had made Kodak happy with her last roll of film, I hadn't made much progress adding anything up.

Deputy Eddie Mitchell arrived less than a minute after we called him, and he and I strung a yellow crime scene ribbon around the pathetic truck and the immediate grounds. When we were ready to leave, Estelle started toward the passenger side of the patrol car. I waved her away. I didn't want to drive. That would mean I would have to pay attention to the world. I plopped down on the passenger seat and gazed out the windshield.

We drove out of the mobile home park, and my eyes shifted to the right-side rearview mirror. By tipping my head a bit, I could see the tangle of trees behind us and glimpse a faint hint of yellow here and there.

"Sir?"

I realized with a start that Estelle had been talking to me. She turned the patrol car onto Grande Avenue and we headed toward downtown Posadas.

"Do you have any ideas?" she said again and I pulled myself out of whatever reverie I'd been in.

"No." I knew that I sounded curt, but that was it. I had nothing. "I've got lots of questions, that's all."

"It should be simple enough finding out how the girl came to be linked up with Orosco. Maybe he really is her uncle. When he dries out a little, we'll get some answers."

"Stranger things have happened," I said, and Estelle shot a quick glance at me.

"No, I'm serious, sir," she said. "There's a possibility that her family in Mexico just sent her up to live with him, maybe assuming that he was well-off or some such."

"Or some such," I said. "You think they just packed her in the back of a truck under a load of watermelons and told the driver to dump her off when he got to the Posadas overpass?"

"Remember last year?"

"Yes, I do remember last year. I remember it very well." And anyone would have who'd smelled the stench when the young state police officer and I had pried the back door open on a van that he'd stopped just across from the motel on the east edge of town. I'd been sitting in the motel's café at the time, drinking iced tea. I saw the stop and knew damn well what was coming, even if the rookie trooper didn't.

By the time the van was unloaded, there had been nineteen confused, sweating, frightened aliens lined up on the shoulder of the interstate awaiting the friendly escort of the U.S. Border Patrol. Three more inside the van awaited the coroner, because heatstroke had killed them deader than desert sand.

Estelle turned onto the street in front of Posadas General, and as she guided the car into a slot in staff parking, I saw Sheriff Martin Holman's brown Buick parked in one of the doctors' spots.

I turned in the seat and rested a hand on the dashboard. "Tell you what," I said, and then stopped. With one eyebrow cocked, Estelle waited for me to finish the thought. "Why don't you drop me off at home."

"Sir?"

"At home. There are a couple of things I'd like to take care of, and sure as hell Manny Orosco is going to wait. Even if your husband pumps him dry, he's not going to be coherent for quite a while." I looked across at the Buick. "And I don't feel like talking to Marty right now. I'm not ready to answer stupid questions." I turned and grinned at Estelle. "I feel too stupid myself at the moment."

She pulled the patrol car in reverse without a word, and in five minutes we turned onto Guadalupe Terrace.

My five acres were overgrown with gigantic cottonwoods and brush, shielding my sprawling adobe house from neighbors and noise. I had always thought of the place as a perfect hideaway for an old insomniac like myself. I did my best thinking either there or in a patrol car, and this time the patrol car wasn't working.

Estelle stopped the car in my driveway. "Is there anything in particular you want me to do beyond...?"

"Beyond what you're already going to do? No. I'll get in touch with you after lunch. By then Francis should have something definite for us about what killed the girl. Maybe we can ream some sense out of all this." Estelle didn't argue with me and she didn't pry. I got out and she backed the patrol car out of the driveway. I couldn't help noticing that she waited until I'd stepped through the front door before driving away.

I closed the heavy, carved wooden door behind me and let the silence and coolness seep in. Diving back in the burrow was all I could manage at the moment. I couldn't remember ever being so angry that I couldn't think straight.

I took off my Stetson, closed my eyes, and rubbed a hand on the stubby bristle of gray hair on the top of my head. Against one foyer wall, its legs resting on elegant Mexican tile, was an old hand-carved wooden bench that had been made years before by Estelle's great-uncle. Folded neatly on one end was an inexpensive Zapotec rug. I used the rug as a place to sit when I pulled on my boots by the door and from time to time in the winter as a seat cover in my Blazer.

As I tossed my hat on the bench beside it, I reflected that the rug was about twice as big as Maria Ibarra's sleeping pad.

12

I had lied to Estelle Reyes-Guzman and she probably knew it. I didn't have "a couple of things to take care of," as I had said in the hospital parking lot. If I had anything at all to do, I sure as hell didn't have a clue what it was. What was worse, I didn't have the gumption to find out.

There was probably a "to-do" list that was a hundred items long in someone's head, but not in mine.

Normally a short nap worked wonders...that was standard operating procedure for keeping my insomnia under control, and I had become adept over the decades at snatching a quick nap whenever the spirit moved me. But even the dark, cool invitation of the bedroom seemed pointless.

I walked down the hallway and into the kitchen. On automatic pilot, my hand was about a foot away from the cupboard where I kept the coffee filters when I stopped.

"Jesus Christ," I said aloud, finally giving voice to my frustration. I stood at the sink with my hands resting on the cool porcelain edge, letting things ebb and flow. Even the idea of coffee, the lifeblood of my existence, was nauseating.

The kitchen window faced north and I gazed out through the six-inch square of dirty glass that hadn't yet been covered by the energetic Virginia creeper vine outside.

If I removed the vine and then a couple hundred cottonwood trees, junipers, elms, poplars, and hollyhocks, I would be able to look across the depth of my five acres and see a vehicle if it drove by on Escondido Lane. Another two hundred yards beyond that were the trailer park, Manny Orosco's truck, and finally the interstate.

The telephone rang and I ignored it. Instead, I walked across the kitchen to the pantry and unlocked the back door. Years before, I had had visions of a wonderful brick veranda outside that door. If I had designed it just right, I could have bricked right around the massive trunk of the nearest cottonwood, including it in the terrace. My youngest daughter had named the huge, sprawling tree "Carlos Cottonwood" for reasons known only to her. Underneath that tree, and on the north side of the house, the area was cool any time of year.

Visions were about as far as I had ever gotten. I stood by the door and looked at the jungle. The Virginia creeper's trunk began on the east side of the house, and the vine had covered thirty feet of adobe wall before taking on the kitchen window on the north side. Encouraged by the cool shade, the vine had created a thick, green mat that was just beginning to brown off with the crisp fall nights.

I turned and looked at the cottonwood. It was an unkempt tree by nature, but the benign neglect contributed by my bachelor residency on the property had resulted in a creation that looked like something out of a British fantasy book.

The tree soared upward, its limbs spreading across the compass, crotches choked with nests whose tenants had come and gone, among them squirrels, ravens, perhaps even children. Who the hell knew. Dead limbs littered the ground and hung perilously from the living canopy, ready to rain down with the slightest breeze.

"Carlos Cottonwood," I said and thrust my hands in my pockets. Beyond a passing glance out the window to check the weather, I hadn't looked at the tree for a decade. Its massive root system was probably a hairsbreadth from plugging my sewer system for keeps.

I turned and looked at the kitchen window again. If the glass ever broke, the vine would find a way inside. They'd discover me one day, choked to death in bed by Virginia creeper.

As if the day held no other urgency, I wandered around the house to the garage, pushed up the door, and slid past all the junk that threatened to landslide down and crush both me and the late-model Chevy Blazer parked there. Deep in the bowels of the garage, in the bottom of a plastic bucket that was home to three sprinkler heads and a half bag of plant food, I found a set of nippers, yellow plastic handles and all.

I had never seen their jaws sprung open. I had no recollection of ever buying them, but knew of their existence in the same vague way that I knew there was a box of wide-mouth canning lids on top of the paint cabinet and a small package of gas lantern mantles in one of the tool boxes.

I went back outside, opening and closing the nippers as if trying to train them before the big event.

Before beginning on the vine, I cleared away the worst of the cottonwood detritus against the back of the house. It all made a neat pile about the size of a bathtub. It would have taken about a thousand of those piles to make a dent around the property.

With access to the back wall, I gently worked on the creeper. I didn't want to make it angry, of course, but I was determined to have a window and maybe even an outside veranda light. There was no bulb in the fixture, but that was a problem easily solved. I left an artistic sweep of vine over the light and let the tendrils drape over the window frame, cascading down on the other side to touch the ground.

With the vine disciplined and the spiderwebs swept away, I had an old-fashioned four-pane window whose glass was intact under the thick crust of time. A sponge and plastic pan were just a few steps away in the pantry and I was eager to see glass.

The grime came away in great streaks, but I worked methodically, changing the water when it threatened to coagulate. By the time I had polished the glass to crystal with several editions of the *Posadas Register*, I could see that the wooden sill and window frame had peeled until there was only a trace of the original blue paint remaining.

With my pocketknife, I poked the wood. It was sound enough. It was still early in the day and plenty warm. Another opportunity might not present itself, and I shrugged. I still had blue paint from the last time the house trim had been painted.

I walked through the kitchen, pausing long enough to pour a pot of water into the coffeemaker and spoon grounds into the filter basket. By the time I had found, opened, and stirred the paint—a color labeled "Alhambra" by some imaginative engineer—and found a serviceable brush buried under my timing light and dwell meter, the coffee was finished.

With a steaming cup of coffee in one hand and the brush in the other, I daubed at the window casing and sill, stopping periodically to critique my progress. The critique was not always good. When my brush touched the glass for the third time, I set down the coffee cup and dug my glasses out of my pocket, then spent some more irritation trying to decide which panel of the bifocals would work best.

By the time I finished a quarter of the window, I had decided that a person could spend a lifetime painting a house. My old adobe, plastered as it was with genuine, hundred-year-old brown mud, saved me that trouble, but it still had an acre of window and door trim. The trick was not to look too closely at the other windows as I walked around the building.

With the window half done, I made another pot of coffee and brought out one of my folding chairs. I sat under the cottonwood and looked at the house, deciding that I liked what I saw.

The second half of the window was tedious. The light was bad, my neck cricked, and the paint was thick and uncooperative on the brush. But I persisted and avoided painting the glass blue.

With six inches of the center mullion to go, I heard footsteps in the house. My hand froze, the brush poised just above the wood, a bead of paint ready to run.

"Sir?"

"I'm out back," I shouted when I recognized Estelle Reyes-Guzman's voice.

She appeared in the doorway but didn't open it. Instead she stood quietly, regarding me. Her eyebrows pulled together in the beginnings of a frown.

"I made fresh coffee," I said, and pointed toward the kitchen with the brush.

"No thanks." She pushed the door open and stepped out. Her deep brown eyes traveled first to the paintbrush, then to the can of paint, and then to the window. She was taking long enough to critique the work.

"What do you think?" I asked.

She looked back at me, and one eyebrow lifted a bit. "Why are you doing that, sir?"

I chuckled. "Because it needed doing. I got tired of not being able to see out the window." I gestured with the brush at the vine. "It wasn't hard. Kind of relaxing, actually." I bent over and laid the brush across the top of the paint can. "What's up?"

Estelle took a deep breath and reached out with one hand toward my sleeve. "You got some blue paint on your revolver." I lifted my arm up and peered down at the gun, not an easy task considering my girth. I frowned. It was the first time all day that I was conscious of being in uniform.

I pulled the flannel paint rag I'd been using out of my back pocket and wiped the drip off the walnut grips and then daubed at another fleck near the buckle of the Sam Browne belt. "I can't believe I did this without changing my clothes," I muttered.

"I tried to call you earlier," Estelle said.

"Yeah, I know. I heard it."

"Five times."

"You need to let it ring more than five times, sweetheart."

"No…I mean I tried calling five times. Once not long after I dropped you off, and then around noon, and then afterward. I figured you were asleep."

I stared at her blankly. "What do you mean 'once around noon'? What time is it?" I said, and looked at my watch. The hands made no sense, stuck at five after four. The sweep second hand swept methodically around the face.

"It's after four."

"What time did you drop me off?"

"About ten…maybe ten-thirty, sir."

"You've got to be kidding."

"No, sir."

I backed up and sat down slowly in the lawn chair, my heart hammering in my ears. Estelle looked back at the window. She stepped up close and examined the glass. "Nice job." She turned and looked at me. "Are you going to do all the trim?"

My hand groped at my shirt pocket, a tick left over from half a century of smoking. "Estelle…" I started and then stopped.

"Do you want me to come back later, sir?"

I shook my head with irritation. "I don't know what the hell I'm doing." I got to my feet and waved a hand at the window. "It just seemed important at the time. I don't know why."

"Sometimes you need a break."

I snorted and toed the paint can with my black boot. "I must be quite a sight."

Diplomatic as always, Estelle didn't respond to that.

"So…what did you find out?" I asked. I pulled a second folding chair out of the pantry and snapped it open for Estelle. She settled into it with a grateful sigh.

"Wesley Crocker left."

"What do you mean, he left?"

"Sheriff Holman suggested to him that maybe he didn't need to stick around the office after all. That maybe he could find himself somewhere else to stay. That's what Bob Torrez told me earlier today." Her mouth twitched slightly. "That's one of the times I tried to call you, sir. The sheriff told Bob that we didn't need to turn the place into a roach motel."

"For God's sakes, what an idiot," I snapped. "Where's Crocker, then?"

"He told Bob that he wanted to ride north of town a ways and investigate an old trail. He said you'd know."

I closed my eyes, trying to imagine the pleasure that strangling the sheriff would give me. "So he's on the loose. What else? What's the rest of the bad news? I hope Manny Orosco is still in custody, or did the sheriff send him somewhere, too?"

Estelle took a deep breath and held it as she regarded me. "Orosco's dead."

"Of what?" Somehow I wasn't surprised, but the news irritated me even more. Drunks seemed perfectly capable of hanging around for years, until everyone was thoroughly tired of them. The day that they might have been of some concrete use, they crapped out.

"Well, sir, that's the interesting thing." She leaned forward in her chair and clasped her hands together. "When we went through the truck, we bagged as evidence the liquor bottle that was lying near the head of his cot."

"The rotgut sherry," I said.

Estelle nodded. "There was no other evidence of liquor bottles near the bed. Up in one of the cabinets, I found a half bottle of that cheap fruit brandy, and a new bottle of peppermint schnapps. Unopened."

"Even Manny might have thought twice about drinking that stuff," I said.

"I don't think so, sir. Anyway, Francis told me this afternoon that preliminary blood tests showed a blood-alcohol level that was right off the charts. Over point three-five. That's enough to be toxic in anyone, sir."

I frowned. "How do you get that kind of blood reading from part of a bottle of cheap sherry, Estelle?" I could see by the look on her face that she hadn't told me everything. The light of the chase was in her eyes, and I took a deep breath, determined to keep up with her this time.

"You don't, sir. The chem lab at the hospital helped me out. The sherry tested out at a hundred and sixty proof."

"That's eighty percent alcohol. That's not possible, unless someone spiked the sherry."

"That's exactly what happened. There was enough sherry for a little flavor. The rest was pure grain alcohol. The stuff that kids like to buy to spike punch when they want a real nuclear buzz."

"Half a bottle of that would kill a person," I said.

"That's exactly what it did, sir."

13

Estelle watched me rinse out the coffeemaker and waited patiently while I dumped the filter, added a new one, and spooned in the grounds. I felt as if I hadn't had a decent cup all day, even though my blood had to be half caffeine. My stomach was growling that it was close to dinnertime. Still, dinner would have to wait.

"Now, let's see what you've got," I said, and joined Estelle at the kitchen table. "And the first thing I want to know is what killed the girl. What's Francis say?"

"She choked to death, sir."

"Choked?" I turned and looked at Estelle. Then I raised my hands as if I were strangling someone. "You mean *choked*, as in strangled?"

"No, sir. It appears that she choked to death on a piece of pepperoni pizza."

"You've got to be kidding."

"No, sir." Her face was sober. "And if that's the case, then it looks like she choked to death somewhere, and then was just dumped."

I stared at the detective and slowly shook my head. "No. There's got to be something else. If she were alone when it happened, she wouldn't have ended up under the bleachers. And who the hell would just dump someone who choked? Jesus."

"That's a good question. We don't know the circumstances yet."

"Yet. All right. What else have you found?"

"We have a list of every student who was in a class with Maria Ibarra," she said, and slid a piece of paper with neatly typed columns across to me. I sat down and scanned the names.

"This won't tell us much," I said. "But it's something. Do we know yet who she was friendly with?"

"The short list," Estelle said, and pulled another piece of paper out of her briefcase. "I talked with the counselor again this afternoon, and each one of Maria's teachers. These names are students who have been seen with her outside of class."

"Not a particularly long list."

"No, sir. Six names."

"Have you talked with any of them?"

"Not yet. I was going to start on that this evening, with the ones who didn't go to the game."

I nodded. "If any. Fair enough. Let me give you a hand. After we eat something."

Estelle smiled. "And we have a list of students who were absent from school today"—she handed me the list of eighteen names—"and absent yesterday."

The names were just a blurred collection of words to me, and I laid the list on the table. "That helps us only if the person or persons that Maria was with when she died were students...and only if that student is in one of Maria's classes...and only if that student chose to be absent from school."

"A lot of if's," Estelle said. "We don't know if any of them are close." She sighed. "And you know, the way she was living, with Orosco and all...there's no way of telling who she was associating with." She looked up at me. "We don't even know for sure if the vehicles that Wesley Crocker saw behind the school were driven by...or occupied by...students. And we don't know if there is actually any relationship between those vehicles and Maria's death."

I shook my head and got up. Enough coffee had run into the decanter that I could slide it out and put my cup underneath the drizzle while I poured it full. "You sure?" I said, and waved the decanter at Estelle. She shook her head.

"What *do* we know?" I asked, and sat back down at the table. "Other than that Manny Orosco didn't kill the girl."

"We don't even know that for sure, sir. He might have been with her last night, panicked when she choked to death, dumped the body, and drained the bottle of sherry after he returned home. Remember, we didn't find him until almost midmorning today."

"That's unlikely. In the first place, Manny didn't have a car. How would he have transported the body?" Estelle raised an eyebrow. "And I'm not sure he would have been strong enough to carry the girl's corpse anywhere. I don't think he would have thought clearly enough to even come up with the scheme. And finally, I don't think he would have bothered mixing grain alcohol, or whatever it was, with sherry. Not only wouldn't have bothered...he couldn't have afforded it."

"Probably not," Estelle said. Her voice was neutral and I looked sharply at her.

"What are you thinking?" She shifted in her chair and grimaced a little, an expression I took to mean discomfort. "Can I get you something?"

"No, no. I'm fine, sir. It's just that I can't imagine anyone cold enough to watch a little girl die and then just dump the body."

"What did Francis say about the bloody finger? The torn nail? Anything there?"

"His first guess is that it might be consistent with the victim flailing around as she was choking."

"*Might* be..." I said. "No other tissue under her nails?"

"No, sir." Estelle frowned. "And there weren't any traces of drugs or alcohol in her system, so that didn't contribute. And there wasn't any sign of a struggle, other than the torn fingernail."

Estelle pulled a small evidence bag out of the briefcase and handed it to me. I held it at arm's length, trying to bring the contents into focus. "Whose hair?" I said, taking an educated guess.

"Bob Torrez found it under the bleachers, sir. There were about eight strands caught in one of the steel angle supports, right where it bolts into one of the girder stiffeners."

"Head height?"

She nodded. "Right where someone would crack their head if they weren't paying attention."

"And we don't know when this nifty little sample was left there, do we?"

"No, sir. We don't know if it is connected in any way."

"Lab?"

"Yes, sir. Part of that sample, and a suitcase of other items. I sent Tony Abeyta to Santa Fe with everything we've got. Jim Bergin flew him up. Maria's clothing, the hair sample, the sherry, the tissue and fluid samples from the hospital that Francis gathered." She smiled. "Hair samples from Orosco, Crocker, and Pasquale."

"Tom Pasquale? Why him?" And then I held up a hand. "Don't bother. I know why him. Anything else?"

"That's about it. I thought I'd do the interviews with Maria's friends this evening. That way, if any kind of pattern develops, we'll be right on it."

I nodded. "One other thing...we don't know yet how Maria got into the country, do we?"

"No, sir."

"We need to find her Mexican connection somehow."

"Eddie Mitchell is working on that. I know that he was planning to meet with Tomas Naranjo of the *Federales* down at the crossing in Regal this afternoon. He took a set of Maria's prints, and a photograph." She pushed herself away from the table and began gathering her papers. Her motions showed signs of fatigue. "We didn't find anything in Orosco's truck that would give us a lead. No letters from Mexico, no photographs. Nothing." She shrugged. "Maybe Naranjo can help."

"And are you going to get some rest?"

"Sure."

I stood up and wagged a mock-stern finger at her. "What about dinner? You want to go someplace and grab a bite?"

"Irma baked a chicken for dinner. She told me at noon that if Francis and I didn't sit down for a dinner together tonight, she wasn't going to vote for me." She shrugged. "So I'm blackmailed. Come join us." She snapped her briefcase shut.

I grimaced and shook my head. "The way I look and probably smell, I don't think so. And it sounds like you guys need a quiet family dinner."

"Take a few minutes to clean off the worst of the paint," Estelle said. She reached out a hand and squeezed my arm. "And you are a member of the family, *padrino*." She glanced at her watch. "We'll look for you about six-thirty."

"One chicken isn't going to be enough anyway," I said, but Estelle was already out of the kitchen and headed toward the front door.

"Six-thirty, sir. Don't disappoint the kid."

I grinned at her reference to her son as the front door thumped closed behind her and the house sank back into its characteristic deep silence. This time, though, the place seemed a little more light and friendly. I turned off the coffeemaker and headed for the shower.

Just as I turned on the water, the phone rang. It was probably Martin Holman, worried about Estelle's hiring Jim Bergin, the airport manager, to fly charter. The county was strapped for funds, but she was right. We were also strapped for time, and we couldn't fax clothing and hair samples.

I hesitated, then stepped into the shower. What the hell, I thought. Life was too short. A baked chicken dinner with the Guzmans sounded wonderful. Anybody else could wait.

14

And they did wait, apparently. The telephone may have continued ringing during my entire shower. I had no idea. When the roar of the water subsided, the damn thing was still ringing—or ringing again. With a heartfelt sigh, I gave in and padded over to the nightstand beside my bed.

I snatched up the receiver. "What?"

"Hello, sir." Estelle's soft voice carried no reproach or urgency. "I was just making sure you hadn't fallen asleep on us."

I laughed. "Not likely, sweetheart. Sorry I barked at you. I figured it was probably the sheriff. I just stepped out of the shower, and as soon as I stop dripping all over my expensive rugs and get dressed, I'll be over. I wouldn't miss fried chili-chicken for the world."

"Baked chicken," she said. "No chili."

I groaned in mock distress. "But that's the next thing to health food."

"See you shortly," Estelle said.

"I'll be over in about fifteen minutes." I hung up, wondering why she'd bothered to call to remind me. To the best of my recollection, in all my sixty-four-plus years I had never forgotten a meal. Skipped a few thousand, certainly, when things got hectic. But never forgotten.

I dressed in my most comfortable civilian uniform—brown boots, khaki trousers, and checkered flannel shirt—and then took my time backing the Blazer out of the garage. I'd owned it for less than two months and hadn't yet put the obligatory scratch on it that would then allow me to treat it like the truck it was.

The Guzmans lived on South Twelfth Street, a street name that made Posadas sound like more than the sleepy village it was. I headed for their place by my usual direct route, under the interstate on Grande, then north to the intersection with Bustos Avenue by Pershing Park.

I wasn't sure what I was looking at, or thinking about. Maybe it was the cloud bank off in the southwest, hanging low over the San Cristobal mountains, promising the first fall storm. Maybe I was wondering what Wesley Crocker had found in his exploration of Bennett's Road north of town. Maybe I was still stewing about Maria Ibarra. Who the hell knew.

Whatever it was that preoccupied my mind, it was a good thing that our postmistress, Carla Champlin, was looking where *she* was going. My shiny new Blazer, with 206 miles on the odometer, sailed right through the stoplight at Grande and Bustos. I realized the light was red only after I'd passed underneath it, commanding the intersection like I owned the road. The spinster Champlin, bless her heart, saw me coming, and had time to stand on the brakes for all her spindly legs were worth.

Her eastbound station wagon screamed to a halt in a cloud of blue rubber smoke, skewed slightly sideways as she wrenched the steering wheel to the left. Her vehicle's bumper missed bashing the Blazer's left rear quarter-panel by inches. I didn't even have time to wave a greeting. As if no one were on the street but me, I continued through the intersection and turned westbound on Bustos.

When my heart started beating again and I stopped swearing, I glanced in my rearview mirror. Her car was pulling away, none the worse for wear except for the flat spots on her tires. It was twilight, and perhaps in the failing light she hadn't recognized me. I knew that was wishful thinking, since she'd had a broadside view of my startled face. Besides that, Carla Champlin never missed anything. I would get the full withering treatment next time I snuck in the post office.

I took a deep breath and muttered a curse-studded prayer of thanksgiving that Posadas was tiny, it was dinner hour, the football game was out of town, and that every other grace had resulted in there being only Carla Champlin and me on the street at that moment.

Estelle Reyes-Guzman opened the door before my finger could touch the doorbell. She took one look at my face and her eyes narrowed. As she stepped aside to let me in, her head cocked a little sideways. Her radar was working overtime, and as usual, it was dead accurate.

"What happened?" she asked, not sounding worried, but rather conversational, as if I were inspecting the sole of my boots after walking past the dog run. Before I could answer, the Guzman's two-year-old son catapulted into the room, saw me, and stopped short.

"*Padrino* is here!" Francis Jr. bellowed and charged toward me. How the genes of two such reserved and quiet parents had produced this tiny human windbag, even Gregor Mendel wouldn't be able to figure out. A lusty roar was the kid's idea of a whisper. I cringed from the attack, not because I didn't like the child, but because I was feeling a little frail around the edges. Estelle gracefully intercepted him and locked him in a bear hug.

"Yes, *kid*, he's here," Estelle said, nuzzling his ear and using my nickname for Francis Jr. The two-year-old squirmed and cackled, but Estelle held him fast. She looked at me, eyes still assessing. "You look pale, sir."

I tossed my baseball cap on their sofa, and like a small two-legged retriever the kid twisted out of his mother's grip and tore after the cap, seized it, and pulled it down on his head to the bridge of his nose.

"I ran the red light at Grande and Bustos," I said and shrugged. Estelle looked puzzled, and I held up my hands. "That's it. I ran the light."

"No one else..."

I shook my head. "Carla Champlin was coming the other way. She managed to miss me. I'm sure I scared the zip code out of her, though." I grinned sheepishly. "If she had scratched my truck, I'd have had to shoot her."

Estelle's smile was only the faintest of twitches at the corners of her mouth. Her dark eyes weren't amused.

"Hey," I said, "it happens now and then."

"Let's eat," she said, and beckoned me toward the dining room.

"Where's the good doctor?" I asked, following her with the blinded two-year-old stumbling at my heels, both hands clutching the bill of my cap.

"He had to run down to the hospital for a few minutes. Cassie Madrid is scheduled for surgery in the morning, and there was some question about her prep meds." Estelle glanced at me. "He said it would only take a minute. You know how that goes." She disappeared into the kitchen.

Before I had a chance to comment on Cassie Madrid's pending cesarean section that would produce child number ten, I heard a car in the driveway. In a moment, Dr. Francis Guzman hustled into the house. In one smooth motion he scooped up his son, tucked him under one arm, and then extended a hand to me. His grip was firm and he was in no hurry to let go.

"Bill, how's it going?" He pumped the hand another time for good measure, just enough pressure that he didn't set off my arthritis.

"I'm hungry," I said. "And this was a nice idea."

"How's Cassie?" Estelle asked.

Francis dismissed that story with a wave of a hand. "Nurse can't read," he said. He put his hand on top of the kid's head as if he were about to unscrew the top of a wide-mouthed jar of mayonnaise. "Do you want this creature in his high chair, or feeding out of the dog dish in the kitchen?" he asked as Estelle reappeared with a load of serving bowls and platters balanced on her arm like a professional waitress.

"High chair, next to you."

Francis Guzman looked eyeball to eyeball with the youngster, both big and little brows furrowed in mock ferocious combat. "But that way he'll get his food all over me instead of Bill." The kid screeched and tried to grab my sleeve.

"That's the general idea," I said.

Francis laughed. We settled in at the table and Francis said grace in Spanish while his left hand clamped his son motionless in the high chair. I don't think that the hand was necessary. As soon as he heard his father start to speak, the kid closed his eyes and froze. The truce lasted as long as the prayer. Then Estelle dolloped the makings of an artistic mess on the kid's unbreakable plate and let him have at it.

"So, how's the painting going?" Francis said. He grinned at me and when he saw the expression on my face he added, "Estelle was telling me that's how you were working out your frustrations."

"Maybe that's what it was, I don't know," I said. I looked at my plate and realized that, despite my best intentions, I wasn't the least bit hungry. I toyed with the food and then spent four times as long as necessary preparing my iced tea with sugar and lemon juice. While Estelle and Francis chatted about this and that and periodically played referee between the kid and his food, I found my mind wandering.

I had enjoyed probably half a thousand meals at this table over the years, and the Guzman home was an adult version of a safe haven for me when I got too disgruntled at the world and the people in it. But that night, it was as if my mind were somewhere else, trying to pick its way through a fog.

"We won't have the full blood run-up back for another forty-eight hours or so, but I think it's interesting," Francis said, and with a start I realized that I had drifted back into hearing range.

"Sir?" Estelle prompted.

"What's interesting?" I asked. "Sorry. I was wandering."

"Francis was saying that the preliminary autopsy showed Maria Ibarra had virtually nothing in her stomach other than the equivalent of about a quarter slice of pizza."

"Really?"

She nodded, and I was aware that Francis was gazing at me, his dark eyes doing their quiet doctor-patient number.

"She was famished then," I said. "She went after the food too fast." I grinned. "Great dinner table conversation."

But with some relief, I focused on Maria's last meal as I laid my fork across my plate, most of the food untouched. With my elbows on either side of the plate and my chin resting on laced fingers, I squinted at Estelle.

"Maria Ibarra couldn't have afforded half a slice of pizza, let alone anything else. So she was with someone who picked up the tab," I said. "We know that much." I pushed myself away from the table and leaned back in the chair. "If she was with kids, what are the odds that it was packaged pizza? The kind you buy in the grocery store?"

"Zero," Estelle said. "That time of night? Kids cruising the village? They're not going to go home and eat microwave pizza."

"Maybe not."

"And not pizza with fresh jalapeños," Francis said.

I turned and grinned at him. "This is getting even better, this conversation. But it gives us a place to start. How many places in Posadas sell fresh pizza? Two?"

"Three, if you count Portillo's Handy-Way."

"And that's just miked packaged stuff," I said. "It shouldn't be hard to track down who sold the pizza...and if we have any luck at all, the counter help will remember who came in and who didn't. It's not that big a town."

"If you can get people to talk," Francis said.

"At the moment, that doesn't matter," I replied. "Remember what it's like to be a teenager? If we find a single kid who remembers seeing Maria last night, even just one, that kid will remember who Maria was with. And a teenager with an adult? That, they'll really remember."

I reached out and stabbed the piece of chicken that I'd been pushing around my plate while my mind was off in the blue. The chicken was tender and spicy, and when that piece was gone I went searching for another. It looked like the others had finished their dinner, so I had some catching up to do. Both Francis and Estelle seemed perfectly willing to keep me company.

15

While the others waited, I finished a dinner fit for a condemned man, and then spent time over coffee, hashing out a battle plan with Estelle. Francis Guzman even spent the better part of ten minutes with us before adjourning to the living room to play with his son. That ten minutes was something of a record for him.

The battle plan should have been simple enough. My brain was clear, the paths of action seemed limited to a handful. The first order of business was to find out who had kept Maria Ibarra company the evening of her death.

What I hoped, of course, was that we'd visit Jan's Pizza Parlor on Bustos and Second, or maybe the Pizza World over on North Fifth, and find out that Maria had been seen with person X, and then we'd go arrest the son of a bitch for failure to report a death. That's not what happened.

The Guzmans' nanny, Irma Sedillos, she of the chililess baked chicken recipe, showed up at the house around eight that evening for the night shift. The kid seemed perfectly attuned to his parents' bizarre life, accepting their sudden comings and goings with complete aplomb. He obviously loved Irma and accepted her as a third parent—probably because she was noisier than he was.

"I can't watch," Estelle muttered as she closed the door on the kitchen. Neither could Francis. The good doctor had locked himself in his study, nose deep in a stack of medical journals. Irma and the kid were about to do the dishes. I didn't bother to ask what kind of team the two of them would make. Irma had to be capable of some magic, though, since the two of them had done dishes many times before and the Guzmans didn't yet eat off paper plates.

After a third cup of coffee, I worked up enough gumption to move out of my chair. We decided to hit Jan's Pizza Parlor first, for no good reason other than that it was the more popular of the two nightspots. With an out-of-town game, business would be slow. There was no reason for this game to be any different from other contests. The cavalcade of cars and trucks that traditionally followed the Posadas Jaguars' game bus out of town would have been long and vocal. The ruckus in the local eateries would start about midnight, when everyone returned.

I drove the Blazer home to its garage with Estelle following in the patrol car. Even as I swung the heavy door down, I could hear a siren far in the distance. Estelle swung 310 into my driveway and I hustled over to the patrol car.

She started to step out. "Do you want to drive, sir?"

"Go ahead," I said, and slid my bulk into the passenger side, simultaneously reaching for the radio's volume knob. The damn thing was turned so low it was an unintelligible mumble and I frowned at Estelle. "Wonderful gadgets, these radios," I said.

"It's a pedestrian accident at the corner of Pershing and Bustos," Estelle said. "Bob Torrez is coming in, but he's about twelve miles west. The ambulance is already en route."

"Where's the P.D.?" I asked, but the radio answered my question.

"Posadas, P.D. will be ten-ninety-seven." I could hear the excitement in Officer Thomas Pasquale's voice, and his radio was picking up enough background noise that I could hear the wail of his patrol car's engine as he flogged it down one of the village's quiet streets.

"Ten-four, P.D.," our dispatcher said, calm as ice. He didn't ask Tom Pasquale where he was, or why he was predicting that he would arrive at the scene before he actually did. Ernie Wheeler took life as it came. Instead he added, "P.D., did you copy three-oh-eight?"

"Ten-four. I'm on North Twelfth. E.T.A. about a minute," Pasquale said, and I wished that he would leave the damn radio alone and put both hands on the steering wheel.

I keyed the mike and told Posadas dispatch that we were responding as well. The ambulance had a block and a half to travel from the hospital to the reported accident site. If Officer Tom Pasquale was on North Twelfth, he had approximately half a mile to cover. We were three quarters of a mile south.

We flew through the same intersection where I'd run the red light earlier in the evening and immediately saw, one block west, the ambulance parked at the south curb of Bustos, near the sidewalk at the intersection of Bustos and Pershing. Two other vehicles were parked nearby, and a small crowd had gathered. Tom Pasquale's village patrol car was nowhere in sight.

"Swing around and block eastbound," I said needlessly. Estelle was already in the process, neatly shielding the accident scene from incoming traffic—including Officer Pasquale, if he ever showed up.

Several people were clustered around a figure lying at the base of a utility pole, but they didn't seem to be paying much attention to the patient. Instead, they were all looking off to the west, and one of them was pointing.

We pulled to a halt and beyond the crowd, fifty feet farther east and well across the intersection of Pershing, close to the curb, was what had once been a bicycle, crushed to junk. The street was strewn with debris. The light was not good, and I wouldn't have immediately recognized the bicycle even if it hadn't been reduced to scrap.

As I got out, one of the well-wishers shouted, "I think you got another accident down there!" He gestured toward the west. "We heard a hellacious crash, and the siren stopped."

"Christ," I said, and Estelle ducked back into the car to call dispatch. She'd take care of the radio, and Bob Torrez would be inbound in minutes. I turned my attention to the figure on the sidewalk.

Wesley Crocker grinned sheepishly as I knelt down. I had to brace one hand on the utility pole to steady myself.

He wasn't bleeding from every orifice, no bones jutted grotesquely through torn clothing, and his limbs hadn't been twisted or smashed into obscene angles. Still, even I could see that he was pale and shaky, despite his attempt at good cheer.

"What the hell happened to you?" I asked.

I moved to one side so that the ambulance attendant could work his magic. Crocker tried to push himself upright and grimaced, and Miller Martinez, the EMT, placed a restraining hand on his shoulder. "Stay put, sir. Let us do all the work."

Crocker turned his head so he could see me. "I fell off my bike, good sir."

"I can see that," I said. "You must have been doing ninety miles an hour." He grinned and then sighed as the two EMTs lifted him onto the gurney and strapped him in. "Did you see who hit you?"

He shook his head. "I surely didn't. I never heard a thing." He grinned. "I wasn't paying all that much attention, either, I confess."

I glanced over my shoulder, and then back at the bicycle. "Whoever it was came up behind you?"

"Yes, sir."

I stood at the back door of the ambulance, and the EMT gave me a few more seconds.

"Did you see the vehicle?"

"No, sir."

"Not even after it hit you?"

"Especially not then," Wesley Crocker said, and managed a chuckle. "I was headed ass over teakettle."

"Were you on your bike?"

"No. I was pushing it. I guess that's what saved me. The bike was on the street side of me. I don't think I would have been hurt much at all if I'd managed to miss that utility pole. That thing's on the hard side, sir."

"We need to go, Sheriff," Miller said, and I nodded.

"Once more, though. Wesley, the vehicle came from the west, is that right? It came down Bustos from the west?"

"Yes, sir."

"And it continued on down Bustos, or did it turn on Pershing here?"

"I couldn't swear either way, sir, but if I was to guess, I'd say it went on down the main drag, there."

I nodded. "We'll catch up with you at the hospital. Don't worry about any of your stuff."

"Oh, I'm not worried about any of that, sir. I just don't think I need to bother the folks at the hospital for a few bruises."

"Sir..." I turned as Estelle touched my arm.

"What's going on?"

"It looks like Tom Pasquale flipped his vehicle down the street. Right at the intersection of Twelfth and Bustos."

"Oh, for God's sakes."

"Ernie Wheeler said the manager of the Don Juan just called. The patrol car is on its top right in the middle of the intersection. Chief Martinez just arrived, and Torrez will be there in a minute."

"Is Pasquale hurt?"

"Apparently not, sir."

"Then let's get busy here. Let the chief call his own tow truck."

I suppose I should have felt more solicitous, but I wasn't in the mood. We cleared away oglers, and Eddie Mitchell arrived to help secure the area so we could see what the hell we had. Then I sent him out to look for a vehicle with a freshly crumpled fender.

We didn't have much. The first clear tire scuff mark showed on the curb about thirty feet west of the corner of Bustos and Pershing. Whoever had been driving the vehicle let it climb the curb on the south side of Bustos, then ran along it for just a few feet, gathering up the bicycle and flinging Wesley Crocker against the utility pole.

The bike had gotten snarled up with the vehicle, which finally spat it out across the intersection.

I played my flashlight over the remains of the bicycle. "After all those miles, some jerk does this," I muttered.

Estelle Reyes-Guzman unlimbered her camera. She knelt down and pointed with the tip of her pencil. "Lots of flat black paint on the bicycle, sir."

"Yep," I said. "Whoever did this is going to show some battle scars. Any other paint souvenirs that you can see?"

She played the light this way and that. "Lots of black. Some bright metal scrapes. We can go over it better down at the shop, with some decent light." She handed me a small plastic object. "And we have this."

It was the plastic trumpet portion of a deer whistler, those little gadgets that folks stick on their cars and trucks to warn deer out of their path. The thing was broken off at the base.

"Maybe," I said. "Or from some other vehicle. Bag it."

Fifteen minutes later, the street was clear and we were as finished as we would ever be.

I leaned against 310, my arms folded over my belly. "We still don't know if it was intentional or not," I said.

Estelle shrugged. "It could have been someone who just wasn't paying attention. They panicked and ran."

"Could have been," I said.

"Do you want to drive down the street?" She indicated westward, and I remembered Tom Pasquale.

"I'm not sure I want to see it," I said, then added, "and sure as hell, Pasquale doesn't want to see me." I looked at Estelle and grinned. "Let's go see."

16

Estelle and I had missed Officer Thomas Pasquale's attempt at high-powered, wingless flight.

The Don Juan de Oñate restaurant, home of the best green chili burritos in the Southwest, occupied the northwest corner of the Bustos Avenue-Twelfth Street intersection. Just north of the restaurant is an arroyo and drainage ditch, and Twelfth Street crosses that deep, weed-choked arroyo by way of an old-fashioned metal bridge.

The bridge is nearly a foot higher than Twelfth Street before Twelfth ramps up on its southbound approach. When patrons of Don Juan's were dining in the restaurant, they could hear the regular clatter as cars bounced from the asphalt of the street onto the old steel plates of the bridge. From the bridge, it was about a hundred feet to the intersection immediately beside the restaurant.

Fortunately no one else had been on the highway or in the crosswalk when Officer Thomas Pasquale experienced his magic moment. When it was over, we heard no call for an ambulance or the coroner, so we were reasonably sure Pasquale hadn't suffered any more injury than a slam-dunked ego.

Estelle slowed the patrol car to a stop on the south side of the intersection and we surveyed the carnage. By that time, Deputy Tom Mears had set up a detour for both east- and westbound traffic. A few patrons of the Don Juan drifted toward the street corner to gawk, but there wasn't much to see...just a trashed police car, on its roof in the middle of the street.

The skid marks and vehicular junk told me all I needed to know about how the car had come to turn turtle. My imagination had no trouble filling in the details.

Always competitive even in the dullest moments, Pasquale had been caught off guard by the dispatcher's call. Maybe he'd been trying to grab a quick sandwich; maybe he'd been in the can reading a magazine. Whatever the scenario, he'd missed the call by a hairsbreadth. Back in the car, he heard the radio traffic and flew into action, trying to beat Sergeant Bob Torrez to the scene...which he could easily have done at a walk, since the sergeant was a dozen miles out of town.

Thomas Pasquale had blasted his patrol car onto the bridge with lights and siren ablaze and awail and his right foot pasted to the floor. No doubt he hoped for a scene right out of Hollywood's best. What he got was something else.

I could picture the village's patrol car, a somewhat long-of-tooth Chevy, launching just fine as it roared up onto the bridge, traveling who knows how fast. Unfortunately, Officer Pasquale had forgotten that automobiles aren't motorcycles. There are no handlebars to haul back on so that the front wheels vault higher than the back for a graceful landing.

The old patrol car had taken the leap, nosed down, and crashed its worn chassis front-end-first on the hard pavement. Various parts gave up the ghost, the front wheels lost interest in working in unison, and after a couple of dramatic swerves that left black rubber cuts in the asphalt, the car tripped over itself and flipped.

I took a deep breath and shook my head. "Just remember," I said to Estelle. "When you're elected sheriff in a couple of weeks, reviewing Pasquale's employment application is going to be one of your first jobs."

"Sobering thought," Estelle replied. "But it shouldn't take long."

Sergeant Bob Torrez was still working the intersection, tape measure in hand. He'd had nearly half an hour to take a few measurements, and he was making it last. It was probably the most fun he'd had in a long time.

Holding the dumb end of the tape was Posadas Chief of Police Eduardo Martinez. With him was a young state trooper whose patrol car was slotted into the patrons' parking area of the Don Juan. If the trooper's dinner was cooling, he didn't seem to mind. He kept laughing about something. Chief Martinez wasn't smiling.

I doubted that Thomas Pasquale was laughing either. I could see a dark shape sitting in the sergeant's county car and assumed that it was what was left of the young officer.

"Give me just a minute," I said to Estelle, and got out of 310. Torrez saw me and I waved a hand at him, not wanting to interrupt his methodical work pace. The passenger's window of his patrol car was up, and I rapped a knuckle on the glass.

It buzzed down. Thomas Pasquale looked up at me, his face pale in the dull wash of the streetlights. He was holding a gauze pad above his right eye, and there was what might have been a speck or two of blood on the collar of his uniform shirt.

"Let me see it," I said, and pulled his hand away. The cut was an inch long, just a nick along his eyebrow. I grimaced with irritation, but it was directed at Bob Torrez and Chief Martinez for letting this kid sit there dribbling blood when he should have been at the hospital.

"I hit the shotgun rack," Pasquale muttered. "It's nothing."

I straightened up and beckoned him out of the car. "Come on," I said, trying for the right combination of fatherly and brusque.

"Sergeant Torrez told me to—" he started to say, and then stopped, remembering the basics of rank.

As we started back to 310, I caught Chief Martinez's eye. "We'll be at the hospital," I called, and the chief nodded, always perfectly content to let someone else orchestrate.

Torrez continued writing on his clipboard as he walked over toward our car. He looked up from his report as I opened the back door and slid in. I waved a grateful Thomas Pasquale toward the front passenger seat. Torrez correctly interpreted the irritation in my expression and said, "He refused treatment."

"That's fine. He'll live, I'm sure. We need to ask him some questions, if you're through with him," I said.

"Who was the pedestrian?" Torrez asked.

"Wesley Crocker."

"You're kidding. Killed?"

I shook my head. "Just bruised, is my guess. Help Teddy clean up this mess. And keep your eyes peeled for a vehicle with damage to the right front, and flat black paint scraped off. If you need us for anything, we'll be at the hospital."

Torrez touched the brim of his Stetson in salute, and flashed a rare grin at Pasquale. I pulled the door closed and settled back.

During the brief ride, the young officer didn't say a word. As we rolled past one of the convenience stores, several younger kids were in the parking lot and stared at us as if we were aliens. I'm sure Pasquale was glad that it wasn't him sitting behind the steel prisoner's screen in the backseat.

Estelle parked in the slot reserved for the hospital administrator. Two slots down, in another reserved spot, was Sheriff Holman's brown Buick.

"Somebody let me out of this damn thing," I said, and Pasquale shot out and unlocked my door. "We're going to need your help, Thomas," I said. "First, let's make sure your eye isn't going to fall out."

"It's fine, sir."

"No, it isn't fine," I snapped. "It won't hurt you one bit to have it checked. And I'll sleep better. Humor me."

He did humor me, and it did hurt. First, an X-ray technician shot a couple of pictures that proved the kid's head was still rock solid, after commenting dryly that it was a "busy night." I took that to mean he had finished a series with Wesley Crocker. Then Dr. Alan Perrone poked in three stitches that were as neat as an old lady's embroidery. Pasquale tried not to flinch.

With the officer sporting a small, rakish bandage that might be mistaken for heroic if one were ignorant of the circumstances, the three of us left the emergency room and tracked down Estelle's husband.

Patricia Schroeder, a young RN who knew my insides like a road map after my own visits to those hallowed halls, met us at the nurses' station and pointed down the hall.

"The convocation is in 109," she said. Her gaze flicked briefly to Tom Pasquale's war wound and she offered the beginnings of a smile. It seemed to me that the young cop walked just a little straighter after that. Maybe he didn't know that Nurse Pat was the wife of our district attorney, Ron Schroeder. It took more than three eyebrow stitches to impress her.

Room 106 was occupied by Peggy Hammond and her nervous husband, Leslie. Les saw us walk by and raised a hand in greeting. I nodded but didn't stop. Les was the dealership service manager where I'd purchased my truck, and I didn't need an awkward conversation about oil filters or about his wife's missing gallbladder. Next door, 107 was empty. Room 108's solitary occupant was an ancient woman with nasal tube, vein tubes, medication drips—the works. She wasn't conscious as the parade went by.

I pushed open the door to 109 with the toe of my boot. Sheriff Martin Holman was leaning against the wall next to the window, his arms folded across his chest, threatening to crease his impeccable blue suit. His head was tilted in his characteristic "I'm listening closely" expression, and Dr. Francis Guzman was ticking a series of points off on his fingers. Standing near the door was a singularly bored-looking Deputy Howard Bishop.

Bishop turned and saw me and grinned, looking heavenward at the same time.

Holman held up a hand to halt Francis in midsentence as he saw us enter.

Bishop glanced at Pasquale and said, "Cut yourself shaving?" Pasquale had the good sense not to rise to the bait.

I took Bishop by the elbow and steered him toward the door. "We need a vehicle with fresh damage to the right front, and scrapes where it's missing flat-black paint...like maybe a grill guard on a pickup. Find it for me, all right? Coordinate with Mitchell and Torrez."

"Yeah, now wait a second," Holman said, and strode across the room toward Estelle and me. Wesley Crocker was lying in the bed, watching the action with keen interest. He sure hadn't had this much entertainment up north when he'd been digging postholes for Thomas Lawton. The crow's feet around his eyes were deep against his tanned, leathery skin. He didn't look like a patient.

Having been missing most of the day, I thought it best at that moment to let Holman finish one complete sentence.

"I wanted the deputy here, just in case," Holman said. He glanced at Estelle and almost immediately flicked his eyes back to me. "I called him in here. I know everybody is tired and working triple time, but it just seemed like a good idea. Just in case."

"Just in case what?" I asked. Martin Holman spent most of his time fighting with the county commissioners over budget, something he was good at. He knew as well as I did how desperately shorthanded we were. The last thing we needed was one of our deputies sitting in a hospital room guarding the bedpans... especially when every one of the officers hadn't slept in a day.

"Well," Holman said, and waved a hand in desperation at my stupidity. "If someone tried to kill Mr. Crocker once, what's to stop them from trying again?"

For a long moment, I looked at Martin Holman. He'd recently given up his gold-rimmed aviator glasses for contacts, and I would have sworn that he'd ordered the shade called "intense blue." And despite the long day, his hair was still perfect. The gray in his sideburns had crept upward, level with the tops of his ears—just right for the campaign. Next to him, Estelle Reyes-Guzman looked about sixteen.

"First of all, Sheriff, we don't know if it was a deliberate assault on Mr. Crocker."

"Well, who's going to just drive up on the curb and hit a pedestrian who's walking along, minding his own business?"

"Anyone who isn't paying attention," I said. "And then they panic and leave the scene. It happens all the time."

"But it could have been an attempt."

"I suppose so. But what we need right now are officers out in the field, looking for the vehicle in question."

"I still think that we should leave a guard."

I inhaled as if I were sucking on a foot-long Cuban cigar and then let it out slowly, finding myself without the energy to argue. "Whatever," I said, and walked over to Wesley Crocker's bedside. "How are you?"

"Just a little sore, sir. The good doctor here worries too much."

A ghost of a smile touched Francis Guzman's face. "He's got a badly torn ligament in his right knee," he said, "and a broken right index finger." Crocker held up the offending digit, now encased in an aluminum splint. "We've immobilized his knee with a cast, but we may have to go in and staple things back together. We'll see."

Wes Crocker frowned, but I doubted that it was the treatment, or even the pain of the injury, that worried him.

"How long is he going to need to stay here?" I asked.

Guzman rested a hand on the bed frame. "Just overnight. When someone his age takes a tumble like that, we want to make sure. I want to hold him for observation, just in case."

And then what? I thought, but I didn't say it. Instead I moved closer to the head of the bed and looked hard at Crocker. "And you didn't see the vehicle?" I asked him.

"No, sir. I sure wish I could tell you what it looked like, but no, sir, I didn't see it."

Estelle Reyes-Guzman padded around to the other side of the bed, and Wes Crocker's eyes tracked her as if she were coming toward him with a hypodermic needle.

"What did you hear?" she asked.

"Well," Crocker said, and hesitated. "Nothing unusual, I guess."

"The vehicle wasn't particularly loud?"

"No, ma'am. In fact, maybe that's why I never turned around. There was no reason to."

"What about afterward, as the vehicle was accelerating away?" Estelle asked.

Crocker grinned sheepishly. "I was too busy goin' end over end to notice, ma'am. But there wasn't any big roar, or anything like that. I remember hearing the bike gettin' all mangled. That was a hell of a screech, excuse the language. But it was."

"What are the chances the vehicle is local?" Holman asked, and I glanced at Estelle.

"I suppose the chances are better than average," I replied. "There isn't much traffic on the interstate this time of year and this time of day, and few of them get off at Posadas to drive around our celebrated downtown."

"What I meant was that if the vehicle is local, we shouldn't have any trouble finding it. How many cars and trucks are there in town, anyway?"

"Probably only a thousand or two," I said. "And now you know why I'd rather Deputy Bishop wasn't tied up here."

"I can stay here," Thomas Pasquale said. He had spent the time standing quietly just inside the door.

"You sure?" I asked.

"Yes, sir." It wasn't the first time I'd saddled Pasquale with chair duty, but this was the first time he had volunteered.

I turned to Holman. "Give me ten minutes to talk with the officer"—I nodded at Pasquale—"and then I'll be back down at the office. We'll spread all the parts out on the table and see what we have."

Holman nodded. "What about Mr. Crocker?"

"What about him?"

The sheriff grunted an impatient monosyllable and thrust his hands in his pockets. "When he's released? Tomorrow morning, maybe?" He turned to Francis Guzman and the doctor nodded.

"Probably," Francis Guzman said.

Holman turned back to me and raised his eyebrows. "Released to what? Where's he going to stay? With you?" He meant it as a joke, of course.

I'd lived alone for more than a decade. I had never taken in a stray dog or cat, and I didn't leave my porch light on at Halloween. Except for Francis and Estelle, I could count on one hand the number of people who'd spent more than a minute inside my front door. I treasured the deep, dark silence of my old house. I wasn't about to break old habits and play nursemaid to a vagrant with a busted leg.

And so I was as surprised as anyone else when I said, "If it comes to that." It was about as gracious an invitation as anyone was going to get.

17

We sat in the little conference room just kitty-corner from the nurses' station. From there we could see down the hallway beyond Wes Crocker's room...not that I expected to see a cadre of hit men in ski masks suddenly plunge out of the janitor's closet at the end of the hall.

I pushed a cup of coffee across the table toward Thomas Pasquale. "You probably would do better with a stiff bourbon right now, but this will have to do."

He accepted it without relish, but the Styrofoam cup gave his nervous fingers something to play with even if he wasn't addicted to caffeine.

Estelle had her small notepad out, and I took a sip of coffee and then got to the point.

"Officer Pasquale, earlier last night, before the call that alerted you to a possible body under the grandstand, you talked with a group of teenagers. In the parking lot of Portillo's Handy-Way."

"Yes, sir."

"Who were they?"

"The names, you mean?"

"Yes."

Pasquale frowned and looked down at the polished Formica of the tabletop. "Jesus Quintana, Garrett Alvaro, Sean Best..." He stopped and ticked names off in his head, rapping his fingers against the tabletop at the same time. "I think one of them was Tiffany Styles."

"That's it? Just the four of them?"

"There were five, I think," Pasquale said. "P. J. House was the other one."

"What were they doing?" Estelle asked.

"Just hanging out," Pasquale replied. "There's a couple of video games at the store there."

"Why did you happen to stop?"

"Someone called in a complaint that the kids were skateboarding in the street and giving the traffic a hard time."

"What did the kids tell you?"

"They said they were just yelling at some friends who drove by earlier."

"Who was that?"

"They didn't say."

"Do you know those kids very well?"

Thomas Pasquale took a minute, then said, "Most of 'em. I know that P. J. House would throw a brick through your windshield as easy as not. He's a punk. I think he does the things he does because he can't keep up with his older brother."

I nodded, knowing the older brother, Ryan House, by reputation. The kid was probably valedictorian of the senior class. He also led the basketball team and played baseball well enough to set people talking about the pros.

"What about the others?"

"Well, sir, Garrett Alvaro would rather live in L.A., but he's just a wannabe. He likes to wear that stupid hair net, and those goofy clothes. It's all fake. The others...they're okay kids."

"We're told that you were a little rough with at least one of them."

Pasquale looked up quickly when I said that. "You've got to be kidding. Alvaro started to shoot his mouth off, swearing at me and so on, so I pushed him up against the front fender of the patrol car and told him to cool it. That's all. It was no big deal." He leaned forward. "Do you think there's some connection somewhere in all of this?"

"I don't know, Thomas," I said. "We're trying to build some sort of profile of the village the way it was last night. We collect names, and juggle all the pieces, and see if anything matches. Right now, we have nothing."

"You don't think the old man killed her?"

"Wes Crocker? No, I don't." If Pasquale thought the mid-fifties Crocker was an old man, I wondered what he called me.

"Or Orosco?"

"No." I stood up. "And right now, it doesn't look like she was killed in the first place. She choked to death on a piece of pepperoni pizza."

Pasquale's eyebrows knitted together until he felt the twinge of a pulled stitch. He reached up and patted the bandage gently. "Is there anything special you want me to do tonight?"

I grinned. "Make sure Crocker isn't bothered. Get some rest yourself. Tomorrow we'll see which direction we want to go."

That was unbridled optimism, of course. Unless Estelle Reyes-Guzman had a magic wand to wave, the only course of action open to us was pounding the pavement, talking to people, and building a list of names.

We left the hospital in Officer Thomas Pasquale's care—in itself a good measure of my frustration—and drove back toward downtown.

"Do you want to stop by the office?" Estelle asked.

"No," I said quickly.

"You mentioned something to Sheriff Holman..."

"True enough, but not yet. Let's get some pizza."

Jan's Pizza Parlor had about three hours before the torrent of game-frenzied teenagers struck. Jan Maldonado knew to the minute when to start worrying, and when Estelle and I walked through the front door, it wasn't the right minute. The place was quiet, with only two patrons. They were sitting off in the corner, happily stuffing starch down their gullets. Only one girl worked behind the counter, and I saw Jan's graying head back by one of the ovens.

I'd been to enough home games and the pizza stuffings that followed to know that when the busy hour hit, there would be ample staff working the joint.

Jan looked up when she heard the door chimes, and I waggled a finger at her. She grinned and approached the counter.

"You two eating?"

"I wish we could," I said. "We need to talk to you for a few minutes, if you can break away."

"That I can do," she said. "How about that booth over in the far corner?"

She brought along three cups and a pot of coffee, but I was the only one with sense enough to accept free coffee anytime it was offered. Jan returned the pot to the kitchen and then slid gracefully into the booth. I pulled out the small photograph of Maria Ibarra that Sergeant Torrez had taken at the morgue. Other than that the victim was obviously dead, the photo wasn't too grim. In fact, Maria Ibarra's expression would probably have been described by an undertaker as "peaceful."

Jan grimaced. "Is this the little girl from last night?"

I nodded. She turned the photo this way and that. "She was pretty, wasn't she."

"Yes, she was."

"I've never seen her before. Certainly not in here. And I work at it."

"I know you do," I said. "That's why we wanted to check with you first." If anyone was an off-campus counselor for the teenagers of Posadas, it was Jan Maldonado. She was a member of every civic group there was, and the fund-raisers she organized were legion. A dozen times or more a year the parking lot of her restaurant became a car wash, with kids raising money for this or that.

"What do her folks have to say?" Jan asked, then held up a hand. "I'm sorry. You probably can't talk about it." But she waited for an answer anyway.

"She was living with Manny Orosco, Jan," I said, and her eyes went wide.

"You're kidding."

"No. What we really need to know is who the girl was with last night. If she was with kids, then it makes sense that she might have stopped in here."

"I know she didn't," Jan said and returned the photograph with a sigh. "I wish I could be of more help. And you know, they might have been using the drive-up window. Or whoever was with her might have left her in the car while he came inside."

I nodded. "We're aware of all the possibilities." I smiled and slid out of the booth with a grunt. "We were hoping that we'd get lucky."

"Do you have an estimate of how many take-out orders of pizza you sold last night?" Estelle asked. She hadn't moved from her seat, and Jan turned and knelt with one knee on the opposite seat cushion.

"Oh, probably fifteen or twenty. It's always slow on Thursday night."

Her answer obviously scotched whatever idea Estelle had been brewing, because she just shook her head with impatience and put her notebook away. She took her time getting out of the booth. We were almost to the door when Jan raised a hand and beamed at her. "How's the campaign trail, by the way?"

Estelle made a face. "I've never seen it," she said and nodded at me. "He makes me work all the time."

"Come on, sir," Jan said. "The first female Hispanic sheriff in the history of the state. It'll put us on the map."

"How incredibly politically correct," I muttered and earned a poke in the short ribs from Estelle's index finger as we walked outside. I grinned at her. "If you were Jewish and gay as well, you'd make a clean sweep."

"I'm Catholic and uncomfortably pregnant," Estelle said. "That's going to have to do."

We drove the three blocks to Pizza World and heard the same story. They had never seen Maria Ibarra before, either in, out of, or around the restaurant.

It was beginning to appear that the young girl had materialized in the middle of Posadas one day and had then gone unnoticed by the entire community—save for the person who had watched her die, and then dumped her body.

"Portillo's," I said, as we settled into 310 outside of the restaurant.

From the parking lot of Portillo's Handy-Way, we could look west and see the domed roof of the school's gymnasium and the bleachers to the north. It was an easy five-minute walk over to the school complex, and I was certain that students took advantage of that, even though it was supposedly a closed campus for everyone except seniors.

Estelle parked along the front curb, away from the gasoline pumps. The place was deserted, and the door chime was loud when we walked in. The place looked like one of those sets for a grade-C sci-fi movie about life after the blast, with everything oddly in place and tidy...but deathly quiet and void of life.

Elliott Parker was working the counter—figuratively, anyway. He was sitting in the shade of the cash register, reading. He glanced up, saw that we weren't armed and dangerous, and took his time marking his place in the magazine.

I had known Elliott Parker for more than twenty years. He had almost graduated in the same class as my youngest son, Kenyon, who had shared his consuming fascination with model airplanes.

For a couple of years, Elliott and Kenyon had been the best of friends. Elliott had stayed overnight at our house dozens of times, and in their basement lair the two boys had built models and talked about aircraft until even the Wright Brothers would have thrown up their hands in despair.

And then it had gradually dawned on my hyperactive son, about the time he turned seventeen, that Elliott didn't actually want to do anything other than talk and read and fuss with models. That was about the time that Kenyon discovered women.

The two drifted apart after that year. Elliott didn't graduate with his class at all, preferring during his senior year to take a job at one of the shops in town where he could talk and read and fuss with models. Kenyon did graduate, married his first date, joined the naval ROTC at the state university, and earned his gold aviator wings five years later.

But all that was a full career in the past. My lieutenant-commander son was stationed in Corpus Christi, and Elliott was looking at me expectantly across the counter of Portillo's Handy-Way.

I purchased a tube of lip balm just to hear the sound of coins clattering on the counter, and then showed Elliott the photograph of Maria Ibarra.

He raised his eyebrows and held his breath. "Yeah, she's been in here a time or two. Is she the one..."

"Yes, she is. When was the last time you saw her?"

Elliott frowned and pursed his lips. "Gee...I don't know if I could swear to a day, Mr. Gastner."

"But you have seen her."

"Oh, yes. She's probably been in here half a dozen times. I think she's new in town, though. I mean she just started coming in a couple of weeks ago."

"What about last night?" Estelle prompted.

Elliott Parker shook his head. "Not while I was here, anyway."

"What time do you come in to work, Elliott?"

"Four. I work four to midnight. Sometimes later, if there's any need."

I retrieved the photograph. "And you remember for certain that she was not in here last night?"

"She was not in here last night. No, sir. Now"—and his face brightened a little—"the afternoon before that, she was in here."

"What did she buy?"

"Nothing. A girl with her did, though."

My heart skipped a beat. "Do you know the girl who was with her?"

Elliott shook his head. "I've seen her a few times, but I don't know her name."

"What did she buy?"

Elliott frowned and looked up at the ceiling. The answer wasn't there, and he shrugged. "I really don't remember. I remember what the girl there in the picture had, though."

"I thought you said she didn't buy anything?"

"She didn't. She slipped a fruit pie into her pocket."

Estelle leaned against the counter and fixed her black eyes on Elliott Parker. He stirred uncomfortably. "She shoplifted?" she asked.

He nodded.

"What did you do?" Estelle asked.

Parker shrugged. "Nothing."

"Why didn't you say something to her?" I asked.

"I don't know. There didn't seem to be any point. She didn't speak much English and I just didn't want to make a scene about it. If she denies it, what am I going to do, search her? And I'm going to call the cops over a fruit pie?"

"Was that the first time you saw her do something like that?"

Parker shook his head. "Two or three times before, when she would come in."

"With the same friend?"

Parker nodded.

"And you never did anything about it."

"No, sir." He returned my gaze steadily.

"Why not?"

"Because, like I said. I just didn't, is all."

"Do other kids steal?" I asked, knowing goddamn well what the answer was.

"Sure."

"And do you do anything about them?"

"Usually not. Unless it's really serious. And they always buy stuff, too, so it's not like they're doing it all the time."

"Do they know that you know?"

"I don't think so. I think they honestly believe they're being really clever." He shrugged again. "It's just easier to ignore it, ignore the hassle, as long as they don't walk off with the whole store."

"Is that the company's policy?" I asked.

Elliott Parker smiled and pointed at the SHOPLIFTERS WILL BE PROSECUTED sign by the door.

I was glad that Elliott had found his niche in life. If he actually owned Portillo's, I wondered if he would put a big neon sign in the window that said STEAL HERE.

"Would you recognize the girl's companion if you saw her photograph?"

"Probably. She was really chubby, you know?" He held up his hands around his face. "Almost perfectly round, like a bowling ball. Perfect teeth. Smiled a lot. Giggled a lot. Looked like she probably had fleas."

"Fleas?"

"Well, you know what I mean."

I didn't know what he meant, but didn't press the matter.

"Elliott, thanks. We'll be back with a yearbook to see if you can give us an I.D. In the meantime, if you happen to think of anything else, let us know." I handed him a business card, just in case he didn't have the energy to look through the phone book.

I left the store thinking it was time to give my son Kenyon a call, even though the official date of Thanksgiving was still a month away.

18

I rang Glen Archer's doorbell at five minutes after ten that night. Under normal circumstances, he would have attended the out-of-town football game. The day was anything but normal, and the principal was about out of starch.

According to our dispatch records, he'd called the sheriff's office on the hour, requesting updates. We hadn't been able to give him much. I was sure that the good folks down at the twice-weekly *Posadas Register* were calling him hourly, too.

The doorbell chimed once before Archer snatched it open.

"Thank God," he said, and I could see his wife behind him. She was hugging a sweater around herself, her hatchet-thin face set in lines of concern. Mrs. Archer looked as if she were counting the days until her husband's retirement. "What have you got?" Archer asked. He waved me in impatiently. "Come in, come in." Estelle remained in the patrol car.

"That's not necessary, Glen. We do need to see a yearbook, though. We need to borrow one."

"Last year's?"

I nodded and stepped inside so he could shut the door.

"I tell ya," Archer said, "when I retire, I'm going to burn everything I own that has to do with education." He walked into his living room and motioned for me to follow. "Then I'm going to buy a big, oceangoing yacht. That way I won't have to live by the side of the road and be a friend to man, as the poet says. I'm getting damn sick of it."

"Would either of you two like something?" Mrs. Archer said. She hovered in the doorway to the kitchen. One hand had released its grip on the sweater and held a glass with amber liquid and ice. It looked good.

"No thanks," I said.

Archer knelt by the bookcase in the corner and selected the last in a long row of high school yearbooks. "Here you are," he said. "You don't have a set of these down at the sheriff's department?"

"No. But about fifteen years ago, we did buy a new dictionary." I grinned. "We like to keep up, you know."

Archer looked at me sideways and cocked an eyebrow. He waved at the couch. "Sit, sit. You have to look at it somewhere, and this is more comfortable than your office."

"I'd like to, but we can't," I said. "We don't know who we're looking for, but we've found a possible witness to make an identification."

"Someone who was seen with Maria Ibarra, you mean?"

"Maybe."

"Well, good luck. And would you call me the minute you know something? I don't care what time of day or night it is." He followed me back toward the front door. I promised Archer we'd keep him posted, and I stepped back out into the night air. The light breeze felt good.

I settled back in the car seat and looked at the yearbook during the few seconds that the dome light was on. On the cover, superimposed across some sort of modern art design that looked like a geranium squashed by a car, was the single word *Promises*.

"Back to the store?" Estelle's quiet voice asked.

"Back to the store. Maybe we'll get something positive. That way there'll be a tidbit to throw to Marty Holman. Otherwise his ulcers will keep him up all night."

The process was easier than I would have imagined. Elliott Parker was still behind the counter, still reading his magazine, still pleasantly vague. He accepted the yearbook without comment and flipped open to the first section of photographs...the class of 2000, the current crop of freshmen at Posadas High School.

In less than two minutes, he said, "That's her, right there."

He spun the book around and pushed it toward me, keeping his index finger on the third photo from the left in the second row from the bottom.

Staring up at me was a blurry image that could have been anybody or anything. I cursed while I fished out my glasses. While I was fussing, Estelle found the name that corresponded with the photograph. With my bifocals on, the image sharpened and became Vanessa Davila.

Elliott Parker's earlier description was accurate. Vanessa Davila was as round as they come, with a wide mouth, great pudgy cheeks, dark eyes almost hidden behind heavy brows, and a forehead that narrowed up into her hairline so that her head looked like an overweight teardrop. While most of the photographs on the page showed amorphous little kids with too many teeth and strange hair, Vanessa's photo promised an imposing figure. Her shoulders jutted out platform-straight, right out of the picture.

Her smile was sweet enough. She looked as if she were about to be handed a bag of jelly doughnuts. She also looked tough enough that if you didn't give her the doughnuts, she'd break your arm.

"Shoplift mostly candy, does she?" I asked, and Estelle elbowed me and frowned. "Sir…"

"Sorry," I said. "Are you sure that's her?"

"Absolutely," Elliott said. "How could I mistake her?"

"And she was with Maria several times? You heard them speak to each other?"

Elliott nodded.

"They spoke Spanish?"

He nodded again.

"Do you understand Spanish?"

He shook his head.

"Is there anything else about her that you know? Where she lives, or who her parents are, or a boyfriend, or anything like that?" Elliott Parker's head wobbled one last time. He was not a well of information, but he'd given us a start.

I closed the yearbook and rapped it on the edge of the counter. "Thanks, Elliott. We'll be in touch." He was still standing behind the counter when we left, probably not caring a lick whether we were ever in touch or not.

On the second visit, Glen Archer met us at the door before I had a chance to reach for the doorbell.

"Success?" He held the door open.

"We have a picture for you to look at, anyway," I said. I opened the yearbook and indicated Vanessa Davila. "Do you know her?"

Archer's reaction was an immediate grimace. "Uh," he said. "I guess I shouldn't be surprised. Vanessa is not one of our rising stars, Bill. I imagine that the instant she turns sixteen, she'll be history as far as we're concerned. And probably just as well." He closed the book. "You know her."

"I do?"

"Or at least you know the family. Remember when her brother killed himself four or five years ago?"

I frowned. "I should, but I don't," I looked at Estelle. She shook her head, and I was glad I wasn't the only one drawing a blank.

Archer continued, "He gave us more than our share of trouble, although I wouldn't have wished an end like that on him. Anyway, his sister is something else, too. She's absent from school more than she's present, which I assume is a plus as far as her teachers are concerned."

"It appears Maria Ibarra linked up with her," I said.

Archer nodded. "I'm not surprised. Vanessa likes to have lots of friends in attendance. That's usually how we see her...in the hallway, the nucleus of a clot of girls, heads together, giggling." Archer grinned with resignation.

"Is she related to the Davilas who run that little used bookstore over on Goff?" Estelle asked. She was seated on the arm of the sofa and was leafing through papers in her briefcase.

"That's her aunt, Orofina Davila."

"And her parents?"

Glen Archer frowned and looked at the floor. "It seems to me that her mother lives down in that trailer park by the interchange."

"That makes sense," I said to Estelle, and then added, "Is there a father in all this mess somewhere?"

"If there is, I've never met him," Archer said. "When we have a conference for disciplinary problems, which is pretty routine with Vanessa, we see either the mother, or likely as not, the aunt.

Not that seeing either one of them makes any difference one way or another."

"Do you know if Miss Vanessa was in school today?"

"Ah, I don't recall..."

"She's wasn't, sir," Estelle said, and both of us looked at her in surprise. She held up one of the papers from her collection. "She's on the absentee list we picked up earlier. She was also absent yesterday."

I straightened up and Glen Archer handed the yearbook back to me. "You might need this."

"I'll get it back to you."

Archer waved a hand in dismissal. "We have more. Start your collection with that one. In fact, Monday morning I'll have the librarian send over a complete set. All the way back to whenever the first yearbook was invented." Archer grinned painfully, wishing his day would end.

***

Each time I settled into 310, it seemed that the seat back hit me just a little bit harder. This time, I took a deep breath, counted to five, and let it out slowly, squinting out through the windshield at the stars. After a minute I realized that Estelle was sitting quietly, watching me.

I turned to look at her and shrugged. "What do you think?"

"About what, sir?"

"About what's-her-name here," and I tapped the yearbook. "Or anything else, for that matter."

"I think I'd like to talk to her. I'd also like to know who was in the vehicle that drove by the convenience store when those five kids were on the sidewalk."

"That shouldn't be hard to find out. At least one of the kids will talk. Eddie Mitchell can do that in between everything else. Just give him that list of names Pasquale gave us."

"Three-ten, PCS."

Estelle reached for the microphone and I said, "You know who that is."

A faint smile touched Estelle's dark face as she keyed the mike. "PCS, three-ten."

"Three-ten, ten-nineteen." Dispatcher Ernie Wheeler's voice was neutral, and I shook my head. I reached over and took the microphone from Estelle.

"PCS, that's negative. We'll be another hour. What do you need?"

"The sheriff wants to speak with you, sir."

"Well, put him on." I was willing to bet that that wasn't about to happen, since Martin Holman went tangle-tongued any time he got within hollering distance of a radio. I would have lost. Holman's voice was too loud, and I could picture him leaning over Wheeler's shoulder, mashing down the talk bar.

"Three-ten, ten-nineteen."

I glanced at Estelle. "He's pissed," I said.

"Well, sir, you told him ten minutes at the hospital, and it's been more than an hour."

"It won't hurt him to be patient. Vanessa Davila is the first person we've found who might have been with Maria Ibarra in the past twenty-four hours. She might be able to tell us something. We can't afford to let her slip away."

I checked my watch. In another hour, the town would come alive with postgame madness, particularly if the Posadas Jaguars had won. "Let's find Miss Davila," I said.

I keyed the mike. "PCS, three-ten will be ten-seven at the Ranchero Mobile Home Park."

Ernie Wheeler signed off, and even as he was saying "Ten-four, three-ten," I could hear Martin Holman's angry voice in the background. I hung up the mike. "Let's go find Vanessa," I said.

Estelle turned 310 south on Bustos and the street's wide, windswept expanse looked particularly empty and bleak. She glanced over at me, but whatever she was thinking, she kept to herself.

19

The Posadas telephone directory told us that Teresa Davila lived at 100 Escondido Lane. She was listed under Teresa...not Bobby and Teresa Davila, or whatever her once-upon-a-time husband's name was. The address was painted on the gate of the Ranchero Mobile Home Park.

As the tires of 310 crunched on driveway gravel, I scanned the rows of trailers. One or two of the twenty-four units had lights burning in the windows. Otherwise the park was dark, with a single sodium vapor light near the entrance. To the north and well above the level of the park, traffic droned by on the interstate, a constant infusion of noise.

A single light burned in the first trailer, where Taylor Boyd had his office.

"I'll go in, sir," Estelle said, and parked in front of Boyd's trailer.

I watched her walk over to the porch and go up the steps two at a time, nimble as a teenager. About the fourth time she pressed the bell, I saw a light go on in the back. A moment later, the front door opened and a wash of light flooded out. Boyd's T-shirt was stretched over a belly bigger than mine, and his boxer shorts somehow defied gravity.

He looked out at our car, frowned, and then squinted at the identification that Estelle held up. Finally he stepped out on the small porch and pointed toward the far end of the park. "About three trailers down," I heard him say. Estelle didn't buy the "about" and said something to which Boyd replied, "That's right, the blue-and-white one."

He said something else that I couldn't hear even with Estelle's window down.

He went back inside and before Estelle had reached 310, the light in the back of his trailer switched off.

"The blue-and-white one," I said.

"Right. In slot three. But he doesn't think they're home."

"Why doesn't that surprise me?" I said. Sure enough, the blue-and-white mobile home in the third slot was dark. There was a porch light fixture, but no bulb. Estelle cranked the spotlight around and illuminated a sorry hulk of a car that was parked next to the trailer, both back tires flat.

"My turn," I said. I didn't take the steps two at a time. In the harsh light from the spot, I watched where I planted each foot. There were only three steps up to the door, and I was glad of it. I rapped on the door, feeling the light-gauge metal bend under my knuckle. Estelle turned off the spotlight so my eyes would have a few minutes to adjust.

No one answered my knock, so I pressed the doorbell. I was surprised to hear it chime bright and cheerful inside. Just after my finger pressed the bell for the second time, I heard a light thud from inside the trailer, and then a voice.

I turned to look at Estelle and nodded.

If I had been Teresa Davila, I'm not sure that I would have opened my door at that hour to a fat stranger on my front porch. But she did and looked up at me with unfocused eyes heavy from sleep. Not counting about a hundred pounds, I immediately saw the family resemblance. Vanessa Davila was a young, heavyweight version of her mother.

I stepped back away from the screen door so she could see past me to the patrol car.

"Mrs. Davila?"

"What you want?" Her voice was flat and featureless.

"Mrs. Davila, I'm with the sheriff's department. Is your daughter home?"

"What?" She said it as if I were speaking Dutch or Greek.

"Your daughter? Vanessa?"

"What's wrong with her?"

"Nothing is wrong with her, ma'am. We just need to talk with her. Is she home?"

"No, she's not home yet."

"Do you know where we can find her?"

"What do you want?" This time a touch of late-night crankies tinged her voice.

"We need to talk with her."

"You want to talk with Vanessa, you come back in the day time." She started to close the door.

I heard the door of the patrol car open and saw Mrs. Davila's eyes dart down to focus on Estelle as she approached.

"Who is this?"

"This is Detective Estelle Reyes-Guzman, Mrs. Davila."

"Is she the one who needs to talk to Vanessa?"

"Yes, ma'am."

Estelle stopped with one hand on the thin aluminum railing and her left foot on the first step.

"Señora Davila," she said, and her voice was soft and musical. *"¿Vanessa...no esta aqui?"* She made it sound as if it were really too bad we were missing the girl.

Mrs. Davila answered in a flood of rapid-fire, slurred Spanish that was far beyond my limited vocabulary. Estelle grimaced and then shrugged.

"Tal vez—" she started to say, and the woman interrupted her.

"Mas tarde, anoche," she said. *"O quizas manana, no se."* She glanced at me, then back at Estelle. *"¿Esta la joven en un aprieto?"*

Estelle smiled and shook her head. "No, I don't think she's in trouble," she said in English, and Mrs. Davila's hand crept up toward her throat, clasping the collar of her nightgown. "But we need to talk to her."

"Is it about that little girl..."

Estelle nodded. "Yes, señora. We think that Vanessa might have seen her sometime yesterday."

Mrs. Davila nodded vigorously. "They plan to go to the game tonight. But now, I don't know..." Her voice drifted off in that delightful habit where the speaker expects the other person to supply the necessary details. But we didn't know details, in any language.

"She went to the game anyway?" I asked, not bothering to add, "Even though her best friend just choked to death?" I didn't say it for two reasons: Mrs. Davila didn't need to hear it, and we didn't know yet what the relationship had been between Maria Ibarra and Vanessa Davila.

"That's what she said," Estelle answered, and then to Mrs. Davila, *"¿Es posible fue con varias amigas?"*

The woman didn't know, or wouldn't say, whether her daughter had gone to the game alone or with a mob, and it was apparent that she really didn't care...or if she did, she was so far from being able to do anything about it that she had given up long ago. We left it at that, and we didn't promise to return...although I had a feeling Mrs. Davila would be seeing much more of us before it was over.

I settled back in the car and looked at Estelle. "I think it's interesting that the girl comes and goes as she pleases, when she pleases. Mama didn't seem the least bit uneasy about not knowing when the kid was coming home."

"Oh, she's uneasy, all right," Estelle said, and swung the car around.

"She is?"

"Sure. But what can she say? What can she do? If she says anything to her daughter, she'd probably be beaten even worse."

"Whoa," I said, puzzled. "Beaten worse than how?"

Estelle shot a quick glance my way, and when she accelerated out onto Escondido, the back tires chirped. "You didn't notice the bruises?" she asked.

I frowned. "No. I couldn't see her well enough."

"Especially around her left eye. A nice shiner."

I hadn't noticed that, and I began to wonder what else I wasn't seeing. For a couple of blocks I just sat, staring out the side window at nothing. "Christ," I said finally. "Remember when it used to be simple? Somebody would rob a store, and we'd chase 'em. Remember that? Or they'd have too much to drink and crash into a tree? Nice simple stuff like that."

"It hasn't been like that for a long time, sir."

"A very long time. Too long." I shook my head. "A horse, gun, and badge, just like Crocker said."

"Sir?"

"Nothing," I said.

"Do you want to go back to the office now?"

"Sure. Why not." What I really wanted to do was go home and go to bed. I picked up the microphone and rapped it against the dashboard, beating out a soft cadence of frustration. "So you think the girl beats her own mother?"

"Nothing would surprise me, sir. That's the simplest explanation."

"And the most depressing. What other explanations have we got, other than that maybe the mother makes a habit of walking into doorjambs?"

"A boyfriend, maybe."

"At her age?"

"Sir..." Estelle said in the tone that she reserved for the times when my Stone Age heritage was showing. "Sir, boyfriends are possible at any age. But bet on the girl."

"She's big enough," I said.

"Yes, she is. And Mrs. Davila doesn't look like she's capable of putting up much resistance."

I keyed the mike. "PCS, 310 is ten-eight, ten-nineteen."

Ernie Wheeler acknowledged, and I wondered if Sheriff Martin Holman was still standing behind him, waiting. It wasn't like Holman to stay up during the night shift unless he absolutely had to. He preferred to meet the public refreshed and well rested, like any good salesman. I didn't have any news to make him sleep any easier.

20

Holman paperback novel as Estelle and I walked into the building. The world might have been ending outside, but it seemed to me that all good dispatchers acted as if they lived completely insulated from the ruckus.

"Where's his nibs?" I asked, checking my mailbox at the same time. It was empty, with no pink slip from the sheriff.

"He took 307 and said he was going to make himself visible."

I stopped short and turned to stare at Ernie. He was a tall, gangly kid, maybe a year or two past thirty, who would have been cast in the lead role of Ichabod Crane had they been filming the remake in Posadas. He bobbed his head as if I were about to lop it off.

"He did what?"

"He took 307, sir."

"Well, he can do that. He's the sheriff." Wheeler wasn't stupid, and he knew I didn't believe a word I said. Holman was sheriff, all right, duly elected. But he wasn't a cop—never had been and probably never would be, no matter how many rinky-dink two-week FBI seminars he attended. Driving around in his personal, unmarked brown Buick was one thing. People could ignore him.

"Where did you say he went?"

"He said he was going to make himself visible, sir. That's all he said."

I gestured at the radio. "Ask him where the hell he is." I glanced up at Estelle. "Goddamn elections."

Wheeler swung his chair around and keyed the mike. "Three-oh-seven, PCS."

After a moment, during which time he no doubt had been groping for the microphone, the sheriff replied much too loudly, "Ah, PCS, this is three oh seven."

"Three-oh-seven, ten-twenty."

There was a pause while Sheriff Holman mulled that over. Perhaps he was looking at the ten-code card on the back of the visor to find out what "twenty" stood for. Or maybe he didn't know where the hell he was.

"Ah, PCS, I'm at mile marker one eight one."

I heard a little chuckle from Ernie but kept my eyes glued to the microphone in front of us just in case Holman should materialize there. "Ten-four, three oh seven. What highway is that?" Wheeler asked. He grinned with delight, but kept the grin out of his voice.

"Ah, roger, PCS. I'm on State seventy eight."

"Ten-four, three oh seven. PCS clear."

Wheeler turned to me, and I shook my head. Estelle said helpfully, "Isn't mile marker 181 a little bit east of the Posadas County line?"

"Yes, it is. And now I know what he means by making himself visible. The school bus carrying the team comes home that way... and so do all the revelers. Actually, except that it's not our county, it's a good spot." I stepped over to the big wall map. "If he's parked about here, just this side of San Pasquale, then traffic will see him before they start down through the breaks. That's dangerous stretch of road." I stepped back from the map. "Maybe they'll think we're out in force and behave themselves." I shrugged. "What the hell."

"What do you want to do about Vanessa Davila?" Estelle asked. "Put somebody on her place?"

I nodded. "Who's on tonight...other than the self-appointed Martin?" I looked at the roster and grimaced. "Shit. Eddie Mitchell and Howard Bishop are on until midnight, then Tommy Mears alone midnight to eight. With Tom Pasquale at the hospital, the only one working the village will be the chief, which means there's no one working the village." I glanced at Wheeler. "You didn't hear me say that, son." He looked appropriately blank.

I looked at my watch. "I don't have anything cooking at the moment. I'll take 310 and go sit in the shadows. If Vanessa doesn't show up by two-thirty or so, then it's a safe bet that she's camped out elsewhere for the night. I don't have a clue where, unless it's with her aunt."

"I'll check there," Estelle said. "And she hangs around downtown a lot. She might be spending the night with friends." She opened the yearbook and showed Vanessa Davila's photograph to Wheeler. "This is the young lady we want to chat with. Vanessa Davila. She's a ninth-grader, and her mother thinks she went to the game with somebody. We don't know who. Tell Eddie Mitchell and Tom Mears to stay central and keep an eye open for her. I'll make copies of her picture from the yearbook. They need to come in and pick those up."

"Do you want this girl taken into custody if they see her?"

"Yes," Estelle said. "We do. Tell them to bring her in for questioning. Call me the *instant* that they do that."

"Me as well," I said. I didn't want to be caught painting windows again.

I parked 310 under a dense grove of elm saplings with the Ranchero Mobile Home Park fifty yards to my right. Escondido Lane was a narrow ribbon of hard-packed dirt, a faint tan strip in the moonlight. The browning leaves of the elms dappled the light from the moon and the park's sodium vapor enough that the car was invisible.

With a deep sigh, I buzzed the window down an inch and then settled back to wait and listen. It would have been a perfect moment for a cup of coffee and a cigarette. I didn't have either one. I tried to will my mind blank, but in a very few minutes, I found myself fretting about Martin Holman.

I didn't care what the voters said—this particular sheriff was a civilian by training and more important, by inclination. Hell, he didn't even wear a sidearm, not that he needed one for most of the county commissioner meetings that he attended. The patrol car he'd heisted included a 12-gauge shotgun in the dashboard rack, but I wasn't sure he knew how to pop the lock.

In his own car, he could observe events and then call in the troops if need be. But folks expected that a marked police car would respond in an appropriate fashion—and not next week. Under normal circumstances, I wouldn't have cared if the good sheriff had ridden a palomino horse through downtown while he was dressed only in his Stetson. But the bizarre deaths of Maria Ibarra and Manny Orosco had trashed all of our normal circumstances.

I considered driving east and baby-sitting, but the last thing I wanted was for Vanessa Davila to slip back home, grab her bag, and head for Mexico.

Radio traffic was slow. Deputy Howard Bishop plodded his way around the county without a word. In sharp contrast, Eddie Mitchell's clipped eastern accent kept the dispatcher busy with routine license plate checks. He was fond of driving through the parking lot of a restaurant or bar and reeling off plate numbers of vehicles he didn't recognize for NCIC checks.

A few minutes before midnight, I heard both Bishop and Mitchell call in their mileage to dispatch and request that the gasoline pump be turned on. Any blockhead with a scanner knew then that the county was lying quiet and wide open.

Tom Mears went on duty a couple of minutes later, and dispatcher Erie Wheeler went home, replaced by T. C. Barnes, a former county highway department employee who'd managed to smash himself in the tailgate of one of the county's dump trucks. He was slow, steady, and as dependable as they came. He worked nights part-time for us while his wife worked at the hospital.

After Tom Mears's initial radio check, the county went quiet...so quiet I found myself wondering if the paint had dried yet on my kitchen window.

At 12:32 A.M., Martin Holman's voice startled me.

"PCS, three-oh-seven. We've got an MVA just west of the Bar N B gate." He sounded reasonably sure of himself. Maybe he'd rehearsed.

"Ten-four, three-oh-seven," Barnes said. "Are you requesting an ambulance?"

"Ten-four, PCS."

"And three-oh-eight, did you copy?"

I could hear the roar of Mear's car in the background as he keyed the mike. "Ten-four, PCS."

I looked across at the dark mobile home, weighing my options.

"Three-oh-seven, this is three-ten."

I breathed a sigh of relief when Holman answered. I could hear his siren in the background. "Three-oh-seven." He was breathing hard.

"Martin, what have you got there?"

"Three-ten, it looks like somebody went off the road just past the Baca place. They hit one of those big boulders. The school bus is stopped, too. We're going to have the whole cavalcade here in a minute."

"Shit," I said and then keyed the mike. "Three-oh-seven, three-oh-eight is on his way. He's about six minutes out. Was the bus involved in the accident?"

"I don't think so, three-ten."

"If the bus wasn't involved, make sure that the occupants stay inside the bus. Inside the vehicle."

"Ten-four."

"If the bus was involved, make sure that all oncoming traffic is blocked, and that ambulatory occupants are escorted away from the bus, and away from the highway. No stragglers. Keep them in a tight group."

"Ten-four, three-ten."

The rest would have to depend on Sheriff Holman's common sense. I pulled my car into gear and cursed again. We didn't need a mess just now. We'd taken a step forward by discovering that Vanessa Davila existed. Now we were running backward.

I accelerated out onto Grande Avenue and turned on my emergency lights. The street was deserted, and I straddled the center line, giving myself all the choice there could be.

The town seemed to drag on forever until I broke free on County Road 43, heading up the hill toward the intersection with the state highway. The road was wide and clear, and I accelerated until an out-of-round front tire began to shake the steering wheel.

State Highway 78 split the northern part of the county as it came in from the northwest, dropping down past the airport and out toward the tiny hamlet of San Pasquale to the east. Ned Baca's

Bar N B Ranch straddled the county line, something that I'm sure drove the assessors of the two counties nuts.

Just west of Baca's front gate, State 78 plunged down through a series of roller-coaster spills as it paralleled the dry washes and arroyos cut deep into the limestone and sand. No cow with any brains grazed there. It was colorful, bleak country—the kind of place where tourists pulled off the road to snap panoramic pictures to send home to Aunt Minnie to prove that, by God, they'd been where other people weren't.

I crested a hill and saw a sea of headlights leading down into one of the deeper draws. It looked as if every car in Posadas County was linked nose to tail, forming an enormous westbound traffic jam. Leading the parade were the running lights of two school buses, and behind the buses were the winking emergency lights of a patrol car.

Deputy Mears had faced the same impressive confrontation, and he'd pulled to a stop squarely in the center of the highway. I pulled up behind him, turning my car diagonally across the highway.

With heavy flashlight in hand, I got out of the car and trudged down the pavement.

With a sigh of relief, I saw that the two school buses were undamaged. In fact, despite the awesome display of rubberneckers, the accident appeared to involve a single late-model pickup truck that had tangled with a boulder the size of a house.

Tom Mears was working inside the cab of the pickup truck with three other men, and Martin Holman was doing his best to hold a light for them. Stub Moore, the driver of one of the school buses, was standing by the door of the first school bus, and I hurried over toward him. They sure as hell didn't need me in the way over by the wreck.

"Did you see this, Stub?"

A sea of eager faces craned from the bus, and I motioned for Moore to close the door of the bus. He did, and then said, "Yep. They passed me a ways back, before the Baca place. In fact, it was about where the sheriff was parked. They wasn't going all that fast. And they was a ways ahead of me by the time we got here. But it looked to me like they might have fell asleep. Just kind of drifted off to the right, and then *pow*." He smacked his fist. "Right through the fence and into that rock."

"No swerve or anything?"

"No, sir. Just drifted over, like I said."

"Who was it, do you know? Did you recognize the vehicle?" I turned and looked ahead toward the wreck. The vehicle was a tangle, resting at odds with the boulder and the highway. It had hit solidly and bounced sideways.

"I'd guess it to be the Wilton boy's truck."

I grimaced. Who was in the truck didn't matter just then, and I stepped back away from the bus and scanned the long line of traffic. "All right. Look, let's get you out of here." I paused as an ambulance crested the hill from Posadas. "As soon as that ambulance has parked, pull your bus as far over to the left as possible and walk it on by."

"You got it."

And as the buses passed, every face was pasted to a window. In another minute, Eddie Mitchell arrived in civilian clothes, and I gratefully passed traffic control off to him. Within three minutes, the spectators were gone and the deputies had room to work.

From the first tire marks off the pavement, the pickup truck had traveled 151 feet before it struck the corner of the limestone boulder's flat face. There were no skid marks, no indication that the driver had yanked the steering wheel. Like a guided missile, the vehicle had tracked straight and true.

After being unlucky enough to fall asleep, the driver had bargained with fate pretty well. The pickup was less than a year old, with all the options. The air bag in the steering wheel had deployed just right and his seatbelt and shoulder harness had been snug. From all appearances, the truck had been traveling nearly sixty miles an hour when it had struck the rock, but the driver had been pillowed enough that the collapsing cab hadn't cut him to pieces or crushed him to pudding.

His buddy hadn't done so well. The truck had struck the rock face just to the right of center. If he'd been awake, the passenger had had one brief moment when his head-on view was nothing but limestone. The truck didn't have a passenger air bag, and if the passenger had been wearing his seatbelt, it hadn't followed him out of the truck. He'd gone ballistic and after blasting through the powdered windshield had made solid contact with the limestone rock. If the truck hadn't bounced to the left after the impact, the kid would have landed right back on the crushed hood.

I winced and turned away. Martin Holman had surrendered his place to the EMTs, and he grabbed my arm.

"It looks like just the two of them," he said.

"Yeah."

"Are you going to call Estelle, or do you want me to?"

"I'll do it," I said. As I turned to walk back to 310, I wondered if Vanessa Davila had been in one of the cars that had filed by the wreckage, or if hers had been one of the faces pressed against the bus window. The thought had never occurred to me to step up into the bus and check. I stopped and turned to Holman.

"You don't need me here," I said. "We're staking out a place at the trailer park for a young girl who was seen with Maria Ibarra earlier. We had information that she might have been at the game." I nodded down the now-dark highway. "While you people are finishing up here, I'm going to see if I can corral her."

"You'll be back at the office later tonight?"

"Yes."

Holman took a step closer and touched my elbow again. "No, I mean…really. You'll be at the office?"

I looked at the sheriff for a long minute, and then nodded again. "If the kid we're after isn't home by now, there's no point in sticking around the rest of the night watching. I'll be at the office."

"Okay, because we need to talk."

"If I'm not there when you get back, just give me a call."

Holman smiled and his eyes narrowed. "I've been doing that all day, Bill."

I didn't have anything to say to that. I climbed into 310 and headed back toward Posadas. Less than three miles from town, Estelle's unmarked county car flashed by, and my radio barked a couple of times. She'd seen me and could figure out easily enough where I was headed.

I reflected that Martin Holman had handled himself with surprising competence. Of course, it was a simple enough traffic accident, but still he'd managed pretty well. And then I realized that I was brooding not so much about Holman's performance, but about having to explain my own.

Posadas was buzzing when I drove back into town. I slowed to my usual crawl, window down and radio low. "All right, Vanessa, where the hell are you?" I said.

21

I idled past Jan's Pizza Parlor, looking at cars and crowds. The place was hopping, and I didn't recognize many of the faces. I wouldn't have even if I had been able to see them clearly. New generations of kids were passing through the school so fast that I had long since given up trying to keep track of them all.

Posadas was a tiny place by most standards. Still, I was discovering that it was startlingly easy to grow out of touch.

All four of my own kids had graduated from Posadas High School, and back then when I saw a kid on the street, odds were ten to one that I would recognize him—and probably in eight of those cases I'd also know the parents, know what the father did or didn't do for a living, know what the closet skeletons were.

Now I was lucky to recognize one out of ten. And that included the two victims of the truck crash that night. I'd heard Stub Moore mention the name, and it had meant nothing to me. Nor had a quick glimpse of the kid's ashen face as he was strapped onto the stretcher. All I'd seen of the passenger was a lump under a blanket. But I was content that I'd find out in due time who they were, and I knew that they'd be just two more faces in a passing crowd.

I swung around the back of the restaurant and parked the patrol car next to the Dumpster. The service entrance was unlocked and I slipped inside.

The smell of fresh pizza and all its possible toppings hit me like a club.

Crowded though the restaurant was, the atmosphere was subdued. The patrons didn't know whether to celebrate the winning game they'd seen or mourn for a lost classmate. But folks eat at both wakes and weddings, so what the hell. The pizza soothed either way.

"Sir?"

I turned and waved a hand in recognition at Jan's assistant manager—whose name promptly escaped me. I handed her a photocopied yearbook picture of Vanessa Davila. "Have you noticed her in here tonight?"

The young lady, a short, stocky, well-manicured gal who looked like she could work sixteen-hour shifts back to back, squinted at the photo and shook her head. "But then, we've been really busy, you know? She could have been in here a dozen times and I wouldn't have seen her."

I nodded, stepped up closer to one of the cash registers, and scanned the faces in the restaurant. There was no Vanessa.

The same was true at the other pizza joint, and at the convenience store. I drove down to the Ranchero, but trailer number three was still dark, with Mama asleep somewhere in the back.

I was no longer feeling gracious. I parked 310 and left the door open so I'd have some light. This time, Mrs. Davila took her sweet time. I knocked, pounded, rang the bell—and finally heard muffled footsteps.

Mrs. Davila opened the door and surveyed me with complete disgust.

"Did your daughter make it home yet, ma'am?"

"What?" There it was again, the automatic bastion of the deaf or the dull.

"Is your daughter here?" I kept my voice down and worked hard at keeping the frustration out of it.

"Does it look like she's here?"

"I don't know, ma'am. I can't see into your home."

She snorted and stepped to one side. "Well, then, come on in and see for yourself. She's not here."

Ordinarily I wouldn't have bothered to press the point—and I didn't think that Mrs. Davila expected my response—but it was the middle of the night, and I had nothing better to do.

"Thanks, I will," I said, and stepped past her. "Where do you think she's staying? With one of her friends in town?"

"I don't know," Mrs. Davila said, her voice winding up and down as if the whole thing was an unfathomable mystery. "I told you that before."

I stood in the middle of the tiny, narrow living room and surveyed the place. The ten-by-twelve room didn't offer much space for decorating. But it was clean and neat, even heated in winter…a hell of a lot more than Maria Ibarra had been looking forward to.

"Mrs. Davila, how old is your daughter?"

"What?"

"How old is Vanessa?"

The hesitation that followed was a bit too long for a mother, even one who'd given up. "Fourteen next month."

"Fourteen." I turned and looked at the woman. "And at fourteen she comes and goes as she likes? When she likes?"

The woman didn't answer my question, but instead asked, "What do you want her for? I deserve to know that."

"We need to talk to her about one of her friends. We told you that before."

"Well, she's not here. You can search the place if you want. She's not here."

"All right," I said. "I'd like to take a look, with your permission." That wasn't what Mrs. Davila wanted to hear, but I didn't wait for another invitation. I had no warrant, and it was my word against hers. The opportunity was there and I took it.

I sidled down the narrow hallway, past the closet door and the doors for the furnace and the front bathroom and then, on the opposite side, a small bedroom. I would have gone further, but there was no need.

Vanessa Davila was sitting in a chair by the window of her little bedroom, rocking back and forth, tears streaming down her face. She was hugging a huge stuffed skunk. She looked up, saw me, and buried her face in the skunk's silky fur. Her body, so large that it overflowed the chair in all directions, shook with her sobbing.

I didn't go in, but turned and beckoned Mrs. Davila. I was acutely aware of Estelle Reyes-Guzman's absence. If she hadn't been busy investigating a traffic fatality, I would have headed for the telephone and let her come and unravel the mess.

Mrs. Davila ducked her head in either relief or embarrassment and shuffled down the hallway until she was within arm's length. I reached out a hand and rested it lightly on her shoulder.

"Mrs. Davila, now listen to me. I know this is hard for you and your daughter, but we really have to talk to Vanessa. And it would be so much easier if you went along."

"She never did nothing..."

"I know that, Mrs. Davila. We're after information, is all. Just give us an hour or so, all right?"

"I got to come, too?"

I nodded. "We really need you to be there. Your daughter's underage. She needs you. She really does."

It was obvious that Vanessa certainly needed something. Mrs. Davila coaxed and got a response that was an odd mixture of rattlesnake venom and abject misery. The two of them slipped into Spanish and left me far behind.

At last, Vanessa rose out of her chair, still holding Sammy Skunk. Through lids puffy from crying, she regarded me as if I were the cause of all her misery. Still, she shuffled across the bedroom toward the door.

I back-pedaled out of her way, taking a step down the hall so she could walk by. Just as she reached the doorway, she turned and flung the skunk into the room. The rejected, soggy thing hit the wall near the head of the bed and tumbled into a corner.

"I'll drive you down and then bring you both back home," I said, and Mrs. Davila nodded.

"My coat's in the kitchen." She didn't say anything about a coat for Vanessa. The girl was wearing a T-shirt and jeans, and I could see her bare ankles above her soiled and stretched athletic shoes.

"Are you going to be all right?" I asked as Vanessa reached the front door. I don't know what I expected, but it wasn't what I got.

Without a backward glance, Vanessa yanked the door open and stepped out into the brisk night. I followed, but she was beyond reach. She ignored the patrol car and set off across the open spaces of the trailer park at a wild gallop.

I bellowed something but I was shouting at the darkness. Vanessa Davila might have weighed enough to squash the scales, but she was only fourteen years old and determined as hell. The last glimpse I had of her was her broad back disappearing around the end of the dark mobile home in slot 12.

Mrs. Davila stood in the doorway, her hands tightly clasped.

"Do you know where she might be going?"

She shook her head. "She doesn't talk to me anymore," she said.

"She's going to talk to us," I said, and forced myself to take the three steel steps down to the car one at a time.

22

There was no way Vanessa Davila could have hidden from me. Her trailer was the better part of a hundred yards from the entrance to the mobile home park, and it didn't take me long to grunt into 310 and slam the gear lever into drive. She had headed for the back of the lot, then doubled back, running along behind the other trailers on the far side. We should have both arrived at the gate at about the same time. I slid to a stop with the patrol car's nose sticking out into Escondido Lane, and I played the spotlight up and down the road. The place was deserted.

I cranked around in my seat and surveyed the nearest trailers. Nothing moved except an elderly, arthritic mutt who leaned his weight against his chain, front legs spraddled. He didn't bark and his tail was motionless. Maybe he was bronze.

Edging out into the street and turning left, I shot the spotlight beam across lots behind the trailers. Unless Vanessa was doing a good imitation of a propane tank, she wasn't there. I probed the dark spots behind cars and wheelbarrows and doghouses as I idled 310 down the road.

A deep hedge of locust, elm, and juniper formed the eastern boundary of the park, and from there the property along Escondido Lane was a hodgepodge of older homes with cluttered yards. I sighed and shook my head.

"Vanessa, Vanessa, Vanessa," I murmured. If she had dived through the hedge, she could be house-hopping all the way out the lane until it jogged north to join State Highway 17.

Dogs barked here and there, but that didn't mean they were watching Vanessa sneak through the darkness. In Posadas, there were always dogs barking. A home wasn't a home without a stupid spaniel or hound in the front yard, barking at the hum of the streetlights.

I accelerated hard and drove quickly east on Escondido, keeping 310 noisy until I reached the state road. There was no traffic, and I pulled out on the highway with a squeal of rubber. It was the sort of sound that would carry, even over the dogs. Vanessa might hear it and relax for a few minutes.

I drove for half a minute, then slowed, drifted the car to the shoulder, and swung in a wide U-turn.

With the intersection of Escondido Lane in sight, I punched off the headlights and let the patrol car coast. The tires crunched on loose gravel as I turned into the lane and I let the vehicle's momentum carry me along. Vapor lights were scarce and there wasn't much moon. I leaned forward, peering into the darkness, until my chin was almost on top of the steering wheel.

As the car drifted to a stop, I pulled over to one side and switched off the engine. Both windows were down and I sat quietly counting the heartbeats in my ears.

I would have felt better if, in a few minutes, I had seen Vanessa Davila's imposing figure materialize out of the darkness. Another car approached, and I turned my head so the bright lights wouldn't rob what little was left of my night vision.

It was an older model pickup, and after it passed I watched it in the rearview mirror. The occupants were silhouetted against the glare of their truck's headlights, and neither person had enough shoulder width to be Vanessa.

With a twist of the key, 310 burbled into life and I drove slowly back on Escondido, sweeping the spotlight from one side to the other. When I reached Grande, I switched off the light and turned right, not the least bit eager to explain to Martin Holman why I didn't have a fourteen-year-old in custody.

I couldn't imagine Vanessa Davila running far—or even walking far. It was just a question of probing the right set of shadows at the right time before I found her. As 310 idled up Grande toward the expressway interchange, I glanced up the steep slope of concrete that formed the sides of the underpass. And there she was.

Vanessa Davila sat on the ledge where the span beams rested. Her legs were drawn up so that she could rest her head on her knees, with arms locked around them. She had to be exhausted after sprinting this far, but I had no illusions about her staying put.

I pulled over and snatched the mike off the radio. T. C. Barnes answered immediately, and I told him to call Aggie Bishop, Deputy Bishop's wife. Aggie worked as an on-call matron for us, and she was just right for this job—big, tough, clearheaded, and soft-spoken in two languages.

I was about to sign off when I thought better of it.

"Three-oh-seven, this is three ten."

Holman's reply surprised me, so immediate he must have been driving with his microphone in his lap. "Three-oh-seven."

I looked up at Vanessa, just to be sure. She was motionless, like a two-hundred-pound pigeon roosting for the night.

"Three-oh-seven, ten-twenty?"

This time, Holman knew exactly where he was. "A mile out on forty-three. You want me to swing down that way?"

"Affirmative, three oh seven. We have a female subject who is sitting under the overpass. We need to talk to her, and she isn't showing much inclination to move." I looked at that steep slope of concrete again, thinking how nice it would be for someone other than me to puff his way up to Vanessa along with Aggie Bishop. "And three oh seven, when you arrive, drive under the interstate, then swing around and park right under the north-bound underpass. I'm going to drive up the westbound on-ramp. That will put me right above her."

"Ten-four, three ten."

I sat back, waiting. Vanessa didn't move, and I didn't want her out of my sight. Sheriff Holman didn't let moss grow under his tires. It seemed only a matter of seconds before 307 appeared southbound on Grande.

As he drove by, he said cryptically, "I see her."

"Keep her in sight. I'm going topside. Wait for Deputy Bishop to get here before you approach her."

"Ten-four."

I pulled 310 into gear and drove out from under the concrete, keeping an eye on Vanessa. The on-ramp curved off to the right, and for half of its distance I could see the girl's dark shape under the beams.

"She's going to be out of my sight now, so keep me posted," I said.

"She hasn't moved," Holman said. "You want me to go up and talk with her?"

"That's negative. Wait for Deputy Bishop." I had visions of Vanessa grabbing the sheriff in a bear hug and both of them toppling down the concrete slope to land in the broken glass and shredded tire treads, Holman no doubt on the bottom.

For fifteen minutes we sat in the darkness, Martin Holman below, me above being rocked by the wake of passing tractor trailers, and Vanessa Davila curled up in the middle.

At five minutes after two, another marked county car idled up behind me. I got out, thinking we had a fair-sized gathering to take one frightened teenage girl into custody. Sergeant Robert Torrez was in civilian clothes, and he came close to smiling.

"Isn't this interesting," he said.

Aggie Mendoza Bishop got out of the car and joined us. She walked carefully between the guardrail and the patrol car, looking over the side. "She's down there? Under the bridge?"

"Yes. Watch your step. There's broken glass and all kinds of pleasant things." I lowered my voice to a whisper. "And I have no idea what her reaction is going to be. She might come without a struggle, or she might bolt again."

"She ain't going too many places from here," Sergeant Torrez muttered.

Aggie Bishop held up a hand. "You two stay well back," she said. "Let me talk with her first. My God, she's got to be frightened to death. Out here in the middle of the night like this. What's her name?"

I told her, and she stepped over the guardrail with considerably more grace than I managed. The footing was treacherous, and when roadside weeds gave way to the steep polished concrete of the abutment, it was even worse. I was perfectly content to stay well back, clinging to one of the rebar bolts for support, my ankles protesting.

Aggie Bishop took her time, but what Robert Torrez had said was true: Vanessa Davila had nowhere to go. After what seemed like an hour, I saw the bright flash of Torrez's light and heard him say, "Watch your step here, now."

The three of them appeared as one huge dark shadow, and I clawed my way back the few steps to the guardrail. Vanessa Davila allowed herself to be steered toward the backseat of the county car without a whimper, and my spirits rose several notches. I still had no idea what the girl knew, but if there was any connection to be made with Maria Ibarra's death, Vanessa Davila was as close to that connection as anyone.

We crossed the median and headed down the off-ramp. Bob Torrez, with Matron Bishop and Vanessa Davila in the backseat, headed for the office, with Sheriff Holman falling in behind. I drove back to the Ranchero trailer park to chauffeur Mrs. Davila down to be with her daughter. I figured, after she had seen Vanessa flee into the night, that she'd be sitting in the kitchen, wringing her hands and worrying herself into a swivet.

I couldn't have been more wrong. Mrs. Davila wasn't waiting for me or anyone else. After a third symphony of pounding and doorbell-ringing, she opened the door, her face puffy from sleep. She rubbed one eye and regarded me with the other as if she had never seen me before.

"Ma'am, we have your daughter in custody. She's safe. I'd like you to come down to the office and be with her while we question her. One of the matrons is with her now."

Mrs. Davila looked puzzled. "What?" she said. I took a long, deep breath. If I had had a bottle in my hand, it would have been a long, stiff drink.

23

"Did she do it?" Sheriff Martin Holman met me at the back door of the sheriff's office, and he spoke in a hoarse whisper.

"Who? And do what?" I asked, pausing on the bottom steps.

"That girl, Vanessa Davila. Do you think she killed Maria Ibarra?"

I looked at Martin's eager face and slowly shook my head. "Martin," I said and stepped up so that I could put my hand on his shoulder. He was four inches taller than I was, and he probably hadn't forgotten that it was his hand that signed my paycheck every month. But he still accepted the fatherly gesture and even leaned forward a little to hear my words of wisdom.

"Martin, every soul that we bring up these steps is not necessarily under suspicion of murder, even if a murder took place. And in this particular instance, to the best of our knowledge, the victim wasn't murdered." I patted his shoulder. "Dumped by some son of a bitch, but not murdered. Stop being so eager."

I gave him a final pat and pushed past. He followed me down the narrow hallway to my office as if I actually had some answers. "She's in the conference room with Torrez and Mrs. Bishop." Just as I stepped into my office he added, "We're waiting on Estelle."

"She may be tied up most of the night out at the accident site," I said, and headed for a chair.

"No, she radioed in that it wouldn't be more than ten minutes. She was at the hospital."

I nodded. "Fair enough. Let me tell you what we have." I sat down heavily. "We have a girl who choked to death."

"That part, I know," Holman said testily. I waved a hand for him to be patient.

"She choked to death on a piece of pizza. Somewhere, we don't know where. Someone, we don't know who, dumped her body under the bleachers. A real good Samaritan that person was. We know where and with whom the victim was living sometime before the time of her death...but not necessarily at the *time* of her death."

"But you don't know what relationship Miguel Orosco is to Maria Ibarra," Holman added quickly.

"Just so. We don't. And you bring up a good point. What we don't know makes a more impressive file than what we do know. In the first place, that girl"—and I pointed in the general direction of the upstairs conference room—"is the only person who was seen with Maria Ibarra outside of regular school hours during the past day or so. Apparently Vanessa Davila and Maria Ibarra might have been friends."

"You don't sound very positive," Holman murmured.

"No, I'm not. It's the word of one convenience store clerk, and not a very dependable clerk at that. Glen Archer doesn't remember the two girls together, but then again he doesn't really remember Maria Ibarra in the first place, alone or otherwise."

"All right, so we don't know who she was hanging out with, other than maybe this Davila girl."

"Right. And before that, we don't know how Maria got herself linked up with Orosco. There's a Mexican connection there that we may never solve, unless we get just plain lucky. We don't know who was in the two vehicles that Wes Crocker reports seeing behind the school. We don't know what kind of vehicles they were. We don't know just when they were there. Do you want the rest of the list?"

Holman shrugged, but it was a bleak shrug. "Sure."

"We don't know if the vehicles behind the school are related to Maria Ibarra's misfortune. We're not sure if she died near there, or somewhere else and was dumped. We received one anonymous telephone tip that reported the body, but other than that, not one word from anyone."

"I just can't imagine someone sitting there, watching a girl choke to death, and not doing something about it," Holman muttered. "I mean, even I know the Heimlich maneuver."

"People are capable of all kinds of delightful behavior, Martin, as you are well aware. And if you don't mind me changing the subject in midlist, we don't know if the hit-and-run incident involving Wesley Crocker was an accident or not. We don't know what kind of vehicle it was, or who was driving it. We don't know if it is connected in any way to Maria's death. Right now, my suspicion is that it is not."

I folded my hands over my belly, leaned back, swung one foot up on my desk, and smiled at Sheriff Martin Holman.

He frowned and looked down at the worn wooden floor, and I tipped my head back, popping the vertebrae in my neck. Every time one popped, the ringing in my left ear changed pitch. Perhaps orchestral tinnitus could be a new hobby for me.

Holman shoved his hands in his pockets and walked across the room to the window, then turned and walked back to my desk, a habit that told me he was thinking as hard as he could and getting nowhere. "Did you make any progress today at all?"

That was a loaded question, and I knew it. But pretending wasn't in my nature, so I settled for a simple, "Other than finding Vanessa Davila? No. But the outlook isn't entirely bleak."

"It's not?"

"No, Martin, it's not. Sometime today or tomorrow or the next day or next week, bureaucrats willing, we may hear something from the state lab. There are blood, tissue, and hair samples that might help us. We'll know exactly what killed the girl, and when, give or take. And when we're finished interviewing Vanessa Davila, we'll have an entire list of details to check out."

I held up my right index finger and thumb, about a quarter inch apart. "Tiny pieces, Martin. Tiny, patient little pieces." I swung my feet down and thumped the chair forward. "The trick is to give Estelle Reyes-Guzman time and room to work. She's the best investigator there is. When she talks with the girl, trust me—if there's something there, she'll find it."

Holman's hands were still jammed in his pockets. "And if there's nothing there?"

I shrugged. "That's the way it is. And by the way, who was the fatal?"

Holman grimaced as that memory replayed itself. "Ryan House." He saw that I was struggling to place the name and added, "He's a senior. Co-captain of the basketball team. All-conference last year. Salutatorian of his class." He waved a hand. "The list goes on. You remember him."

"Uh," I said, committing to neither a yes nor a no. "That's interesting. His younger brother is the kid who was giving Officer Pasquale a hard time the other evening. How about the other one? The driver?"

"Another senior. Kid by the name of Dennis Wilton. His father works for the state highway department."

"Ah, Wilton," I said, remembering the name that the school-bus driver, Stub Moore, had given me.

Holman nodded. "Right. He's a lucky kid. Apparently he suffered just a few bruises, a couple little cuts. That's about it. The driver's-side air bag worked just like it was meant to. And he was wearing his belt. Estelle was going to talk with him for a few minutes at the hospital before the sedation puts him out."

I rubbed a hand over the sandpaper bristles of my short-cropped gray hair. "That's what I need, a sedative habit." I closed my eyes for a moment and then blinked at Holman. "But why are they keeping him if it's just cuts and bruises?"

"A few hours for observation," Holman said. "Apparently he's not doing very well," and he tapped the side of his skull. "It would be rough for anyone, but I'm told that the two boys were close friends." Holman had been edging toward the door and he looked sideways at me. "Is everything all right?" He didn't accept my shrug as an answer. "No, really. Are you okay?"

I settled for a simple nod.

He reached for the doorknob and glanced at his watch at the same time. "If Wesley Crocker is released later this morning, are you going to let him stay with you?"

"Why not?" It was easy keeping the enthusiasm out of my voice.

Holman smiled. "I always got the feeling that you prized your isolation and privacy out there in the woods."

I chuckled and stood up too suddenly for my middle ear's sake. I had to rest the knuckles of my right hand on the desk until my vision cleared. If Holman noticed, he didn't say anything. "I'm not sure twenty trees make a woods, Martin. And I do value it," I said. "But everything else is shot to hell, so that might as well go, too."

Voices out in the hallway interrupted us, and Holman turned and looked past the doorjamb. "Detective Reyes-Guzman is back," he said. It may have been the middle of a long night for everyone else, but Estelle Reyes-Guzman looked like she'd had her twelve hours of sleep. She appeared in my doorway, black briefcase in hand.

"Puzzling, sir. Really puzzling," she said by way of greeting. She set the briefcase down on the straight chair just inside the doorway and ran both hands through her black hair, then froze in position with a hand on each side of her head. For the first time I saw the black circles under her eyes.

"What's puzzling?" I said. "And sit down for a few minutes."

She didn't argue, but crossed the small room and sat in the leather chair by the wall map of Posadas County. Sheriff Holman drifted back into the room and closed the door.

"I had the pickup truck secured in the county shop so I can take another look tomorrow. Maybe you'd take a look, too, sir."

I sat down, letting the old, familiar swivel chair soothe the tired bones. I'd been standing for two minutes, and that seemed long enough. Estelle was frowning and looking at the fingernail of her right index finger. She picked the cuticle without knowing what she was doing, and at the same time her lower lip pursed out. I'd known her long enough not to interrupt the patient thought process that was going on in that pretty head. Even Martin Holman knew better.

Finally she looked up at me. "Do you remember Ryan House?"

I shook my head. "Marty here told me that House was the one killed. The passenger. But I can't bring him to mind. Show me a yearbook picture, and it'll click."

"It probably doesn't matter. But that's right...he wasn't driving. Dennis Wilton was."

"So I heard."

"Ryan House was thrown out on impact. Through the windshield."

"I saw that," I said. "But Wilton is all right?"

Estelle nodded. "Physically, I guess. They were close friends. And Wilton is blaming himself."

"That would be expected," I said. "So what's puzzling?"

"Stub Moore, the driver of the lead bus, says that the pickup truck that Wilton was driving passed his bus on a long downgrade. Although the truck was going faster than the speed limit, Boyd said that the speed wasn't excessive for passing."

"And then he lost it somehow, and went off the side of the highway," I said.

"It sounded pretty cut and dried to me," the sheriff added, but Estelle shook her head.

"Moore said the pickup was half a mile or more ahead of him when he saw the lights just drift off the road to the right." She swept her hand out in front of her, and then held it suspended in space. "He said it looked like the driver maybe fell asleep."

"That could happen," Holman said. "That late at night? Why not."

"It could, but put yourself in that pickup truck. Sure, it's late. They're heading home from an exciting football game. It's about an hour-and-a-half drive. The boys might have stayed in Sierra Linda for a few minutes after the game to get something to eat. They caught up with the buses somewhere near Baca's ranch. And a few minutes later, when the bus started into that section of highway that looks like a roller coaster, Wilton decided to pass."

"What's your point, Estelle?" Holman asked abruptly. He glanced at his watch.

"Dennis Wilton might not have known the road very well," I said. "He might not have had occasion to drive it often."

"That never stopped most teenage drivers from passing," Holman said.

I hooked my hands behind my head and regarded Estelle. Her thought processes had always amused me, running in nice, true lineal lines from A to B to C. In the eight years I'd known her, I couldn't recall a single incident of her engaging in idle chatter.

"True." Estelle nodded. "And think about them passing. Maybe some of the kids in the bus were asleep, but probably most of them weren't. They're too wired after a conference win. And the driver said that they were noisy. He had trouble getting them to stay in their seats. So, as the pickup drives by, we've got kids looking out the window, probably responding to waves or honks or what have you from the two boys in the pickup truck."

"Remember last year," I said, "when one of the Posadas wrestlers hung his butt out the bus window and mooned half a mile of downtown Belen?"

Estelle nodded. "With all that kind of behavior that we expect, it seems odd to me that a minute or so after the pickup pulls back into its lane ahead of the bus, the kid who's driving just simply falls asleep."

The room fell silent as both Martin Holman and I regarded Estelle Reyes-Guzman.

"But..." Holman said when the silence stretched too long.

Estelle raised an eyebrow and waited.

"How else?" he added and held up his hands.

"I don't know how else," Estelle said quietly.

"What are you going to do?" Holman asked, and he sounded a bit nervous.

"I want to talk with Dennis Wilton some more," she said. "I want to hear what he has to say. And the bus driver gave me names of some of the kids who were riding on that side of the bus, kids who would have seen the pickup go by. I suppose it's entirely possible that the two boys were half asleep when they cruised by the bus. I just find it strange that the very act of passing a game bus wouldn't stir the adrenaline just a little bit and keep them alert for a while longer." Estelle pushed herself out of the chair. "I asked the parents for a blood test and they agreed. We didn't need to go through the hassle of a court order. We'll see what those results say."

"You think they might have been on something?" I asked.

"It's possible. We didn't find anything like that in the truck, but it's possible."

"Do you think they were drinking?" Holman asked.

"Maybe. I couldn't smell anything, but you never know. I don't think the doctors would have given Dennis Wilton a sedative if he'd been drunk."

"That would make it vehicular homicide, if he was intoxicated," Holman said.

"Yes, it would, sir."

He sighed loudly. "Jesus Christ," he said and looked heavenward. "That's all we need. First the girl, now this."

I had been gazing at Estelle during the exchange, watching her expression. She turned and when our eyes met, I knew that she'd told us most of what she knew. Most.

The anticipation did more for me than ten cups of coffee. I pushed myself out of the chair and said, "One case at a time. Dennis Wilton isn't going anywhere. We caught up with Vanessa Davila and she and Mama are waiting for us upstairs. Let's go chat with them for a few minutes. Then we'll take a look at that truck." I turned and smiled at Martin Holman. "Then maybe we can have a domestic knife fight or two. Maybe even a rabid dog. Spice this evening up."

Holman looked long suffering. "It's three ten in the morning," he said. "The evening was shot to hell a long time ago."

"You'll get used to that, Sheriff," I said.

24

Vanessa Davila cried. It didn't matter what the question was, or who asked it. She cried. Sometimes the tears leaked out from tightly squinched eyelids while she bit her lip. Sometimes her body heaved and the tears flowed openly. At one point she got the hiccups so badly that I could feel the floor jolt every time one of the spasms shook her.

Sheriff Holman fetched her a glass of water, but she ignored it.

At first I handled the tears by simply pushing the box of facial tissue close to Vanessa's elbow and waiting. She ignored those, too. For the first ten minutes, Estelle did most of the talking, and most of it was in Spanish, between Estelle and the girl's mother. Vanessa Davila didn't utter a word.

She didn't answer questions about her relationship with Maria Ibarra, nor about her activities that night. She would have known about the girl's death, given the efficient way that word travels around a school. It was impossible to believe that she could *not* have known. Still, she had elected to go to the football game anyway. Perhaps that was her way of grieving for a lost friend.

She wouldn't tell us how she got to the game, or how she got home. The list of students riding the spectator bus included fifty-five names, and none of them was Vanessa's. I was impressed. No witness called to testify in front of a senate subcommittee ever stonewalled any better.

I watched the girl's face closely, and what I saw was pure misery. I'd watched my own four kids grow up, and a time or two there had been an emergency when something was *really* wrong, not just a minor ouch where the tears came and went. Vanessa Davila was being wrenched this way and that by her own private hell, and she had elected to keep it to herself. Most kids weren't that tough.

She didn't nod answers, she didn't use her hands. She didn't focus on the picture of Maria Ibarra that Estelle slid in front of her. She just sat and waited us out while the tears flowed.

During a silence while Vanessa ignored a question from her mother, I glanced at the wall clock. In another two hours it would be dawn. Posadas would wake up and folks would have a lot to talk about. A little girl whom few of us knew had died a lonely and dirty death; the man she'd been living with had poisoned himself with a lethal alcohol mix; a harmless itinerant had been the victim of a hit-and-run; and one of the community's top students had tried to fly through solid rock. The past twenty-four hours were something of a record for the tiny community.

At least we'd won the football contest. I gazed at what was left of Vanessa Davila and wondered how she'd managed to sit through the game, because it wasn't the thrill of victory that had reduced her to jelly.

Her mother began another set of rapid-fire exhortations with the word *basta* sprinkled through it and I held up a hand.

"Mrs. Davila, I don't think we're getting anywhere," I said. I didn't take my eyes off her daughter. The mother subsided, and I leaned back in my chair, rapping my ring lightly on the edge of the table. It had been a long time since I'd been a practicing parent, and none of my four youngsters had strayed very far from the straight and narrow. Still, barring a family tragedy, I could think of only one reason for a fourteen-year-old to be so consumed by grief.

"Vanessa," I said, "how well did you know Ryan House?"

Vanessa answered that question, but not with words. The name caught her off guard, and she sucked in a quick breath at the same time that her eyes closed. The flow of tears increased to a gusher, and she buried her head in her crossed arms, her thick black hair cascading around her face.

I nodded. "Well, well," I said quietly.

"Sir?" Estelle asked.

I glanced at the detective and saw that she was frowning at me. If I was one step ahead of her, it was the first time in days. The late hours were really catching up with her.

"She wouldn't go to a football game feeling like this," I said. "She won't tell us who she rode with, but she either saw, or heard about, the wreck." I gestured toward Vanessa, whose head was still down on the table. "And she heard that Ryan House had been killed." And when I mentioned the name, Vanessa flinched. It wasn't much, but Estelle saw the slight hitch of the left shoulder and the snuffle from down under.

The girl's emotions had opened a door for us, but that was the extent of her cooperation. She obviously had learned early on, and learned well, that if adults gave her a hard time, the simplest solution was just to refuse to talk to them.

We pursued her apparent acquaintance with Ryan House for several minutes without progress. Finally there appeared to be nothing else to say. I turned to the girl's mother.

"Ma'am, if we let your daughter return home with you, are you going to be able to keep her there?"

Mrs. Davila started to say "What?" but thought better of it. She couldn't meet my gaze and looked at Estelle instead.

"We're going to need to talk with her again," I said. Mrs. Davila's chin started to quiver and tears came to her eyes. "We need to know that she's available."

The woman's response surprised me. Instead of apprehension, I saw a glimmer of relief in her tear-filled eyes. "She never does what I ask," she said. "I can't make her mind me." She looked at her daughter. "But she's a good girl, mister."

That sounded more like something said in self-defense than from any basis in truth, but I nodded sympathetically. I had my glasses on, and I tipped my head so I could scrutinize the older woman's face through my bifocals. "Those facial bruises, Mrs. Davila. How did you get those?"

"Oh," she replied, and her hand crept up to her face. "I fell down," she added, and then stopped. She wasn't a good liar. Her daughter had lifted her face from her hands and was busy wiping her eyes. Every now and again, she shot her mother a glance, just a quick look to keep tabs on the situation.

"Maybe," Estelle Reyes-Guzman said, her voice almost a whisper, "maybe it's all just too much." She reached out and touched the back of my hand lightly, a soothing gesture that couldn't have been lost on anyone. "Before the Davilas go home, maybe I can talk with Vanessa for just a few minutes alone?"

I pulled at my earlobe and grimaced. "Hell, why not." I stood up and gestured toward Mrs. Davila. "Let's give the detective a few minutes alone with Vanessa, ma'am. It won't hurt." I glanced at the girl in time to catch her gaze. "Of course, it probably won't do any good, either, but it's one last chance for her."

With great shuffling of papers, the sort of thing lawyers do before a trial begins, we cleared the room, leaving the five-foot-six-inch, 110-pound Estelle Reyes-Guzman with five-foot-seven, 210-pound Vanessa Davila.

When my back was turned, I couldn't help grinning, because I knew the two were no even match.

25

I was as surprised as Estelle Reyes-Guzman was baffled. "The girl just won't say a word," she said. Estelle had spent another twenty minutes with Vanessa, and then another session with mother and daughter before giving up in frustration. Matron Aggie Bishop stayed with the pair for a few minutes until Estelle, Holman, and I could figure out a game plan.

"She knows she doesn't have to talk," the sheriff said in one of his rare moments of clear thinking. "There's nothing we can do to her, and she knows it."

Estelle watched as I poured the last cup of what passed for coffee out of the pot. "Sir, did anyone actually see her at the game?"

"I don't know." I spooned in creamer and watched it swirl on top of the oil slick. "Her mother said she went. No...I take that back. She said she *thought* that Vanessa had gone with the crowd. That's the only word we have."

"Oh," Martin Holman said, and it was close to a groan. "Now we're saying she may not even have gone to the football game? That she was just roaming around town? What do we have to do, interview two hundred kids now to find out something as simple as that?"

"Maybe so, Martin," I said, and tossed the plastic spoon in the trash. "That she went to the game is an assumption on our part, and not a particularly bright assumption, either, as it turns out."

Holman frowned. "Why is it so important, anyway? Do we suspect this girl of anything? Do you think she had a hand in what happened to Maria Ibarra?"

"It's possible." I grinned at Holman. "If we knew what actually happened to Maria, we'd be farther ahead." I sipped the coffee, and then tossed the remainder in the trash can. "It would be more fun that way...actually making progress before the snow flies."

"It doesn't look like she's ever going to tell us," Holman said. "Vanessa Davila, I mean."

"Unless it begins to suit her purpose," Estelle Reyes-Guzman said.

Holman blinked at her, then snapped his mouth shut when he realized how stupid he looked. "I don't follow," he said.

"Well, Martin," I said, and sighed long and loud. "Think of things from Vanessa's position. If she's just mourning the death of a good friend—Maria Ibarra—then talking to us isn't going to do Vanessa any good. There's nothing we can do to make her feel better."

"And if she knew Ryan House, then she's mourning him, too. And there's nothing we can say or do to help," Estelle added.

"But I've never seen a youngster just sit and ignore the world like that," Holman said. "God, if either of my daughters were caught up in trouble, they'd babble out such a string of stuff that it'd take a week to sort things out. But this gal...she just sits there and ignores us. It's almost like she's got something she's guarding from us. Something important that she doesn't want us to know."

Estelle nodded, and I saw the ghost of a smile touch her face. "Exactly, sir."

"Do you want someone to watch her for a while?" I asked. "Find out where she goes and who she sees?"

Before Estelle had a chance to answer, Holman yawned and shook his head, trying to clear the cobwebs. "You mean like a tail? Surveillance?" I nodded. "That's expensive," he said. "And for a fourteen-year-old kid? It seems like a waste of time."

"That's what we're good at...wasting time," I said. "It won't hurt, and it'll give Tom Pasquale something to do."

"Why him?" Holman asked.

"For one thing, it'll do his ego good," I said. "He'll enjoy playing secret agent man after spending a night at the hospital listening to Wesley Crocker snore. For another thing, I don't want to spare one of the deputies. We don't have enough manpower to go around as it is. And third, if Pasquale does the stakeout, the village will eat his overtime, not us."

Holman grinned. "By all means, then."

I glanced at my watch. "Give Pasquale a call at the hospital and fill him in. Tell him to use his own car, and to be discreet. If Vanessa slips out, we don't want to interfere in any way. We just want to know where she goes and who she sees."

Estelle nodded and left to telephone the good news to Thomas Pasquale. I chauffeured mama and daughter home, and when I opened the door for them to alight at their trailer, I said, "Are you sure you don't have anything you want to tell us?" Vanessa didn't bother to glance my way. She trudged up the steps to the trailer, opened the front door, and disappeared inside.

I handed one of my cards to Mrs. Davila. "Call me if you think of anything." She accepted the card, but my hopes didn't soar.

Dawn was beginning to streak the sky when I pulled into the graveled driveway of the county maintenance yard. I saw Estelle's unmarked car parked over by our secure garage and I pulled 310 in beside it. The lights were ablaze inside, and I opened the heavy galvanized steel door.

The remains of Dennis Wilton's truck sat in the middle of the floor. I walked slowly around it until I reached Estelle, who was sitting on a shop stool off to one side. I thrust my hands in my pockets and stood silently beside her, gazing at the remains.

The truck had hit the rock outcropping so hard that the frame had folded at the spot where cab and bed met, forced downward far enough that the truck actually rested on the two back tires and the bent frame members rather than all four wheels.

I walked around in front and cocked my head. "If it had hit center on, both kids would be dead now, air bag or no," I said. The left half of the truck's front, although bent and twisted by the forces tearing at the passenger side, had missed the rock. Incongruous with the rest of the mangled mess, the left headlight and parking light were in perfect condition.

"What year was this thing?" I asked.

"Nineteen ninety-five," Estelle said. "Just over sixteen thousand miles on the odometer."

"And the driver said that he dozed off?"

"That's what he claims."

"And the House kid must have been asleep. Otherwise he would have had time to make a grab at the steering wheel," I said. "The bus driver would have seen them swerve. If they traveled more than a hundred feet on the shoulder, and even ripped out a fence, either one of the occupants would have had plenty of time to make a frantic wrench at the wheel."

"That's why I ordered the blood test, sir. It's routine for the autopsy, but I want the driver's, too."

"That's what you wanted to show me?" I said.

"Well, no." She pushed herself up, moving like she had a crick in her back.

"You need to go home," I said.

"In a few minutes. Let me show you a couple of things. Then we can both brood on them for a while."

She walked around the truck and pulled the driver's-side door open slightly more than it already was. The deflated air bag hung from the core of the steering wheel.

"The bag functioned perfectly, and the driver was wearing his shoulder harness," Estelle said. "That, combined with most of the force of the impact being on the far side of the truck, accounts for his relatively minor injuries."

"And there was no air bag on the other side."

"No, sir. And worse than that, the passenger's seatbelt wasn't buckled."

I leaned against the cab of the truck and squinted at the interior. The dashboard had collapsed back so far that the section including the glove compartment was buried in the fabric of the seat, crushed backward by the heavy V-8 engine as it crashed off its mounts. When the firewall folded backward, the cab of the truck had ovalized, with the roof folding upward.

There wasn't much blood inside. Ryan House had been fired through the windshield during the first microseconds of the impact, taking out part of the roof framework with him.

"He had his belt on," I said, and pointed. The belt was indeed deployed, tangled in part of the dashboard so that the retract mechanism couldn't reel it in.

"But it wasn't buckled, sir."

I turned to look at Estelle and she lifted an eyebrow a fraction. "That doesn't make sense," I said. "Did the buckle fail?" I slid into what remained of the driver's seat and pulled the passenger-side belt free from the twisted steel and plastic. The shiny chrome buckle insert was undamaged. The slots stamped through the metal for the locking lug were clean and unmarred.

Estelle reached out and pointed at the edges of the larger cutout with her index finger. "If the buckle had been securely latched, and then torn from the locking clasp, we would expect to see some marking on the metal. There would have to be some distortion if that happened. If the belt itself gave way, we'd see obvious evidence of tearing or stretching of the fabric."

"Yes, we would," I said. I pulled the belt toward the center and inserted the buckle into the lock. It snapped into place with a crisp, definite "click." I yanked on it, knowing full well that I could never exert the kind of forces generated by a crash. "It feels normal enough to me," I said. "But who's to tell? Actually, the way these things are made, I'm not sure that buckle failure is even *possible* if the thing snaps in place properly."

"I wouldn't think so," Estelle said. "I've never seen one fail that was properly latched...at least not on newer vehicles. The forces just aren't there. It's not like a jet plane crashing into the side of a mountain at six hundred miles an hour."

"And even in airplane crashes, it's not uncommon for investigators to find victims still strapped in their seats, hundreds of yards from the plane. The seat tears out of the floor, but the belt doesn't fail." I shook my head. "No, the most likely answer is that the thing wasn't latched properly," I said. "Ryan House wasn't paying attention and didn't push it in far enough."

"That's the most likely explanation."

She beckoned me out of the truck. "It just seems to me that there are several possibilities. But all things being equal, the explanation you gave is the most likely. Having the buckle itself fail just isn't in the numbers, sir. The belt was not fastened properly and came loose at the critical moment of impact. That's probably what happened."

I recognized that particular tone of voice, and I turned to frown at Estelle. "You still don't sound convinced."

"Well," she said, "there is a third possibility. Maybe it was fastened properly and was then unlatched."

"Like maybe Ryan House had dropped something on the floor and was in the process of unbuckling when the accident happened. He never had the time to jam the buckle back in, even if he had thought to do so."

Estelle nodded. "I've done that myself on occasion."

"I can imagine that maybe House had something in his hands—like a cup of coffee or something—and managed to spill it. He leans forward to get away from it and unbuckles his belt so he can squirm away from the mess."

"That's the most likely scenario. But it doesn't make sense with the way the accident happened. If they were awake and alert, they might let the truck drift off the pavement and onto the shoulder, but not for so long, and certainly not straight as an arrow through a fence without any attempt at correction. After all, the most common pickup truck accident is running off the shoulder, overcorrecting, and then flipping. The occupant gets pitched out and crushed by the truck as it rolls. That sure isn't what happened here."

I straightened my back with a grunt and rested my hand on the side of the truck's bed. "And that's what has been bothering you all night?"

"Yes, sir. Dennis Wilton says that he fell asleep. Maybe they both did. Maybe it's as simple as that. Maybe it's as simple as Ryan House not properly snapping his seatbelt."

"The wreck would have killed him anyway, probably," I said. "That's small consolation, but it's true."

We stood and looked at the cab of the mangled truck. Finally, Estelle sighed. "Yes, sir, that's true."

She stepped away from the truck and walked around the front. "Can I show you something else that bothers me?"

"Sure." As I joined her, I could smell the tangy odor of gasoline and antifreeze mixing in a puddle under the truck, soaking into the sand that one of the county employees had spread on the floor when the truck had been brought in.

Estelle knelt by the right front side of the truck, reached out, and pointed at the tangle of metal that had been the fender. The front end had collapsed to within inches of the door post, crushing up in sharp, torn metal that folded back on itself in waves, like bizarre yuletide ribbon candy. Buried in the folds were bits and pieces of rock, headlight rim, grille, and front bumper.

I bent down with my hands on my knees, cricked my neck back so I could see through the lower portion of my bifocals, and pursed my lips.

"This, sir, is flat black paint."

26

"Well, I'll be damned," I breathed. "Let me see that." I went down on one knee, at considerable price, and got close. The truck had originally been metallic blue—a bright, deep tone a squirt or two lighter than royal blue. The primer under the blue was gray. Nothing else on the truck was black, flat or otherwise, except that one smear.

The pickup had been hit at one time or another by something carrying a coat of black paint. One sharp dig was visible in the metal. The rest of the impact had been obliterated by the later damage done by the rock outcropping.

"What hit him?" I said.

Estelle smiled, a rare thing in itself. She put one hand on my right elbow and ushered me along toward the front of the wreckage. "Right here, you can see the mounting bracket, sir. Or what's left of it. It's easier to see on the other side where there was less damage."

"A grille guard, you mean?" And that's exactly what she meant. The mounting brackets were bolted to the frame. The right side bracket was twisted and ruined like the rest of the hardware that had lost the fight. The mount on the driver's side was still in one piece, flat black paint and all.

"It's been recently removed," Estelle said. "On this side you can see the wrench marks. They scuff the black paint, and the marks haven't been there long enough to collect road dirt or rust."

"We don't pay you enough," I mused. And then, because it was easier, I let myself slump back until I sat down on the hard, cold concrete. "What you're leading me to think is that this is the truck that smacked Wes Crocker."

"I've considered that," Estelle said. She knelt down on one knee and rested her right hand on the bottom rim of the undamaged left headlight. Her fingernails rapped a quiet dance on the glass of the light. "Everything fits, even this." She reached out and for a moment her body blocked my view of what she was doing. When she turned around, she held out a small object to me.

I reached out and took it. The little black plastic trumpet was as undamaged as the headlamp. "A deer whistler," I said. "And let me guess. The other side is missing one."

"The other side is missing, period," Estelle said. "There's no way to even tell anymore what piece of metal held the little plastic mounting bracket. We didn't get that lucky."

I dug out my notebook and rearranged myself on the floor so I could attend to flipping the pages without toppling over. "Wes Crocker was hit sometime around eight P.M. yesterday," I said. "It's a nice theory, but it doesn't fit the timing of the events. This pickup truck hit the rock at thirty-two minutes after midnight."

Estelle nodded and waited.

"And so," I said, "if they were going to a night football game that started at seven all the way over in Sierra Linda, why would they still be in town at eight?"

"I don't know, sir."

"If the two boys had decided to go to the game, they would have been out of Posadas long before that in order to be in Sierra Linda in time for the kickoff."

"That's if they decided to go to the game, sir. Only one of them was in school yesterday."

"Which one was that?" I asked.

"Dennis Wilton, sir. He was one of the front office aides."

I frowned and looked back through my notes. "I didn't write that down."

"There was no particular reason you should have, sir," Estelle said. "You did remind Glen Archer that you didn't want students handling material that we asked for. The Wilton boy was the student aide who photocopied the parking permit list for us."

"Son of a bitch," I said, more in irritation at my memory than anything else. "And Ryan House was absent from school yesterday?"

"Yes, sir. He was."

I leaned back and put both hands on the cold concrete floor behind me. "Let's assume again that this is the vehicle in question... its passenger misses the day in school, its owner doesn't. So we assume that sometime in the afternoon, the two boys get together, for whatever reason."

"That's easily done, sir. Dennis Wilton only attended classes until noon. He normally works from one to six every school day at Guilfoil Auto Parts."

"All right, so he even has time to go to work yesterday."

"He didn't, though."

"You checked?" I asked, knowing it was a waste of breath. Estelle nodded. "So the pair link up sometime in the afternoon, perhaps. We don't have a clue what they did between the time Dennis Wilton left school and the time of the encounter with Wes Crocker. If that happened at all, we can then suppose that they hightailed it out of town. If they wanted a place to hide, then an out-of-town football game is as good as anyplace."

"The complication is the grille guard, sir."

I nodded. "If it was on the truck at eight P.M., when Crocker was hit, then it was taken off sometime before midnight thirty-two, when they crashed the truck into the rock."

And that was as far as my fatigued brain would go. I put the notebook back in my breast pocket and turned over on my knees so I could push myself upright. That accomplished, I brushed the dirt and sand off my trousers and hands.

"I don't like any of this," I said. "And I'll tell you why. No matter which way we go, there's a fork in the road."

"For example..."

I shrugged. "If this is the truck that hit Wes Crocker, and if one of the boys was driving it at the time—and by the way, we don't know *that* for sure yet—then we've got a fork in the road." I pointed off to the right. "One choice says that they meant to hit him."

Estelle leaned her head the other way and finished the thought. "And the other route says it was an accident."

"That's right. If it was intentional, then we've got ourselves a wonderful mess, with all kinds of nasty questions. And lots of forks in the road, by the way. And if it was an accident..." I shrugged. "Either way, they took off. Maybe it took as much as half an hour in someone's garage or backyard to yank that bent grille guard off and clean up the truck." I waved a hand at the right side. "They missed a little slash of black just above the scrape where the guard bent back and dinged the fender. And then, because it's a tiny town and they know the cops will be out looking for them, they slip out to the east, figuring to get themselves lost in the sporting crowd. If somebody asks, hell, they were at the game all night."

"We're not that stupid, sir."

"God, I hope not. But kids think we are. And right now, I'm so tired, I think I am."

"We don't have to make a move right away," Estelle said. "If this is the truck, it'll be around for a while. I've got some fingerprints to match, and I was able to pull a paint tracing off that black mark on the fender. We can send it to the lab along with paint from Crocker's bicycle. That will give us an absolute match. And later today"—she held up the deer whistler—"I'm going to ask Bob Torrez to take a microscope to all this pot metal and see if he can find the spot where the right-side whistler might have been. If we can make some kind of match there, that's it."

"It's part of *it*, anyway," I said wearily. "If this is the truck, we don't know why they hit Crocker and ran. And if it's not the truck, we're no further ahead than we were." I glanced at my watch. "I'm going to swing by the hospital and see what time they're going to release Crocker. I'll put him in Camille's old room."

"The one with all the stuffed toys?"

I grimaced. "Uh-huh. That way, he might not want to get too comfortable and stay too long."

"It's really sweet of you to do this," Estelle said, and I shot a quick glare at her, sure she was kidding. She wasn't.

"What's the choice?" I said, and started toward the door of the garage. "You ready for some breakfast?"

She declined, claiming "a couple of things to do." I didn't know what, but I didn't twist her arm. My little notebook told me that I'd been going around in circles since Thursday evening, when I'd eaten too much green chili at the Don Juan de Oñate. I was ready to fall off the carousel.

Estelle locked the door of the steel building and was driving out of the county yard before I'd even untangled my keys. The patrol car started instantly and settled into its usual smooth idle, waiting for me to select a gear.

With my hand on the gear lever, I frowned and looked over my shoulder at the little trail of dust from Estelle's car.

"What fingerprints?" I said aloud. She had told me that she had some fingerprints to match. I looked ahead toward the garage where the broken truck rested. There had been two occupants. One was headed toward the autopsy slab; the other was riding a wave of sedative at the hospital. We knew who had been driving, and who had gone flying.

I frowned again. There was little comfort in knowing that if Estelle Reyes-Guzman had wanted me to know about fingerprints, she would have told me.

27

I went home and slept for three hours. That was something of a record, and it should have rejuvenated me. It didn't. I awoke feeling awful, with ears ringing like the carillons in the *1812 Overture* and a vague, general ache that puddled in an arc above and behind my left ear.

I showered in the hottest water my aging hot water heater could brew, and then managed to shave without cutting my throat—although that might have been an improvement.

Breakfast didn't hold much of an attraction, so I settled for coffee, taking a steaming mug with me to Posadas General Hospital.

Sometime during my three-hour nap, a couple of ideas had begun cooking inside my thick skull. One in particular had leaked to the surface and refused to go away. If an answer was to be had, Wesley Crocker had it...and then several forks in our tangled road would close like magic.

I walked down the hall to Crocker's room and was surprised to see Ernie Wheeler sitting outside the door. Even dispatching was more exciting than counting floor, wall, and ceiling tiles. Posadas General was as quiet as the village it was named for...no one shouting "stat," no crash carts charging down the hall, no buxom nurses threatening to heave their bosoms out of their white uniforms.

Ernie looked up at me and his eyes focused on the coffee cup.

"You want some?" I held up the cup.

He shook his head. "No, sir. I've had enough to float my kidneys as it is."

I glanced at my watch. "Why are you here?"

Wheeler shrugged and yawned. "The sheriff thought it was a good idea to have someone around after he pulled Pasquale off."

I nodded and pushed open the door. Crocker was up and dressed, sitting easily in a wheelchair. That didn't surprise me. That Estelle Reyes-Guzman hadn't beaten me to the punch did.

Crocker grinned at me as I stepped in the room.

"Well, good morning, sir," he said, and nodded vigorously. He thumped the arm of the chair. "They won't let me walk on out, so I got to sit in this thing."

"Beats crawling," I said. "When are they going to spring you?"

"The good doctor said the minute you walked in the door." I grunted something not particularly gracious, and Crocker's good humor faded. "They got me those fancy iron crutches, over there, and I can manage just fine. Maybe there's a little room somewhere's that I could rent for a week or two."

I rubbed my eyes wearily and shook my head. "No. In the first place, a wrecked knee isn't for a week or two. And if you try and bounce around on it too much right away, it'll be for life."

Crocker looked stricken. "Well, I sure don't want to cause no trouble."

"Things are what they are," I said. "I think the best thing to do is call your sister to come and fetch you."

If I had stuck an electric cattle prod up Crocker's ass, the reaction wouldn't have been more immediate. His face collapsed into a grimace and he held up both hands as if to ward off another attack, leaning back in the wheelchair so far I thought he might flip the thing.

"Kind sir," he said, and I swear there was a tremble in his voice, "don't ask her to do that."

"Real close family, are we?"

Crocker took a deep breath, keeping his hands up to fend off any more punches. "Sir, if you talked to my sister, well, then you know what kind of woman she is."

"I have an inkling."

"Sir, she just cannot"—he stopped and fumbled for words—"she just..." He looked up at me. "In all these years, anytime I'd call, all she could think to say was some comment about when I was going to stop 'this silliness.' That's what she called it. 'This silliness.' She couldn't bring herself to ask me how I was, or ask what I'd seen, or ask where I was goin' next." He lowered his hands to his lap and stared at them. "And that's why I just stopped callin' her ever, don't you know."

"Well," I said, and then let it trail off.

"She'd fix it somehow so's I could never leave again. I know she would," he said. "I'd rather make my way along the road on crutches than face her."

"We can't let you do that," I said. "You got in the way of traffic once already. But I guess there's no hurry. We need you around for a few days until we work out a few details. Maybe that will give you time to think of an alternative."

"I could always steal a car or something, and get myself thrown in jail," Crocker said with a lame smile.

"Theft is not your style," I said.

"No, sir, it's not."

"Then we'll think of something." I picked up his fancy aluminum crutches and laid them on the bed. "Don't forget those. I'll go get the nurse. And then we can get out of here."

And fifteen minutes later, we were out in the fresh October sunshine, Crocker sucking air from the exertion of swinging from the wheelchair to the front seat of the patrol car. The cast around his injured knee was a small, light, high-tech thing made out of aluminum and fiberglass that accomplished with a few ounces what the old thigh-to-ankle plaster had done a decade before.

I waited patiently until he had settled into the seat.

"I haven't had any breakfast yet," I said. "How about you?"

He waved a hand. "Oh, now, they gave me a little something."

"I bet they did," I chuckled. "Let's go get something decent. You think you can hobble into the restaurant?"

"I should think so," he said, "but really, don't go out of your way on my account."

"Don't worry. You're going to pay for it this time," I said, and pulled 310 out of its parking slot. Wes Crocker apparently didn't know what to say in reply, and I noticed that he rubbed his jaw with that nervous tic so many of us use when our brains are racing pell-mell trying to puzzle out an answer.

❧❧❧

There was something about a good breakfast that always brought out the best in me. I could cheerfully skip any other meal of the day or night—and frequently did. The time to make up for those omissions was over a breakfast burrito as only the Don Juan de Oñate could serve it. I ordered two, and the platter must have weighed four pounds when it came.

The aroma of the fresh green chili cleared my head. Even the ringing in my ears settled down a decibel.

Crocker and I ate in silence for a few minutes until the worst of the wolves were at bay.

"How do you make out on your travels?" I asked, resting my fork for a while.

"Well, now," Crocker said, and wiped his lips, "the good Lord has seen fit to bless me with my health, so…" He shrugged.

"That's not what I meant." I reached over with a fork and indicated a sausage link that he had pushed to one side. "You going to eat that?"

"You just go ahead," he said and started to lift his plate.

I speared the tidbit and wrapped it in the tail end of the burrito's blanket where the stuffing had ended. "A man's got to eat. And food costs quite a bit of money these days. What do you do, work a few days here and there to pay for things?"

Crocker ducked his head and frowned as if he were expecting a broadside from his sister.

"I'm just curious about the logistics of life on the road, is all," I added. Shari arrived with the coffeepot and we both waited until she left. "I mean, you're obviously fit. You're not starving."

"Well," Crocker said slowly, "I take work now and then, but say, I don't do it for the money. No." He shook his head. "That just don't appeal."

"What about when you worked for Tom Lawton? What made you decide to stay on there and work?"

"The wagon place? Well, now, that's an easy one, sir. You see, I stopped at this little café in Button—that's Button, Utah—just down the road from where his place is. And there on the bulletin board on the wall behind the cash register they had one of his flyers tacked up. I read it, and I got to thinking about a man who'd make a living today working on something that hasn't seen regular use for a half a century."

"And so you rode out to his place."

"I did that. Yes, sir. And the good Lord provides. He was working on his tractor when I rode up, and I could see his new fence, just about half finished. So I figured"—Crocker paused and sipped his coffee—"so I figured that this man, this Thomas Lawton, could tell me just about everything a man would ever want to know about wagons and such."

"And that took three days?"

"Well, I didn't see no reason to head on out until that fence was just the way he wanted it. We talked about wagon trains, and freight wagons, and buckboards, and buggies—" He waved his hand at the wonder of it all. "It's interesting to know just what kind of hardware moved things along, don't you know."

"You haven't worked since leaving Lawton's place?"

Crocker pursed his lips and thought a minute. I knew it wasn't a hesitation to refresh his memory. "No, sir. See," and he leaned forward against the table, his coffee cup between his rough hands. "I get a little something every month from the government. It ain't much. Tied in with my days in the military. But it's all I need." He grinned. "I don't go in much for buying souvenirs. You'd be surprised how far two hundred bucks will take you when you don't spend much of it."

"I can imagine," I said, and almost added, Especially when you panhandle a few meals along the way. "How does the government get the money to you, if you don't have a permanent address?"

"Well, now, that's one thing my sister will do, bless her heart. Every now and again, I send her an address where I'll be for a few days. Then she up and sends along whatever money's come in. Every two, three months, maybe."

"What are you going to do for a new bike?"

Crocker grimaced. "I ain't thought that one through yet," he said. "Got to find a used one somewheres." He shook his head. "I sure hated to see the last one go. My, that was a brute of a machine. Would have lasted another century."

I leaned back to give the burritos room to settle. "Do you make plans for where you're going to travel, or do you just make up your mind each morning?"

"Oh, I get notions."

"Notions?"

Crocker smiled and looked down at his coffee cup. "They don't always work out just the way I'd plan 'em, but say, it's all been interesting."

"For instance."

"Well…it isn't the sort of thing to bore another man with, but there've been times." He grinned again. "Like last summer. I got a bee in the bonnet to see Death Valley. You know, in California? I'd been reading this magazine that I got in a little town outside of Yosemite. It had a story in it about a wagon train getting stuck out in Death Valley in the middle of summer time. And I got to wondering just what that might have been like."

"And so you rode your bike down into Death Valley?"

He nodded. "I rode into Stovepipe Wells on June 30. It was so bright out I was near to blind, and so hot that my bike tires sounded like they were rolling through molasses. Folks thought I was crazy, needless to say."

"Needless to say they were right. Your sister also mentioned something about you getting stuck in a blizzard in the Dakotas."

Crocker's grin turned electric. "That's about the only time I ever thought that maybe I'd made me a big mistake. See," and he leaned forward again, "I just got done reading this book about the pioneers and how they managed to survive through some of those north country winters. Now me, I'm from down this way, and the only time I ever saw the North was in the finer times of the year. So…" He leaned back and shrugged. "I rode into Bismarck, North Dakota, on December 23. I'd had me a fair enough trip, comin' up from the south. Hit a little storm in Kansas, and another one right at the Nebraska–South Dakota line, but neither one didn't amount to much. I kind of got to thinking that all the stories were just that…stories. Well, I figured to take one of the back roads north out of Bismarck and visit old Fort Mandan. You ever been there?"

I shook my head.

"Well, it's kind of along the Missouri River, there, just east of Washburn a hair. I got me about fifteen miles out of Bismarck, and I tell you what. That old wind commenced to rage down from Canada, and those big old storm clouds lowered right down on the prairie"—he smacked the table with one hand—"and snow pellets about the size of golf balls start shooting right down the road, right into my face. Let me tell you, I got to know real quick why some of them settlers never made it where they was going."

"But you obviously did."

"Well, it's ranching country. I found me a barn and snugged down on the lee side, between a big old combine and an old semitrailer. Long as a man's got something to break the wind, it's not so bad. So I sat there, listening to that storm and watching that snow snake and curl around the buildings. It got dark, and the only thing I could see was the vapor light right by the barn. Watching that blizzard dance around that light was about all the entertainment I had for the better part of twelve hours."

"Makes me cold just to think about it," I said. Shari Chino appeared at my elbow with more coffee, but I waved her off. Wesley Crocker tried his best not to look relieved when I picked up the ticket.

"Well, it was worth the wait. The storm broke, and I guess I had dozed off for a while, because when I woke up it took some work to shovel myself out of the snow that had drifted around all that machinery. That's when the man of the house saw me. They were fit to be tied. They was mad that I hadn't just come to the house, instead of waitin' it out wrapped in a blanket under the snow."

Crocker stretched his bad leg out, trying to find a comfortable position. "They fed me more'n two men could eat, but the best part was they hauled out two big old scrapbooks that they'd kept over the years. Showed me some pictures of blizzards that were *storms*. That's what the wife told me. She said, 'This wasn't no storm. It's when it don't stop for a week that things get bad.' I believed her."

I thumped the table. "Let's get you somewhere more comfortable. I've got a couple other things I'd like to ask you about."

Crocker nodded eagerly, thinking that it was his traveling that piqued my curiosity.

28

I opened the massive, carved oak front door and held it for Wesley Crocker. Even as the first wash of familiar aromas wafted out to greet me, so too did the curse of my life—the distant jangling of the damn telephone far out in the kitchen. I ignored it, knowing that it would go away if it wasn't important.

"Now say, sir," Crocker murmured as he stood in the tiled foyer. "This is..." And he stopped for want of anything better to say.

"It'll do," I said. "Let me show you where you're going to be staying."

"Is that your phone, sir?"

"I suppose." I led him down the short hall. "Watch the step," I said when we reached the living room. He maneuvered his crutches carefully on the polished tile, trying to divide his attention between where he was hobbling and the view.

I used my eldest daughter Camille's bedroom as a convenient guest room—it was the farthest from my own burrow on the other side of the house. And since I rarely had overnight guests, the linens went untouched for months at a time.

"Here's a place to sleep," I said, and Wesley Crocker leaned against the door, a wistful expression on his grizzled face.

"Ain't seen that many teddy bears in one spot in some time," he said.

"My daughter's. She takes a few every time she visits. She doesn't visit often. Anyway, it's a comfortable bed. Let me show you the bathroom." I turned and realized the telephone was still ringing. "It's right here on the right. Let me get the damn phone."

I crossed the living room quickly and picked up the phone from the kitchen counter. I knew who it was before I heard the voice, since only one person had the patience to let the thing ring thirty times.

"Gastner."

"Good morning, sir," Estelle Reyes-Guzman said as if we hadn't spent most of the night together. She sounded bright and efficient. "Do you have Wesley Crocker with you?"

"Good morning, and yes, I do. Why?"

"I just wanted to make sure that he got from there to there in one piece."

"He did."

"Actually, I wanted to tell you what Bob Torrez found out. I got him to dig around in that pile of scrap metal, and he found the two-sided tape that sticks the deer whistler base to the truck."

"What about the plastic base itself?"

"No, sir. But he said he and Eddie Mitchell would scour the intersection again and come up with it. If it's there, they'll find it."

"What else did he have to say?"

"He said that the bolts holding the front bumper on didn't come with the truck. They're longer than they should be, for one thing. For another, they're not chrome, and the bumper was. He said the bolts always match the bumper."

"Huh," I said. "So if the kid bought a grille guard, then it stands to reason it came with mounting bolts that would replace the originals."

"Yes, sir. And if he was in a hurry to take the guard off after a collision, he might not have had time to hunt up the original bolts."

"Or might not have thought of it."

"Yes, sir."

"Have you talked again with the Wilton kid?"

"No, sir. I wanted to stay clear of him until we had something definite to go on. I told the deputies the same thing."

"And the sheriff as well, I hope."

"He went home to bed, sir."

"Smart man. So should you. What about Tom Pasquale?"

"He's been checking in regularly with dispatch, sir. Vanessa Davila left the trailer shortly after you took them home. She walked as far as MacArthur Street, then turned around and walked home."

"That's almost a mile, round trip. She isn't the type for exercise. I wish we knew what's going around in that head, if anything."

"That's one of the reasons I called, sir. I came home for a little bit...just in time to fix breakfast for Francis and the kid."

"I'm sure they appreciated that."

"One can only hope. But I went through Maria Ibarra's things again."

"There wasn't anything there, Estelle."

"Well, sir, there was, but not where we looked the first time. Can you stand a visitor for a few minutes?"

"Sure. I was just about to put the coffee on. I was giving Crocker the tour."

She chuckled, but didn't say what amused her. I hung up and turned to see Crocker hobbling across the living room. "Kitchen," I said, sweeping my hand around. I pointed at the refrigerator and then at the stove. "Food." I pointed at the telephone. "Sister in California when you get around to it." I realized I was sounding like a parent, and grinned. "I'm no nurse, so you're just going to have to make yourself at home."

I stepped down into the living room. "The television works, and I have one video. And books, since you like to read. I have lots of books."

Crocker hobbled just far enough to reach the first set of bookshelves, where the multivolume set of New Mexico statutes gathered dust. "You know, a man can learn a lot of history just through readin' the laws," he said.

"Sure. Given enough free time."

He moved slowly along the east wall bookcase, from statutes to natural history to Grant's memoirs and the rest of my Civil War collection. He turned and grinned at me, nodding. "I guess I could just kinda sit here and read for a bit," he said.

"Make yourself at home. I come and go at all hours, so don't wait on me for anything. You want some coffee?"

"Why, that would be fine," he said absently, but I could see he was lost in the book titles again.

As I put the grounds in the filter and filled the pot, I watched him inch along the shelves, now and then stopping to pull a volume toward himself a quarter of an inch. He hesitated in the Civil War section.

"That book on Joshua Chamberlain is particularly good," I said as I walked back into the living room and grunted into my leather chair.

Crocker frowned. "I'd like to look at that," he said. "It always surprised me that he lived to be such an old man after being so terribly hurt in the war." He said it quietly, just as an observation in passing, not to impress me. But I was impressed.

I tented my hands and waited until he moved another couple feet into the section of Revolutionary War and War of 1812 books. In order to reach those, he had to step past a collection of family photographs. I saw his brow furrow.

"Did your wife pass on?"

"Yes."

He nodded as if that was all he needed to know, which indeed it was.

"You have a passion for military history," Crocker observed.

"I've always believed that our wars define us," I answered. "And that's not an original observation by any means. But let me ask you a question, Mr. Crocker." He turned with one hand still resting on the shelving. "How is it that a man who has spent his life traveling, observing, learning"—I paused, my hands still in front of my mouth—"and *remembering*...How is it that you can spend so long doing that, and when it comes to suspicious, maybe violent, activity within one hundred yards of you, you see nothing?"

Crocker dropped his hand to his crutch and stood quietly, eyebrows knit.

"And how is it that you can walk down a quiet street," I continued, "and not see the single vehicle that struck you? Not see it either coming or going. Now how is that? Someone who can see the faint wagon rut traces of Bennett's Road from a mile away doesn't notice whether it's an automobile, a pickup truck, or a tractor trailer that hits him. How is that?"

I hooked my hands behind my head and let the leather recliner cradle me. Crocker looked back at the books, but I knew I was right. He sure as hell wasn't thinking about the War of 1812.

29

"You know, in thirty years I ain't done anything illegal, except maybe a little trespass now and then." Crocker leaned against the oak fascia of the bookcases and looked down at the floor. I kept quiet. "Nothing would please me more than you folks finding out who murdered that little girl."

"A small point," I said. "She wasn't murdered."

Crocker looked at me blankly. "I thought that's what everyone was thinking."

"Only in the beginning. But the autopsy shows that she choked to death. A piece of pizza crust with a big gob of cheese and pepperoni."

"My Lord," Crocker whispered. "And then somebody just dumped her there under those bleachers?"

"It appears so. It would be a hell of a dismal place to have a picnic."

"Now who would go and do a thing like that?"

"That's what we want to know, Mr. Crocker. And I think you know more than you're telling us."

He stepped away from the bookcase, holding himself on his crutches. "Now this is the God's honest truth, Sheriff. I camped under those trees, and sure enough I noticed there were two vehicles parked behind the high school, there. I could even hear a voice now and then, but I couldn't make out what was bein' said. That's a dark place, and the only thing I could see was taillights. I couldn't tell you what those lights belonged to, car or truck."

"And no one opened a door while you were looking?"

"No, sir. At least, if they did, no inside light came on."

"And you didn't see one or both of the vehicles go over toward the bleachers?"

"No, sir. And that's the God's honest truth."

"What about later, when you got hit?"

After just a couple heartbeats' hesitation, Crocker said, "That was a Ford pickup truck."

"Color?"

"If I had to say..." He paused and frowned. "Real dark color. Maybe blue, or brown, or black, or dark green. Something like that."

"Just one color?"

"Far as I saw." He bit his lip, sheepish.

"How did you know what make it was?"

This time, Crocker smiled. "Because it said so in great big letters on the tailgate, sir."

"That's always a sure giveaway," I replied and pushed myself out of my chair. "Coffee?" Crocker nodded. "Take anything in it?" He shook his head. A couple minutes later, when I handed him the cup, I asked, "So tell me, why didn't you tell us this twenty-four hours ago?"

Crocker set the coffee cup down and lowered himself into one of the other leather chairs. "Well, sir, I just got to thinking. I didn't figure I was hurt bad, and I thought I could fix up the bike or get another one easy enough. But if I said anything, then I'd get all tied up with the law somehow. Hit-and-run is pretty serious business, ain't it?"

"A felony."

"See there? And I got to thinking about me having to testify and all that...and if the driver got himself a good lawyer, then there'd be delays. My soul, I could end up here in this fair little town for a year. Maybe longer."

"And that's surely a fate worse than death," I said. "Did you see the driver? You said if the driver got *himself*..."

Crocker shook his head quickly. "No, I didn't see who it was. That was just a manner of speakin'. But I think there was two in that truck. As they drove away and turned up that street on the other side of the park, I could see what I thought was two heads, there, silhouetted by the streetlights."

"They went up past the park?"

"Yes, sir. Turned at that first left and went up that way."

"Is there anything else about the truck you remember?"

Crocker sipped coffee and closed his eyes. Finally he said, "No, sir."

"Couldn't see a grille guard, or lights out, or anything like that?" He shook his head, but he was still frowning. "What else?" I prompted.

"Well, now, sir, I couldn't swear to this, so I hate to say it."

"Say it anyway."

"Well, it seems to me that I saw the truck earlier in the afternoon, when I was ridin' back into town from the north, there."

"Tell me about it."

"Well, that's all there is to tell. I was ridin' back into town, ridin' on that county road that comes in from the north."

"Forty-three."

"That's the one. Goes on out of town and up the mesa past the village dump. That truck came out of town, passed me by, and then went on up the road a quarter of a mile or so, and turned around. They drove back and passed me kinda fast. Didn't seem like they give me much room, neither."

"And you think that truck was the same one that hit you?"

"I think it was. Like I say, I wouldn't swear to it. But I think so."

"And you didn't see any distinguishing features then, either?"

"None that I noticed. Just looked like a common truck to me."

"And you didn't notice who was in it?"

"No. But I think there was maybe just the one person driving. That's the way I remember it."

"What time was all this?"

"Oh, I suppose just about sundown. I was just startin' to think it was a good time to get off the road. Maybe find myself something to eat."

"Huh," I said and gazed into my coffee.

"You're thinkin' that there's some connection between that little girl dying and that truck, is what I see in your face."

"We don't know that yet. We have two isolated incidents, and the only common factor to both of them is you...maybe." I looked at Crocker, unblinking. He didn't know what to say and settled for a helpless shrug.

"What I've told you is all I know, sir. God's honest truth."

Estelle Reyes-Guzman's light, rapid knock on the front door startled me, and she opened it and stepped into the foyer before I could pry myself vertical. I waved her into my den, leaving Wesley Crocker in the living room to wonder by himself what we were up to.

"I should have known to look here before," Estelle said by way of greeting, and she laid her briefcase on my desk and snapped open the locks.

"Look where?"

She opened the briefcase and pulled out the blue notebook that we had found among Maria Ibarra's few belongings in the truck. She laid her hand flat on the cover and looked at me. "Kids write notes and all kinds of things in their notebooks," she said.

"Sure," I said.

With one fingernail, she flipped the notebook open. On the inside cover, in tiny, neat script, was Maria Ibarra's schedule—all eight periods, including the names of the teachers. Below that were three numbers: 39-17-50. I tapped them with my finger. "Her locker combination?"

"Yes. And her locker is basically empty. A few books, is all. Nothing else. This first section is her math, and you can see that she kept each day's problem set, or sets, in order. The math teacher checks them right in the notebook, so she didn't have to tear them out. She did problem set 19 on October 2. That's probably either the day she arrived, or the day after."

"All right.

"The next section in the notebook is history, and again, we can see how neat she was. It's hard to tell from what little is there what kind of work she was doing, but it's neat. The next section is language arts. Vocabulary words, reading assignments, things like that."

"Where is all this going?" I asked.

"To the back cover, sir. We go past language arts, and the next section, her biology notes, are all on one page."

"If she didn't speak much English, it's hard to imagine her being able to do much in a science class," I said. "They're hard enough if you speak the language."

"Right. And then there is a section for her afternoon classes, including Spanish." She didn't tour all the pages, but rifled through quickly. "As we might expect, most of the notebook is still blank." When she reached the back cover, she said, "And she's so organized and fastidious that she keeps the inside covers clean. Most kids doodle all over the place."

"Maybe she wasn't a doodler."

"She was, in the appropriate place." Estelle backed up through several pages. "Actually, more of a graphics designer." I looked at the drawing in front of me.

"Huh," I said. The ballpoint pen drawing was a thoroughly detailed three-dimensional rendering of a massive stone crucifix with rose vines twining around it. Each of the five rose blossoms was deeply shaded, somber flowers that would have been appropriate for any funeral. "Pretty good. You see that kind of thing on T-shirts and in the back windows of low-riders."

"And in many notebooks, I'm sure," Estelle said and turned the page. "Along with this sort of thing, as well." Scattered around the page, with other, smaller crosses here and there, were the ubiquitous badges of what teenage girls thought was important... the love matches.

I'd seen them spray-painted on every highway underpass in Posadas, and on half of the blank back walls of businesses. *Paco y Esmeralda*, or *Tiffany 'n Sammy*, or *Freddy loves Tomasita*. They came in endless variations.

In her notebook, Maria Ibarra had tried out only one combination of names, but in ten or twelve styles.

In script varying from simple block to balloon to old English, the legend was always the same: *MI y RH*.

"Maria Ibarra and Ryan House," I said.

"Or Maria Ibarra and Richard Hiliger," Estelle added, "or Maria Ibarra and Richard Hernandez."

"You're saying that those are all of the RH combinations at Posadas High School?"

Estelle nodded. "Richard Hiliger is in the special education program for students with profound learning disabilities. He's wheelchair restricted and needs help feeding himself." Estelle grimaced. "Odds are good it isn't him. Hernandez is a sophomore. Right now he's on a week-long field trip with the FFA program to Kansas City. The high school principal knows him well, since he's always on the top honors list. Archer's comment was that if Hernandez got within five feet of a girl, he'd probably dissolve with fright."

"That too shall pass," I said. "But it's more interesting to think that 'RH' means Ryan House. And if it's House, then we've got a good reason for a pickup truck with Ryan House in it to be interested in Wesley Crocker."

I stepped away from the desk and toed the door of my den closed. "If Ryan House was somehow involved with the Ibarra girl's death, and if he thought that Wesley Crocker had seen them...or had even caught a glimpse of their vehicle in the dark..."

"Maybe, sir."

"Let's say that Ryan House was riding in the truck driven by Dennis Wilton when it hit Crocker. Why, exactly, we don't know. They go home and panic, seeing the bent grille guard. So, being the clever souls that they are, they take off the damaged guard, clean up the truck, and take off to the game for cover."

Estelle nodded, but said nothing. I continued, "Impact with that boulder did a pretty thorough job of erasing evidence of the collision. In most people's minds, entirely adequate, unless you look really close." I stopped and frowned. "No one would take that kind of risk," I said when the silence began to thicken.

My stomach growled, but I ignored it. Estelle reached into her briefcase and pulled out a small manila envelope. She produced three finger print cards and laid them side by side on the desk. One set was so clear it looked like it had been rolled at the office. The other was smeared and appeared to be only the bottom portion, across the lower third of the finger pad. The third was a print taken at the autopsy for Ryan House.

"This one," Estelle said, and indicated the complete print on the first card, "is from a drinking glass used by Dennis Wilton at the hospital earlier today. It matches ten for ten with prints on file when the Wiltons applied for passports two years ago when they went to England. This one I lifted from the seatbelt buckle of the crash truck this morning."

"It's not very clear."

"No, it's not. But if you look in this area," and she pointed with a pencil while she handed me a magnifying glass at the same time, "you'll see enough similarities that you could imagine a match. Maybe one and a half, maybe two out of ten."

I bent and studied the prints. "I'd like to see this under a stereo," I said.

"That doesn't help much, but some."

I stood up with a grunt. "And so what. It's the kid's own truck. You'd expect to see his prints all over it."

"This was taken from the passenger side seatbelt buckle, sir." She indicated a point beside her left hip. "The lock side."

"So?"

"This is a thumbprint, sir. It's just about impossible to press the release of your own belt with your thumb. On either side, you'd do it with your index finger. Unless you were releasing the other person's belt. If he reached across to unsnap the passenger's buckle, he'd use his thumb, no matter which hand he used. If he reached across with his left hand"—and Estelle did so—"he'd use his thumb. If he reached down with his right hand, he'd use his right thumb."

I sat down on the edge of my desk and crossed my arms over my belly, regarding Estelle skeptically. "What would be the point?"

"The point, sir, would be to kill Ryan House."

30

Estelle Reyes-Guzman sat quietly while I mulled over that bombshell. Finally I said, "Do you have some reason to suggest that Dennis Wilton may have wanted to murder his best friend?"

"No."

"He'd have to be halfway suicidal to go about it like that, anyway. There are a thousand and one ways something could go wrong."

"That's true, sir. And I've been thinking a lot about that in the past few hours. The crash of that pickup truck into that rock is interesting in all kinds of ways. It's an interesting set of circumstances. First, it appears that the truck was aimed at the rock, from the beginning. It never swerved, even after tearing through a fence."

She stopped and looked at me, left eyebrow raised while I digested that information. "I've never tried it, sir, but I would think it would actually take some work to keep a vehicle going on track while it bumped and banged across a rough shoulder, through a fence, and then another hundred feet to the target."

I shook my head skeptically. "We've both been to a number of accidents where the driver apparently just froze at the wheel, Estelle. That's almost as common as jerking the wheel and causing a rollover."

"Maybe. But in this case, it's interesting that the impact was entirely on the passenger's side."

"That's not hard to imagine, if you remember how the boulder was located, Estelle."

She shook her head doggedly. "Second, the driver had the advantage of both an airbag and a shoulder harness-seatbelt combination. The passenger had neither. Third, the truck was traveling at a reasonable rate of speed. Plenty fast to be lethal without protection, but a pretty good gamble with protection, if the driver was the gambling sort."

I shook my head. "Be reasonable, Estelle. There are lots of ways to murder people. I don't think driving head-on into a boulder is high on the list."

"Why not, if you were reasonably sure of getting away with it?"

"You could never be sure."

"Not if you were an experienced adult. But a kid? They think in absolute terms, sir. And who would ever know?"

I laughed. "Well, if you're right about all this, you know, for one."

"But some kid, maybe with a touch of arrogance, who thinks police are as dumb as the one he comes in contact with all the time?"

"Thomas Pasquale, you mean?"

"Sure. If he's the law enforcement experience level held to be typical, then the kid has every reason to be confident."

I gazed at Estelle, trying to sort pieces. "I'll ask it again: why would Dennis Wilton want to murder his best friend?"

Estelle put the fingerprint samples back in the briefcase along with the notebook and closed the lid.

"I don't know, sir."

"Any guesses?"

"Well, sure, I can imagine all kinds of things. Maybe the two boys picked up Maria...she was pretty enough. And in this day and age, you never know what's going through the minds of two young men in rut. Maybe things didn't go so well, either through intent or accident. It doesn't take much imagination to figure out what they might have had planned. She chokes and they panic."

"And dump her under the bleachers? Christ," I said. "Why wouldn't they take her out into the middle of the prairie somewhere?"

"Because when the body was found, if it ever was, that would make it look like murder, sir. If the body was never found, you're still looking at foul play. This way, by dumping her under the bleachers, police would be more apt to write it off as some sort of bizarre accident...especially when they discovered Maria Ibarra's curious lifestyle."

I looked at Estelle as all the jumble rolled through my mind. "What about the phone call? You think they called the village P.D. so that a cop like Tom Pasquale would respond?"

"That may be part of it, sir, but I think it's simpler than that. The office number that was called isn't recorded. Anyone who watches television knows, or at least believes, that all 911 calls are. By calling the P.D., they didn't have to worry about a voice match."

"We haven't heard from the state lab, have we."

"No, sir. But I called Lieutenant Bucky and asked him to expedite the processing of the hair samples that Bob Torrez found under the bleachers. I sent samples of both Dennis Wilton and Ryan House's hair to the lab by courier earlier."

"Where did you get Wilton's?"

Estelle came close to smiling. "From his hospital pillow case."

I frowned and let my chin drop down to my chest. "It doesn't figure, does it? You're saying now that, based on the initials in the notebook, maybe Maria Ibarra was going with Ryan House. That's an unlikely match, somehow."

"But I'm not suggesting they were 'going together,' sir. Maria might have had a crush on House from afar. Girls do that, you know."

"I know, Estelle, I have two daughters of my own. And boys have crushes, too. But think on it. If you're suggesting that they somehow got together...that it was House who was with Maria when she choked to death...it was more than a one-way crush from afar. And that's not too likely, either. He's a senior, she's barely a freshman. She doesn't even speak much English. She lived like a goddamned troll in an old truck body under the interstate. House is from a good family."

"Good, sir?"

"You know what I mean."

"No, sir, I don't," Estelle said, and I looked up quickly, hearing the snap in her voice. "If Ryan House was with Maria when she choked, apparently he didn't do anything to help her. And then she was dumped like a sack of garbage."

I shrugged and nodded. "You're right. That's subhuman behavior, if that's what happened."

"*Someone* was with her when she died."

"Yes," I said. "Someone was. Otherwise she wouldn't have been dumped. An innocent passerby would have called the police the minute she was discovered. I can't imagine that she was eating pizza under the bleachers. For one thing, she had no money to buy it with. If it was Ryan House who was with her, that leaves us with what appears to be the single essential question...Why did Dennis Wilton want Ryan House dead?"

"I don't know," Estelle said. "Jealousy, maybe."

"Jealous about a fifteen-year-old Mexican illegal alien? I think not."

"Fear of discovery."

"That I can imagine. If Wilton was somehow involved in Maria Ibarra's death, and Ryan House was going to blow the whistle, then murder makes sense."

Estelle looked up suddenly, her mouth forming a small *oh*. "What if it was Ryan House who called the village police to report the body?"

"And Wilton figured that was the first step toward stepping forward to admit to what they'd done."

"Maybe."

"But if she choked accidentally, dumping the body isn't much of a crime. It's a simple case of concealing an incident, compounded with failure to report an attended death."

"We know that, sir. A couple of kids don't."

I slid off the desk and walked around it, to thump down into the old chair. It let out a squawk as the springs compressed. "With everything Ryan House had hanging in the balance—scholarships, awards, honors—he might have panicked. And Dennis Wilton was no slouch in his own right."

"Glen Archer said that he'd just been accepted at a couple of premed programs out of state. Prestigious schools."

I shrugged. "Well, maybe. And maybe we're just inventing ghosts to chase. What about Miss Davila? Suppose *she* was the one with Maria when she died."

"They were at least acquaintances, maybe even best friends, sir. Vanessa may well have been the only friend that Maria had."

"So what? Jealousy rears its ugly head, Estelle. Maria is Vanessa's best friend, and suddenly Maria is mooning over a senior. Vanessa isn't blind. She can see that Maria Ibarra is a cute kid—maybe in need of a shower and a perm, but a cute kid nevertheless. And Vanessa looks in the mirror and knows damn well that she *isn't* cute, in any way, shape, or form. And so there she goes, tricked and ridiculed by fate once again."

Estelle smiled and looked up at the ceiling beams. She reached up and clapped a hand over her face in mock frustration. "I want to go to bed."

I laughed. "That's the first time I think I've ever heard you admit to fatigue, sweetheart. Join the club." I leaned forward and indicated the briefcase. "Anything else?"

Estelle sighed. "Sheriff Holman came back into the office a few minutes ago. He asked if there was anything he could do. I had him shag Glen Archer back to the high school so he could go through the four lockers...Maria's, Vanessa's, Dennis Wilton's, and Ryan House's."

"Anything?"

She glanced at her watch. "I'm sure they're still at it, sir. They were going to go through every notebook, everything they can find."

"All right, that's good. Keep Pasquale after Vanessa Davila. If he gets tired, rotate someone in. I still have a feeling that she's more than just a grieving friend. Grieving friends talk to people... they don't clam up like that. That leaves us with young Mister Wilton."

"I'd like to talk with him again, sir. I talked with him briefly right after the crash. Holman was busy with Mr. and Mrs. House, and I had only a few minutes at the hospital to talk with Wilton's parents."

"What did you think?"

"They're terrified, sir."

"Terrified?"

"I asked them for consent for a blood test. They agreed, and then afterward, when it was too late, they put two and two together. They know that if anything shows up, Dennis will be sued for wrongful death...and he's a minor, which means it falls back on them."

"How thoughtful and compassionate they are," I mused.

"I'm sure they managed to work a little grief in there somewhere," Estelle said.

"Maybe. Now listen. When you talk with this kid, don't spook him." I realized as the words were being uttered that they were a waste. Estelle was a far more competent interrogator than I.

But she just nodded and said, "I won't, sir. I'm really curious to hear how he's going to describe the accident, now that he's out of the sedative. And now that we know a few more details."

"Or at least we think we know," I said. "Crocker says now that it was a dark-colored pickup truck that hit him. He didn't want to say anything earlier for fear of being caught up in something that would keep him in town."

Estelle cocked her head and looked at me askance. "That's what he says?"

I nodded.

"Well, maybe," she said.

"Something nags about that?"

"No, I guess not." She looked at the door, as if she could see Crocker through the oak panels. "Wesley Crocker is a person far, far beyond my experience, sir. I'm not sure that those of us who are nest oriented can ever understand him." She pushed herself out of her chair with unaccustomed effort. "If it was Wilton's truck that hit him, the paint samples will prove it."

"If you get a match, then we need a warrant to search for that bent grille guard, Estelle. Five gets you ten that it's tucked inside his dad's garage."

"Or at the bottom of the lake up at the old quarry."

"Maybe so," I said. "He's not going anywhere, but it wouldn't hurt to have Tom Mears or Tony Abeyta park themselves down the street and keep an eye peeled. Tell 'em to use their own vehicles. And keep someone on Vanessa. Nobody is going anywhere, so we can afford to sit back and watch and wait for some lab reports to tell us which way to go."

"If anything comes from the locker search, I'll let you know," Estelle said, and I followed her back out into the foyer. Wesley Crocker was still in the living room, resting with his leg up, his head back and eyes closed. At the sound of the door, he turned his head and grinned, waving a hand at Estelle.

"Good to see you again, miss."

Estelle nodded and glanced at me, the crow's feet at the corners of her eyes just a little deeper than they needed to be. She didn't say "What a pair," but I had a suspicion she was thinking it.

31

The sun's schedule had very little to do with my own. I had learned that simple lesson over the years, and that's probably what had contributed more than anything else to my colossal insomnia. After Estelle left, I glanced at my watch, thinking that a two-hour nap might be the proper medicine. But other things nagged, and seven minutes after ten on a late-October Saturday morning was as good a time as any to find normal folks at home.

When I walked back through the living room, Wesley Crocker didn't bother to open an eye, and his lower jaw was going slack as he sank into the comfort and quiet of the place. It was enough to make me yawn, but I plodded on into the kitchen and thumbed through the phone directory.

Stub Moore answered his phone on the tenth ring, and he didn't sound alert. I glanced outside through my newly trimmed, painted, and cleaned kitchen window and saw no sun filtering down through the bare limbs. With the weather chilling and the sky gray, people were going to start hibernating.

"Stub, this is Bill Gastner."

"Yo," he said, and let it go at that. He knew damn well it wasn't a social call. I didn't need to keep him long. Like so many expert school-bus drivers, he knew the youngsters and he knew their habits. He gave me what I needed in less than two minutes. Estelle had said that Moore had given her a list of students as well, and when the bus driver hung up the phone, he was probably shaking his head, wondering if the investigating cops ever talked to each other.

With his short list of names in hand, I went into my bedroom and changed clothes, donning the most comfortable and least threatening civilian clothes I could find—a pair of heather-green corduroy slacks and a wool checkered shirt that my daughter had sent me for my birthday. And like the honest soul she was, she hadn't bothered to try to stroke my feelings by sending something several sizes too small. It was a checkered tent, and it fit my mounds like an absurd, huge glove.

With a light tan jacket to hide the threat of gun and cuffs, I left the house to a sleeping Wesley Crocker.

A few minutes after ten-thirty, I pulled into a driveway on Hidalgo Loop, behind the middle school off MacArthur. I parked 310 behind a late-model foreign sedan and beside a Volkswagen bus.

I had known Maryanne Scutt for twenty years. She had two daughters, and hadn't seen her husband since the older daughter turned three. She'd probably sold more real estate in Posadas County over the years than any other two Realtors put together. She answered the doorbell, and when she saw me her eyebrows came together quickly, and then her face smoothed as she composed herself.

"Sheriff, good morning," she said. She didn't open the screen door.

I smiled faintly and nodded. "Morning, Mrs. Scutt. We're still in the process of investigating that fatality from last night." I waved a hand aimlessly off toward the east. "The one out on 78."

"Wasn't that awful," she said, and meant it.

"Yes, it was. We're doing some routine follow-ups. The school-bus driver said that your daughter was a passenger on the game bus. Is that correct?"

"Yes, she was."

"I wonder if I might talk with her for a few minutes." I saw the worry on the woman's face. "Apparently she was sitting on the side of the bus where she would have seen the vehicle when it passed. There're a couple things I'd like to ask her. And I'd like you to be present," I added.

"Well, sure," she said, and pushed open the screen door. "She isn't up yet, but let me get her." She indicated the living room, and I walked over to a padded straight chair that sat beside the blocked-off fireplace whose wood and brickwork were painted gloss white.

The place smelled like a mix of a hundred different perfumes and powders. I could feel my sinuses starting to swell shut. The chair looked as if it was sturdy enough, and I eased myself down onto it to wait.

In a few minutes Mrs. Scutt reappeared with young Gail, a pretty towhead high school sophomore, plainly embarrassed at having a stranger see her dressed in a bathrobe.

They both perched on the sofa. "Gail," I said, "I'm Undersheriff William Gastner." I smiled. "I think the last time I saw you was when you were about this long." I held my hands a couple of feet apart, but Gail didn't care when I'd seen her. She shifted nervously and tried a brave smile.

"I know it's been a rough night for you," I continued, without the vaguest idea what sort of night she'd had, "but I need to ask you a few questions about the truck accident."

She nodded and clasped her hands together between her knees. Her eyes followed my hand as I slipped a microcassette recorder out of my pocket and placed it on the footstool in front of me. I leaned forward, locking my eyes on hers. "I'd like to record, if it's all right with you." I smiled ruefully. "My hands get so lame in this cold weather it'd take me all day to write down a few notes." I glanced at Mrs. Scutt. "Is that all right with you, Maryanne?"

She nodded and put her hand over her daughter's.

"Good. Now, Gail, the bus driver, Stub Moore, says that you were one of several students sitting on the left side of the bus last night. Is that right?"

She nodded and said in a hoarse whisper, "I was sitting three seats behind the driver."

"By the window?" I asked.

She nodded and then, like the sharp little kid she was, said for the benefit of the recorder, "Yes."

"All right, Gail, I'm most interested in what you saw when the pickup truck passed the school bus. The truck that later crashed into the rock. Where you looking out the window when it passed the bus?"

She nodded. "Yes."

"Is there any particular reason you looked out just then?"

"Well, I heard somebody behind me, and they're all, 'Here comes Denny and Ryan.' So I turned to look. There was lots of cars passing us on the way home."

"Could you see clearly?"

"Yeah, pretty."

"And was it them? Was it Dennis Wilton and Ryan House?"

She nodded and frowned.

"Was the truck going very fast?"

"No. Not really." She moved her hand from side to side. "It just went by, like."

"And you could see them clearly?"

"Yeah."

"Could you see who was driving?"

"Well, I could see Ryan, so I guess it was Denny behind the wheel." She bit her lip.

"You could see Ryan House clearly?"

She nodded and I could see tears in her eyes. Her mother slipped an arm around her.

"Gail, can you remember what Ryan House was doing? Did he look up at the bus, was he waving, what?"

"He was asleep."

"He was asleep?"

"Yes, his head was leaning against the thing there," and she tipped her own head and indicated with her hand about where the passenger window's rear post would be. "He's all with his jacket, or something, wadded up like a pillow."

"And he didn't appear to wake up when the truck went by the bus?"

"No, sir."

"Were you able to see Dennis Wilton?"

"Not really. Only for a second as the truck came up beside us."

"And not after that?"

She shook her head.

"Now I'd like you to really bring that picture back in your mind, Gail. Could you see, or did you notice, whether Ryan House was wearing his shoulder harness?"

She frowned and looked at the rug. "Yes, he was."

"You noticed that particularly?"

She looked up at me. "Yes. Because I could see that he had his coat all squished under the belt where it went by his neck, like it was holding it in place. His jacket."

"Okay. Did the person sitting with you see them, too?"

"Yes."

"Who were you sitting with?"

"Melissa Roark. She leaned across me to wave, but they didn't see her."

"Do you remember if Vanessa Davila was on the spectator bus?"

Her pretty little eyebrows twitched a hair when she heard the name, as if puzzled that I would think that she'd know Vanessa. "I didn't see her."

"And one last thing. Did you see the truck veer off the road?"

This time her reply was just a small, strangled croak that I took for a "no." She wiped her nose. "I heard the driver shout something, and then all of a sudden we slowed down and stopped. He was all shouting for us to stay in our seats, and then he grabbed the fire extinguisher and ran up ahead. I couldn't see very well."

I nodded and reached for the tape recorder, then hesitated. "Gail, did you know Maria Ibarra?"

"Who?"

"Maria Ibarra. She was a student from Mexico who just came to Posadas High a few weeks ago. She's a freshman."

"You mean the girl they found under the bleachers?" She scrunched her shoulders together, making herself as small and inconspicuous as possible. "I knew who she was, is all. A couple of times, I knew some of the kids were all talking about where she lived and stuff like that."

"Where she lived?"

"They were just stories, I think. And they're all, 'She lives in an old truck out in the arroyo,' but..." She scrunched a little more, as if she were trying to touch together the outboard ends of her young, pliable collarbones.

"But no more than that?"

"No."

I stood up amid a cracking of joints and creaking of belt leather. "Mrs. Scutt, thanks. And Gail, you, too. You've been a big help. I shouldn't have to bother you again."

Gail Scutt was all too happy to head for her room, and Maryanne Scutt saw me to the door. I thanked her again, mostly because she had the good sense to let me leave without badgering me with questions that I wouldn't be able to answer.

An hour later, I had three nearly identical copies of my interview with Gail Scutt. Her seat partner, Melissa Roark, confirmed what Gail had seen.

Sitting directly behind the driver had been a sleepy high school junior, Bryan Saenz. He'd seen the truck go by, had remembered a vague image of Ryan House snoozing, and then had been jarred into full wakefulness when the bus driver shouted and spiked the brakes.

Three rows behind Gail, Tiffany Ulibarri, a sober-faced senior, had seen the pickup glide by as well. She'd seen the somnolent Ryan House, even noticed a small patch of breath condensing on the side window by his slack mouth.

That was as far as I cared to go. I didn't need sixty adolescent bus passengers to tell me that Ryan House certainly had been sound asleep when the truck passed the school bus and then pounded itself and him into the limestone.

32

I drove past the high school, saw the deputy's car parked in front along with Glen Archer's station wagon, and on impulse pulled into the circular driveway. I got out of the car. The gray sky was unusually bright even though the sun hadn't been able to crack through the solid high overcast. The light breeze had died, leaving just the leaden, uncharacteristic sky like a pewter bowl inverted from horizon to horizon.

The sidewalk, a full sixteen feet wide, led from the curb to the quadruple glass doors under the lunging gold jaguar that was the school's mascot. For a moment, as I started up the walk, I thought I was looking through my bifocals with one eye and through cloudy water with the other. The sidewalk's neatly clipped margins appeared to converge.

Before I had time to pause and reflect on that odd visual aberration, a sudden and vicious pain lanced through my skull from back to front, traveling in an arc over my left ear. With a yelp, I staggered sideways, tripped over my own feet, and sprawled on my hands and knees, partially off the concrete.

"Jesus Christ," I muttered and remained frozen, waiting for my skull to crack into little pieces. But the pain subsided as quickly as it had come, and with a grunt of relief I pushed myself up to my knees. I reached up with an unsteady hand and wiped the tears out of my eyes.

Apparently no one had seen my swan dive, or if they had, they figured I could pick myself up. I did so, grimacing at the rip in my left trouser knee and the skin scrubbed off the heel of my left hand.

"Absolutely goddamned wonderful," I said. I considered the mishap a sure sign that I wasn't needed inside the school. Sergeant Torrez could search through lockers all day long without help from me. I turned and walked back to the car, still rubbing my bruised hand. I plopped down in the car and just sat still for a few minutes.

"Well, shit," I said finally, not sure of my next step. That in itself was irritating. Usually dogged persistence, if nothing else, had always saved my day. Now I didn't know what to doggedly pursue.

I swept my right hand up to pull the gear lever into drive and missed it by three inches, instead making a ridiculous motion with a clawed right hand like I was trying to catch flies.

The second attempt did the trick, and I pulled 310 out of the school's driveway. Even without making any stops, it seemed an inordinately long distance back to the house. I parked the car, called dispatch and told them where I was, and went inside. I could see Wes Crocker still out cold in the living room, and that seemed about the right decision.

I headed for the dark, quiet confines of my bedroom, closed the door, and shed jacket, hardware, hat, and anything else with hard corners that might disturb me. I could play the waiting game as well as anyone. The bed felt cool and wonderful, and before I'd exhaled ten times, I was hard asleep.

As was usually the case, my brief sleep was a colorful parade of ridiculous dreams. This particular session was dominated by my youngest grandson, Kendall, who was trying to persuade me that yes, his old wooden toboggan had front-end steering. I looked down the slope at the thick forest of Douglas fir through which he proposed to slalom the thing and tried to convince him that his plan was idiocy.

I was irritated that he was right, all along. As soon as we started down the hill the trees disappeared, giving way to thick pasture grass that somehow hadn't been bent by the snow burden.

When I awoke, we still hadn't solved the riddle of the grass. I didn't bother to look for my watch, but swung out of bed and plodded toward the bathroom.

I didn't remember leaving the bathroom and returning to bed, but the dreams started up immediately, and even more ridiculous than before. Wesley Crocker's face refused to come into focus, and he kept making suggestions that really had nothing to do with the problem at hand…whatever that was.

The light seemed harsh, and suddenly, as if something had tripped a switch far inside my skull, I could see the bottom of the bathroom sink, its porcelain slightly dimpled, with a strand of cobweb running from one side over to the center drain trap.

"What the hell's this?" I said, because I'd never had a dream quite so stark and clear. Movement above the sink attracted my eyes, and there was Crocker again, his face more or less in focus.

"I'll call someone," he said, and this time I heard him clearly.

"What the hell?" I said, quite loudly. I was lying on the floor of the bathroom, my head under the sink pedestal, my feet by the commode. It wasn't a resting spot I normally would have chosen, and the concern on Crocker's face echoed that.

"I heard you fall," Crocker said, and then repeated, "I'll call someone." He turned and started to hobble off.

"No, wait, damn it," I said. Like most people, I had preferences about where strangers might find me and in what condition, and lying under a sink wasn't a top choice. I twisted around until I could draw my knees up, flailing for purchase with my hands at the same time…no doubt looking a good deal like a beached whale.

"You probably oughtn't to move," Crocker said helpfully.

I grunted something rude and continued to flail. Crocker reached down a hand and I waved him off. I didn't care for the vision of him slipping and falling on top of me, the two of us forever tangled on the floor in the bathroom of my master bedroom.

With enough effort to set my pulse hammering in my ears, I managed to roll the right direction and push myself to my hands and knees. I reached up and rested my left arm on the sink's rim.

"I still think I ought to call someone," Crocker said. "I was just thinkin' about stretchin' out for a few minutes, and I heard this God almighty crash, so I come on in."

"Well, here I am," I said. I lifted my head up and pushed against the sink, driving myself upright. My right leg tingled. Shakily, I rested both hands on the sink and looked at myself in the mirror. "Shit." I didn't much care for the aging, fat, old man that stared back at me, a little tremor pulling at the right side of his mouth.

I stood up straight and buttoned my shirt, then ran a hand through quarter-inch-long hair that didn't need combing no matter what acrobatics I performed.

Crocker stood in the doorway of the bathroom, hands on the jamb. Evidently he'd left his crutches behind. I tried a grin at the sight of his worried reflection. With an effort I turned around, one hand still on the sink.

"You want some coffee?" I asked.

"You ought to call somebody," he said, and I grimaced with irritation.

"I'm fine." I let go of the sink and hobbled past him to make my way to the kitchen, thankful that the walls were holding still so that I could find them for support.

Once in the kitchen, familiar things worked their magic. I put on coffee without making a mess even though I had to hold the decanter under the faucet with my left hand. By the time I snapped the "on" button of the coffeemaker, I was feeling human again. The clock on the stove told me it was five minutes to four, and I had to look at it several times before I could believe I'd managed to turn a nap into a major crash.

I walked into the living room and thudded into my leather chair. My stomach growled.

Crocker had made his way along the hall wall from my bedroom to the living room, keeping his weight off his knee. He reached the sofa and eased himself down.

"I don't much care for this getting old business," I said.

"Well, no," Crocker said slowly, as if he didn't quite know what to say.

I leaned my head on one hand and regarded him from across the room. "What are you going to do when you're too old to ride a bike?"

The question surprised him and he smiled. "Walk, I guess. It's slower, but I got time."

"I suppose you do."

He nodded. "I ain't got anything I just have to finish," he said. "So I got time. How much ever I got, it's what the Lord gave me."

"Wouldn't that be nice," I said, not in the mood to discuss personal theology. The only mental image I could conjure was Maria Ibarra, maybe happy for one of the few times in her life, reaching eagerly for a big piece of sloppy, greasy, pepperoni pizza, the food offered to her by a good-looking American kid whose motives were probably not obvious to her. She wouldn't have understood anything about theology if someone had told her that she had only seconds to enjoy life.

My lapse into silence worried Crocker. "How are you feeling?" he asked.

"A little woozy, but otherwise all right," I said. "You never said if you wanted coffee or not."

He shrugged and I took that for a yes, even though I knew damn well what was going through his mind. I suppose that's why it seemed necessary to me to push myself out of the chair with what I thought was my usual vigor and go to the kitchen.

The cups were sitting on the counter, and I had only to pick up the pot from under the machine and pour. My right hand went exactly where I sent it, but from there the signals were botched. With perfect ease, I drew the full decanter off the hot plate and swung it just enough that when my right hand spasmed, the pot crashed to the tile floor.

Glass and hot coffee sprayed into every corner of the kitchen. The string of oaths was painful for the gentle Crocker to hear. I bit off another curse and stood silently regarding the mess on the floor, on my shoes, even on the Navajo rug that lay just beyond the step down into the living room.

"You really ought to call someone," Wesley Crocker said.

"What I need is a goddamned maid," I replied. The broken glass seemed very far away. "Shit," I added, and went into the pantry for the sponge mop, broom, and dustpan. I managed to sweep the most lethal of the glass shards into the dustpan, surprised and not a little alarmed at how useless my right hand had become. I opened the cupboard door under the sink and missed the trash can with the dustpan. The broken glass cascaded back onto the floor at my feet.

I rested with my hands on the sink, a posture that had become familiar to me. Wesley Crocker watched the performance in silence. Without looking up, I said, "How about a beer?"

"No, no," Crocker said hastily, no doubt imagining the havoc I could wreak with a zip-top can. "No, beer and I don't get along so well." And then, like a recording, he added, "But I still think you ought to call someone."

"I dropped the goddamned coffeepot, for God's sakes. Why should I call somebody?" I regarded the mess again, the lake of coffee puddling nicely on the vinyl flooring, various tributaries and extensions and inlets spreading here and there, some of them scuffed into lines by the broom.

"To find out what to do," Crocker said.

I looked at him and frowned. "What's to do is clean up this mess."

"You have a seizure like that, you got to take care of yourself."

I stared at him. "I didn't have a seizure," I said with more irritation than necessary, partly because I knew that Crocker was right. It didn't take a doctor from the Mayo Clinic to figure out what a flash headache with loss of consciousness and partial numbing of one side meant. That didn't mean I had to dwell on it.

I glanced at the stove clock, then at my wristwatch. Estelle had had all afternoon, and there was no way of telling what I had missed by napping away those hours.

The telephone was only a step away, and I picked up the receiver, ready to punch in the number. My mind was blank. I closed my eyes, but that didn't do any good. I had called Estelle Reyes-Guzman so many times that I hadn't even bothered to write her number in the back of the phone directory.

"Shit," I said again. The Reyes-Guzman number wasn't listed, not surprising considering their occupations. Even if it had been, my reading glasses were on the nightstand beside my bed, now about a thousand miles away. Instead, I punched the number for the sheriff's office. Ernie Wheeler was working dispatch.

"Ernie," I said. "Is Estelle in her office?"

"No, sir. I think she's home."

I chuckled. "What the hell is her home number?"

Wheeler didn't make an issue out of his boss's senility, but just rattled off the number. I reached for a pen to write it in the back of the book where it belonged.

"Wait a minute," I said, but Ernie Wheeler could have waited for an hour. My right hand refused to drive the pen, and I made a pathetic series of hen scratchings. With another curse, I tossed the pen across the counter. "Thanks, Ernie," I said and hung up. I quickly punched in the number before it seeped out through the holes in my head.

Francis Guzman answered the phone with his characteristic "Yup?"

"Francis, is Estelle home?"

"Sure, Bill. I think she's out in the kitchen hatching something with Irma. Hang on a minute."

"No, wait," I said, then hesitated. "Don't bother her."

"Can I give her a message?"

"No, that's all right. Listen..." I stopped. "While I've got you on the phone..." I fumbled and stumbled, finding it harder to talk with the professional side of Francis Guzman than it was to mop up coffee-and-glass soup. "I, ah, passed out in the bathroom a while ago, and—"

"You did what?"

"Well," I said offhandedly, "I think I got up from a nap a little too fast or something. Next thing you know I'm lying on the floor, looking at the bottom of the sink."

"And that's it?" His voice was calm, the sort of tone he would use to talk patients into letting him crack open their chests and switch hearts.

"Pretty much. I got some tingling in my right hand. Can't seem to hold on to anything."

"Stay put," he said, and then before I could ask him what he meant, he added, "Here's Estelle, by the way." I heard mumbling in the background for a few seconds, and then Estelle's soft, melodious voice came on the line.

"Sir," she said, "Ron Bucky called me this afternoon, about an hour ago. The hair sample that Bob Torrez collected from the steel frame of the bleachers matches Maria Ibarra's."

"You're kidding," I said. "How could it match hers? I thought Bob found the hairs higher up than what her head would be."

"Unless she was being carried, sir. That's what it looks like. And it fits. If they carried the body from a vehicle to under the bleachers, it's not surprising that in the dark they'd crack a head somewhere along the way."

"Too bad it wasn't their own," I said.

"The most interesting thing is the blood workup."

"No, the most remarkable thing is that Bucky got someone to come in and work on a Sunday," I said.

"Saturday, sir."

"Whatever. What did they find out?"

"Maria Ibarra was clean. No drugs, no traces, nothing. No alcohol, even, which surprises me. Dennis Wilton was clean as well. No alcohol, no nothing."

"And let me guess. Ryan House was..." I stopped to let Estelle fill in the blanks.

"His blood showed a moderate dose of temazepam."

"What the hell is that?" I asked.

"It's a sedative. Francis says that it's similar to Valium. The sort of thing someone would take if they couldn't sleep."

"Prescription?"

"Most likely."

"That's interesting, because this morning I made some house calls."

"So I understand."

I stopped short, amazed yet again at the workings of a small town's communication system. "Who did you talk to?"

"I saw Maryanne Scutt at the drugstore." Estelle chuckled. "She said her daughter was scared to death."

"She should be," I said. "That accident was a horrible experience."

"No, I mean of you."

"Oh," I said. "I'm crushed. I was perfectly civil."

"I'm sure you were, sir. What did you find out?"

"A whole handful of kids sitting on the left side of the bus saw Dennis Wilton's truck pass by. Every one of them said that Ryan House was sleeping."

The phone went silent.

"Every one of the kids I talked to, Estelle. The Scutt kid even remembers seeing the seatbelt holding Ryan's jacket in place. He was using the jacket rolled up as a pillow. One of the other kids remembers seeing a patch of fog on the passenger-side window, right in front of Ryan's mouth. Where he was breathing."

"So he was sound asleep."

"And helped on by the temazepam, no doubt," I said. "I wouldn't..." and I stopped at the sound of the doorbell.

"Someone's here," I said. "Can you hang on a minute?"

I rested the receiver on the phone directory, shaking my head at the interruption.

"You want me to get it?" Crocker called from the living room.

"No, I want you to sit still," I said. By the time I had reached the foyer, the front door was already opening. Dr. Francis Guzman stepped inside.

I stopped short, frowning. "You didn't have to come over," I said.

"I hope not," he replied cheerfully. "But as long as I'm here..."

"Your wife's still on the phone," I said. "I'll be right back."

The young doctor followed me toward the kitchen. He glanced down at the mess on the floor and then I could feel his eyes on me as I picked up the receiver. My left hand worked just fine.

"Your husband just arrived," I said testily. "What did he tell you to do, hold me hostage until he showed up?"

"You were asking the questions, sir."

"Well, it was a slippery trick," I said.

"Behave, sir," she said, and hung up. I turned to face Guzman. He wasn't smiling.

33

"This isn't a stubbed toe, *padrino*," Dr. Francis Guzman said. "You don't get to take a pain pill and feel perfect come morning."

"I had a stroke?" I asked, giving in finally. He had marched me into the bedroom, seated me on the edge of the bed, asked me a thousand questions, and poked and prodded.

"Yes, an episode of some kind. You aren't on blood pressure medication?"

"I used to be."

"But you haven't been taking it, I gather."

"No."

He sighed and shook his head, holding up his hands. "You know what a stroke is, Bill. If the heart pumps blood too hard through a weak vessel in the brain, the vessel pops. Or a vessel gets clogged with cheese from all those burritos and a portion of the brain suffers. It's that simple."

I clenched my right hand. "It feels a little better."

Guzman's mouth twitched in a smile, but there wasn't much humor in his dark eyes. "You have a good imagination, *padrino*."

"So what, then? What do I do?"

"The best and safest thing is to admit you to the hospital and run some tests in the morning."

"I don't think so."

"Then out-patient testing," he said. "We can't rummage around much inside the head, but an MRI will tell us something. It'll give us something to go on."

"That's the gadget the hospital got last year?"

He nodded. "All two point six million dollars of it."

"And all on my tab, too," I said. "Can it wait until next week?"

The doctor stood up and looped his stethoscope around his neck. "I don't know, *padrino*. You might not have another episode for years, or you might have thirty seconds left on the clock."

"That's an encouraging thought."

Guzman thrust his hands in his pockets. His heavy dark eyebrows knit together and he chewed on the corner of his lip as he assessed his patient. "It puzzles me why you're so stubborn, I suppose," he said quietly.

"It's not just a question of being stubborn, Francis. Right now, we're in the middle—"

He cut me off with a shake of the head. "No. Now look. Do you trust me?"

"Trust you? Of course I trust you."

"No, I mean do you *really* trust me? Do you trust me not to exaggerate, not to be just an old maid worrywart?"

"Of course. If I needed a new heart, you're the one who would zip it in."

"Well, then, picture it this way. You're hanging from a loose rock at the edge of a five-thousand-foot cliff. Do you trust me to drop you a rope?"

"Sure." I knew damn well what he was driving at, but that didn't mean I wanted to hear it.

"And as I was handing you the end of the rope, would you say, 'Hold it, Doc. I've got things I have to do?'"

"This isn't the same thing."

"Yes, it is, *padrino*. There are always going to be 'things to do.' That's what life is…'things to do.' Right now, your 'thing to do' is to trust us to do what we do best, and then take care of yourself. Trust Estelle."

"I do trust her."

"Then let her do it," Francis said, his voice taking on an edge. "The Posadas County Sheriff's Department can function without you for a little while." He saw me winding up to say something, and added, "Eventually it's going to have to function without you, my friend. Period."

I looked at him steadily, like an old bulldog figuring the chances of catching the neighbor's cat. Guzman didn't flinch.

"What do you want, then?" I said.

"I want you admitted to Posadas General right now. This evening. I want you monitored, and then first thing in the morning, I want to run you through a battery of tests so we're not flying blind."

I turned and looked out the window at the wooden shutters, closed over the panes so I could sleep anytime day or night. My mind conjured up an image of an old fat man sitting in a wheelchair, drooling from the right side of his mouth, the fingers of his right hand clawed into the cuff of his pajamas.

"Shit," I muttered.

"Yes," Francis said gently. A light knock rapped on the bedroom door, and he stepped over to open it.

I heard Estelle murmur, "I'm here," and he nodded and closed the door again.

"For God's sakes, what is this, the gathering at the wake?" I snapped. I stood up and straightened my clothes, glancing at Francis with irritation. He stepped to one side as I headed for the door, the burst of anger giving me some momentum. I knew that if Estelle saw the mess in the kitchen, she'd be down on her knees, cleaning.

But she had outfoxed me. She'd cleaned the floor before she'd come back to the bedroom to let her husband know that she was in my house.

She saw me standing in the archway to the kitchen and held up the handle of the coffee decanter. "Do you have another one of these, sir?"

"No," I said. I gestured at the floor. "And you didn't have to do that."

She shrugged. "How are you?"

"Fine," I said. "And did Bucky have anything to say about the paint chips?"

She shook her head. "No, sir. He said they might have trouble with that. What we sent him wasn't much more than a little powder...he said it's going to be a hard call."

"Black is black, for Christ's sakes," I said. I noticed that Francis was the only person in the living room. "Where's Crocker?"

"He went into his room, sir."

I grinned. "Family squabbles bother him, sweetheart."

"What did Francis say?"

I glanced at Guzman, who was standing with his hands behind his back, examining the titles of the books on the shelf beside the television. "He wants to commit me."

"Admit," he said from across the living room. "You don't need mental help yet."

"It amounts to the same thing," I said. I lowered myself onto one of the kitchen chairs. I had no sooner touched the chair than the telephone rang. Estelle reached for it, one eyebrow up in question.

"Go ahead," I said.

"Detective Reyes-Guzman," she said, and I got the impression that she had been expecting the call. She listened for several seconds, then said, "Is Sergeant Torrez standing by?" Apparently he was, because she nodded at the response. "Good. Tell Pasquale not to do anything. Just sit tight. Have Sergeant Torrez park on the opposite side of the block, just in case."

"What's going on?" I asked, but Estelle held up a hand, stalling me while she listened. I could feel my blood pressure inching up another notch. Dr. Guzman was still looking at books.

"No," Estelle said, "tell him not to leave his car. Period. And tell him to keep his windows rolled up so she doesn't hear the radio. Sound carries."

I couldn't stand it any longer and pushed myself to my feet.

"I've got a handheld with me, so have him call me directly on car-to-car. Make sure he understands that. A lot of people have scanners."

She rang off, and I tried my best to be civil. "Well?"

She glanced first at her husband, and faced me. "That was Ernie Wheeler. He's on the radio with Tom Pasquale. Pasquale says that Vanessa Davila left her trailer and walked to a house a few doors down on Escondido Lane. Number 135. Just a minute ago. From where he's parked, he can see her. She apparently has broken a side window and has gone inside."

"What?"

"B and E a neighbor's house, sir."

"You said you had a radio. Where is it?"

She pointed over on the counter where she'd put her purse and jacket. She crossed the kitchen and picked it up, then handed it to me. I fumbled the buttons and then keyed the mike.

"Posadas P.D., do you copy?"

"Ten-four." Tom Pasquale's voice was loud in the kitchen. If he'd opened the window and shouted, we could have heard him through the small forest that separated my house from Escondido Lane.

"Is the subject still in the house?"

"Ten-four."

"Any other activity around there that you can see?"

"Negative, sir."

I let the radio rest on the table. "Do we know who lives there? One thirty-five is about Toby Romero's place, isn't it?" It was dark outside, and I tried to imagine what Vanessa Davila might be doing, thinking that she could get away with something as stupid as residential burglary.

"She's still inside," Pasquale's voice said. "Do you want me to move in?"

"That's negative," Sergeant Torrez's voice barked before I had a chance to move my hand. "Stay put. We want to know what she's up to. I'm working my way around there. She isn't going anywhere."

"Bob," I said, keying the mike, "is that Toby Romero's place?"

"Affirmative."

"What the hell is she doing?" I said to Estelle, but she just shook her head.

"There's a light on inside now," Pasquale said, his voice hushed.

None of the rest of us responded.

The seconds ticked away, and I could measure their frequency against my pulse, two heartbeats for every tick of the second hand.

34

"The light went out," I could hear the tension in Patrolman Thomas Pasquale's voice, and I could imagine him hunched over the steering wheel, eyes locked on target, knuckles of his right hand turning white on the microphone.

I had felt that same rush of adrenaline myself, hundreds—maybe thousands—of times. This time, I sat at my kitchen table staring at a black handheld radio, like an old man listening to a favorite baseball game.

"She's at the window," Pasquale said, his voice hushed into a hoarse whisper.

I glanced up at Estelle. "You want to take a stroll through the woods and go over and have a look?"

Her smile was sympathetic.

"P.D., three-oh-eight is entering Escondido from the east."

"Hold back, three-oh-eight. If she hears you, she'll run."

"Ten-four."

I could easily enough imagine Vanessa Davila outrunning me...but I couldn't imagine her losing either Thomas Pasquale or Robert Torrez.

"P.D., can you see her yet?" I asked and released the switch.

"Negative."

I looked at Estelle. "There's a streetlight there somewhere," I said.

"Posadas, she's coming through the window right now. It looks like she's got something in her hand. It could be a gun." There was a moment's hesitation. "That's what it is. She's putting it under her coat."

I cursed and jumped to my feet. I could picture several ways that a confrontation between an armed Thomas Pasquale and an armed Vanessa Davila could turn out, and any one of them was enough to give me the willies.

"P.D., hold back and see if she's heading toward her trailer. Three-oh-eight, did you copy that?"

"Ten-four, 310."

"Thomas," I said, hoping that switching to his name would snuff out any chance of error, "do not approach her, do you understand?"

"Ten-four. It is a handgun. I saw it clearly just a few seconds ago."

"All right, hang back. Don't do a thing. Now listen, Thomas," and I realized I was pressing my nose into the speaker face of the handheld. "If she goes to her trailer, just let her go, do you understand?"

"Ten-four." He sounded disappointed.

"If she goes anywhere else, we'll handle it at that time. Do you copy?"

"Ten-four."

"And three ten," Torrez said, "I'm going to swing around and get myself on the north side of the interstate on Grande, in case she decides to head downtown."

"Ten-four," I said. I looked over at Estelle. "Vanessa Davila with a gun," I said in wonder.

"Dennis Wilton," Estelle murmured. "That's the only thing that makes sense."

"And even that doesn't," I said. I heard a discreet clearing of the throat in the living room. Francis was leaning against one of the bookcases, hands still in his pockets, watching us. Estelle caught the exchange. "Your husband thinks I'm going to drop dead," I said.

"That's not funny, sir."

"Indeed not," I replied.

"She's heading across the trailer park toward her place," Thomas Pasquale said, and I pushed the talk switch twice. Pasquale continued, "She's up on the porch, door open, and she's inside." I half expected the kid to add, "Touchdown!"

"Sit tight," I said into the radio and beckoned to Estelle. "Let's get over there."

She didn't move. "Sir..."

"What?"

"We don't need to do that, sir."

I stared at her incredulously. "What are you talking about? That kid's got a gun. And the closest cop to her is Thomas Pasquale."

She nodded. "And in another minute, the supervising sergeant will be there. And so will experienced backup, sir. Thomas Pasquale isn't even going to get close to the front door of that trailer by himself, if at all. Sit down and relax."

I stood rooted, not knowing what to say. As if to break the silence, the radio barked. "Three-oh-seven, three-oh-eight. Ten-twenty?"

Eddie Mitchell's voice, even over the scratch reception of the handheld, was calm and unperturbed. "Three-oh-seven is just turning onto Grande at Bustos. ETA about a minute."

"Ten-four, three-oh-seven. You'll see the P.D. just inside the entrance to the park. Park there and approach on foot."

"Ten-four."

"I'll pull right through the place and park on the north side of the trailer. That way we'll have spotlights on both sides."

"Ten-four."

Estelle looked at me as if to say, "There, you see?"

I sat down again and leaned forward, keeping my voice down. "Estelle, now listen to me. Remember a long, long time ago there was a day when you helped me escape from a goddamn hospital when I needed out of there the most? Do you remember that?"

She nodded slowly. "And you ended up back there again, too."

"I know that, but not before we did what needed to be done. Now look. This is important to me. It really is. Tell your husband there that I'll check myself into his goddamn hospital at 8 A.M. sharp, Monday morning. Then he can do whatever he wants. Brain transplant, fiberglass hip joints—hell, I don't care." I lowered my voice even more. "I just figured something out about Vanessa Davila."

I sat back and Estelle mused at the expression of satisfaction on my face. "What's that, sir?"

"She'll talk to us now."

"You think so?"

I nodded vigorously. "She didn't before because she had plans." I held up my right hand and made a pistol with thumb and index finger. "She was after someone. She decided to go get them… him…whoever…in her own way. We arrest her tonight and even she has to know that she isn't ever going to get to do that."

"On the way over, there's something else I want to tell you, sir. Something that I found out this afternoon."

My smile was like the Cheshire cat's as I got up from the table. "But one thing, sir," Estelle added, reaching across and putting her hand over mine. "No going solo."

"What's that mean?"

"It means you don't drive yourself, you don't chase, and if there's a medication that Francis wants to give you to even the odds a little, you'll take it. Deal?"

At that point, I would have agreed to anything.

35

"We can't let an off-balance teenager walk around with a loaded firearm just to make it convenient for us to find out who she wants to kill," I said, and Officer Tom Pasquale nodded as if he'd thought the same thing, even though seconds before he had suggested that we let Vanessa Davila go about her business, leading us to her intended target.

If Vanessa had looked out the curtained window of her trailer, she would have seen a fair-sized convocation. We waited in the darkness for fifteen minutes while elsewhere in Posadas Judge Lester Hobart scribbled his signature on an appropriate warrant. When the paperwork arrived via Deputy Eddie Mitchell, we kept the performance low-key. No lights, no sirens, nothing to disturb the neighbors from their dinner tables.

Vanessa never looked out, and her mother appeared genuinely surprised when she opened the door. Sergeant Bob Torrez was so tall he nearly had to duck going in, but he didn't wait for an invitation.

He snicked a set of handcuffs on an already blubbering Vanessa and helped her to the living room sofa. Her mother stood in the kitchen, wringing her hands. If I had been in a worse mood, I would have suggested snapping a set of cuffs on her, too. But it had been Vanessa who had done the burglary, and I fervently hoped that the awful sound of handcuffs would frighten her out of any last resolve.

"Vanessa," Estelle Reyes-Guzman said, "where's the gun?"

"I ain't got no gun," she said, and it was the first time I had heard her voice—low, husky, and really quite pleasant. She would have made a good announcer for an airline.

"You were observed breaking into a residence on Escondido just a few minutes ago," Estelle said. She sat on the sofa beside the cuffed Vanessa, and she was just about half Vanessa's size.

"Just a few minutes ago," she repeated. "Do you understand that you will be charged for breaking and entering and for aggravated burglary? When you broke into that house and then armed yourself with a stolen weapon, you got yourself in considerable trouble." Vanessa Davila didn't react with any great contrition, but I got the impression that Estelle made the speech more for the mother's benefit.

"I didn't," Vanessa said.

"We got you on video," Tom Pasquale said from the doorway, and I turned, surprised to see him holding one of those small video cameras that's not much bigger than a sandwich. I tried to keep the surprise off my face.

"Well, I didn't take nothin'."

"We saw you remove a handgun from the premises, Vanessa. Now before you get into more trouble, play it smart," I said.

Vanessa shook her head, still crying.

Estelle took a deep breath. "Mrs. Davila, do you know anything about your daughter's activities?"

"What?" Mrs. Davila said, and Estelle glanced at me and then heavenward. She stood up.

"All right. Begin with the girl's room," Estelle said. Torrez, Mitchell, and Pasquale clumped down the narrow hallway, back into the dark confines of the trailer. Estelle turned back to the women.

"Do you understand that if we find stolen items in a search the penalties are more severe than if you cooperate?" she said, but Vanessa was playing her last cards, figuring that maybe we'd go away.

But we didn't go away. It took ten minutes before I heard Bob Torrez say, "Okay, here we go."

He walked out into the living room holding an enormous stuffed kangaroo. In its pouch, a small stuffed joey snuggled up beside a semiautomatic pistol. By this time, Mrs. Davila had made her way over to the couch, where she sat on one of its arms and hugged her daughter.

"Oh, Vanessa," she said. That about covered it.

Sergeant Torrez slipped his pen into the weapon's barrel and lifted the gun out of the pouch. Thomas Pasquale was at his elbow, holding a large evidence bag. "The cocking indicator says it's hot, so handle it gently until we get prints off it," Torrez said, and Pasquale nodded as if he'd thought of that, too.

By this time, Vanessa had sagged sideways into her mother's arms and rocked and quaked with sobs. Estelle reached out a hand and put it on top of Vanessa's, just holding it, a slight contact that told the girl she was there.

"Vanessa," she said finally, "did you take anything else from your cousin's house?" It was the first time I'd heard that connection, but it didn't surprise me. Half of Posadas was related in some fashion to the other half. Vanessa shook her head and for the first time turned and looked squarely at Estelle. I saw the muscles of Estelle's forearm flex as she squeezed the girl's hand and said, "You took just the gun?" Vanessa nodded, and Estelle turned to look up at Bob Torrez.

"Would you please uncuff her now?" Estelle had a handcuff key somewhere on her person, but Vanessa didn't know that. Torrez nodded and bent over, removing the cuffs none too gently. That helped, too. Estelle kept her hand on Vanessa's.

"Let us talk for a while, Officers," she said, and Torrez nodded, ushering Tom Pasquale toward the door. Deputy Mitchell followed, the ghost of a smile crinkling around his eyes when he glanced at me as he went by. I closed the door and made my way toward a chair that looked like it would hold me.

"Vanessa," Estelle said, "we know you've been upset since your friend died. Since Maria died." She brought her other hand over and held Vanessa's. "And you have every reason to be. But you can't try to settle things by yourself."

Vanessa sniffed and Estelle handed her a tissue. "Do you understand what I'm saying?" Vanessa nodded. "Was it Denny Wilton, Vanessa? Was that who you were going to go after?"

Vanessa nodded again, and the relief of knowing at least one small answer swept over me.

"Vanessa, were Ryan House and Denny Wilton with Maria the night she died?" Vanessa had experienced good luck with the nod, and she stuck with it. "Were you with them?" This time she shook her head. "Did you see them together?"

"Yes," Vanessa said. "I saw them drive in to where Maria stayed."

"How did you happen to see them?"

Vanessa shrugged. "I was walking over to see if Maria wanted to go downtown for a while."

"And did they see you?"

"No." Vanessa heaved a great breath and sat up a little straighter, shrugging off some of her mother's weight. "I don't think so."

"Was it Denny Wilton's truck that you saw? The dark blue one?"

Vanessa nodded.

"Did you see them again that evening? Thursday night?"

She shook her head.

"When did you hear about Maria?"

Vanessa took another shuddering breath. "Next morning at school."

"You didn't try to see her again that night? Thursday night?"

"No." This time the reply was small and faint, as if Vanessa realized she'd made a mistake by letting her friend go off with the two boys that night.

"Why didn't you come forward and tell someone, Vanessa?"

The girl shrugged and her lower lip thrust out. "'Cause."

"Were you afraid?"

Vanessa shook her head. She didn't look like the type who was afraid of much.

"You left school on Friday, didn't you? Right after homeroom, when you heard the news? When you saw all the commotion?"

Vanessa nodded.

"Where did you go?"

"Home."

"She was here all day," her mother barked helpfully, apparently forgetting our earlier visits.

"Did you go to the football game Friday night?" I asked, and Vanessa leveled expressionless eyes at me and didn't respond.

"Did you?" Estelle prompted.

"No."

"Where did you go? You weren't home most of the day, and certainly not that evening. We stopped by and talked with your mother a couple of times. You didn't come home at all Friday night."

"I was sitting up by the highway, watching cars."

"By the interstate, you mean?" I asked, and she nodded. "All day and most of the night?"

She nodded again. "Until I walked uptown. When I thought everybody would be coming back from the game."

"Were you trying to decide what to do, Vanessa?" Estelle asked, and on the surface it sounded like a monumentally dumb question... a rarity for Estelle Reyes-Guzman. Why else would a fourteen-year-old sit hidden in a bunch of elm brush, I thought, watching others travel on with their lives? Vanessa nodded, and Estelle patted her hand. "And when did you decide to go after Denny Wilton?"

"After I heard about him killing Ryan."

"Who gave you the idea that he killed Ryan, Vanessa? It was a truck crash. They had just passed a school bus. The bus driver thinks that Denny fell asleep."

"He killed him. I know he did." She said it with simple finality.

"Who told you about the crash, Vanessa?" I asked.

"They were talking about it at Portillo's."

"The convenience store, you mean. You went there?"

"For a little while."

"Why would Denny want to kill Ryan House, Vanessa?" Estelle pressed gently. "Why would he want to do that?"

"'Cause Ryan woulda told on them sometime about Maria. He couldn't keep quiet very long. And somebody was saying how he'd heard that somebody had killed that old bum that was in town...the one that got arrested when they found Maria."

The grapevine was a marvel of efficiency if not accuracy, I marveled.

"And you think that Denny Wilton killed Ryan House because he was afraid that Ryan would tell someone about Maria, and about the old bum, is that right?"

Vanessa nodded with absolute certainty.

"But Vanessa, Maria choked to death. She wasn't killed by anyone. The boys may have panicked and run, but they didn't kill her. And the old man wasn't hurt badly. Don't you think Denny Wilton might have known all that? Is that a reason for him to kill his best friend?"

Vanessa choked back a sob. "He don't have best friends," she said, and the venom fairly dripped.

"Do you think he would risk crippling or killing himself, just to get at Ryan? Why would he do that? They were friends."

"He started hangin' out with Ryan House this year 'cause Ryan broke up with Julie Hayes. That's all. And..." She hesitated, as if she was afraid to give away too much. "Even last year, he and Ryan got into a fight right during class. So they weren't no best friends."

I heaved a sigh myself, not ready to try analyzing the why of teenage relationships. And from my own experience with my two sons and their friends, I knew that kids could be sworn enemies on Monday and best buds on Tuesday.

"Why do you think Ryan and Denny Wilton wanted to go out with Maria, Vanessa?" Estelle asked.

"'Cause."

"Because why?"

"Her and Ryan were in Spanish together."

"That's all? They shared a class?"

"She had this crush on him. One day her and me were in the hall, and she tried to say something to him. She talked Spanish at him, and Denny Wilton was there and called her 'the truck girl.' He was real mean."

"And yet they all went out together," I said.

"A bet, maybe," Estelle said quietly. "That and the fact that Ryan House didn't have a car. Vanessa, do you know anything else about that night? The night Maria Ibarra died?"

She shook her head.

"And you still think Denny Wilton killed his best friend? You don't think that the crash was an accident?"

Vanessa nodded. "I know he did."

"How do you know, Vanessa? He could just as easily have been crippled or killed as well." Estelle didn't bother to mention the functioning air bag and seatbelt–shoulder harness.

"'Cause he killed my brother, too. And he didn't never get caught either."

36

By the time we had pried the story out of Vanessa—and tried and failed to pry corroboration from her mother—it was after seven that Saturday night.

Estelle argued vehemently against charging the girl. I didn't think that formal charges would be such a bad idea, but I certainly balked at the idea of jailing an emotional basket case like Vanessa in our crude, outdated lockup, and Judge Hobart balked with me. After a brief preliminary hearing, both the girl's mother and the old judge agreed that we could transfer Vanessa to the juvenile facility in Las Cruces, where she'd be properly cared for.

With that compromise, I agreed with Estelle. If Vanessa's story held water, there was no point in pressing any kind of charges for burglary...and Toby Romero didn't care, as long as he got his gun back and his window fixed. He and his girlfriend came home from a day trip to Albuquerque to find a yellow crime scene ribbon tacked across the window and a deputy parked out front. Deputy Tom Mears said Romero shrugged when he heard the story and said, "Whatever you want to do, I mean, you know."

It was the part about the girl's story holding water that bothered both Estelle and me.

Back at the office, we spread out every scrap of paper that we could dig from the files that was remotely related to the death four years before of Rudy Davila, Vanessa's brother. The event had occurred during a brief period when Estelle Reyes-Guzman had been working for a sheriff's department in the northern part of the state...a period I preferred to forget.

It was the same summer that Sheriff Martin Holman's house had burned to the ground, a summer he no doubt would have liked to have forgotten as well.

When the school principal, Glen Archer, had mentioned Vanessa's brother as being cut from the same cloth as his sister, he had been guilty of understatement if anything.

The file told us that Rudy Davila had been a real piece of artwork. Some of the arrests I remembered clearly. His first arrest had come at age nine, when he'd helped a friend break into a car dealership to steal several expensive tools. He'd been caught, much to his dismay, when a neighbor saw and reported them.

That lesson lasted for almost a year, until he was arrested for assaulting his school-bus driver. The details were sketchy, but the incident apparently involved something about a lunchbox being knocked off a seat. Young Rudy had lost his bus-riding privileges for the remainder of the school year. That wasn't much of a penalty, since Rudy attended more sporadically than did his younger sister, Vanessa.

The string of petty events continued pretty much unbroken until he was apprehended during a paint-sniffing incident under the interstate overpass…and I tapped the report.

"Maybe that's why Vanessa likes her troll spot," I said.

"No doubt," Estelle replied. "He almost killed himself that time."

A year later, in October, Rudy Davila took a bottle of pain pills to school—pills taken from his aunt's medicine cabinet—and during an eighth-grade social studies class downed the whole mess. He popped the pills like candy, so quietly that no one noticed until he fell out of his chair with his eyes rolled back in his head. Posadas General pumped his stomach and sent him home, suggesting at the same time that the school counselor might take a whack at the kid.

Rudy's middle-school career managed to last another six months, during which time he cut his left wrist once and drank himself into oblivion on numerous occasions. By the spring of his eighth-grade year—the last time school officials saw him—he was a scrawny, vacant-eyed little hoodlum.

At that time, the Davilas were living at 198 North Fifth Street in the back apartment of a three-unit, story-and-a-half rental. Mrs. Davila was still working, although only part-time, at a grocery store down the street. Vanessa was in fourth grade.

I wondered if Vanessa had been an elementary school version of the oversized bully she'd managed to become since. Maybe back then, before the hormones kicked in, she was still playing with clay and cutting out paper chains and hearts and doing all those other things that elementary kids did.

On a hot August evening that year, Rudy Davila was in his gable bedroom of the small upstairs apartment. He had drunk enough cheap bourbon that he thought he felt no pain. Mrs. Davila was home, watching television downstairs in the living room. Vanessa was somewhere, Mrs. Davila had told police, but she wasn't sure just where. According to the report taken by Posadas Chief Eduardo Martinez, Vanessa was two doors down the street, playing with friends.

A few minutes after nine that night, the report said, Rudy Davila sat down on the edge of his bed, the window open so that he had an unrestricted view of the neighbor's garage roof. He loaded a semiautomatic .22-caliber rifle with ten rounds. The police report indicated that he might have had trouble managing the process in his inebriated state, since .22-caliber shells were scattered over the bed, some even rolling onto the floor.

Rudy had almost made a hash of the final process, too. He'd managed to shoot himself three times before he could no longer control the gun, and the condition of the room indicated that he'd thrashed around a good deal—enough to attract his mother's attention away from the television.

He'd locked his bedroom door, though, and by the time his mother and a neighbor had gained access, Rudy Davila had made peace with this world.

Vanessa Davila hadn't told Chief Eduardo Martinez much. He accepted her account at face value. She had come home when she heard sirens and saw police cars parked in front of her house. She was not overwhelmed with grief to the point that she cared to tell Martinez what she told us four years later…Perhaps at that time, her distrust and fear of her brother were too fresh in her mind.

Chief Martinez had accepted Mrs. Davila's bewildered account, maybe because no one in the village had ever seriously expected Rudy to make it to his eighteenth birthday anyway. The .22 rifle was his, Mrs. Davila was quoted as saying. She'd signed the affidavit to that effect. Maybe so, but four years later, Vanessa Davila put a different slant on things. The rifle had been given to her brother, Vanessa said, by a friend.

I sat down and rested an elbow on the table, rubbing my forehead. "Have you ever heard of a youngster who gives away something like a .22 rifle? I mean, those things are next to sacred to a kid." I reached out and nudged the bagged cassette that held Mrs. Davila's interview. "Let's hear what her actual words were," I said.

And after twenty minutes of start and stop, we found the right spot on the tape recording and heard Chief Teddy Martinez ask, "Did the rifle belong to Rudy, ma'am?" His voice was soft and dripping with sympathy.

"I don't know," Mrs. Davila said. "I think so. I guess so."

"Do you remember him buying it?" the chief asked.

"No," Mrs. Davila said, "but you know, he goes about his own business. He don't listen to me. So, maybe. I don't know. Maybe he got it, or traded for it, or something."

And at that point, Chief Martinez dropped the subject. The "or something" covered all the bases.

I reached over and punched off the tape player. "So we go from a resounding 'I don't know' on the tape to a written, sworn statement that has her saying the gun was Rudy's. Outstanding."

"It won't be hard to trace, sir," Estelle said. "If Dennis Wilton purchased that rifle, or if it was purchased by someone else and given to him as a gift, then it won't be hard to trace."

"What remains is to find out who actually pulled the trigger of the rifle," I said. "Vanessa claims that she saw the Wilton kid slip out of her brother's upstairs window shortly after the three shots." I held up two fingers. "She says that number one, the rifle was Wilton's. Number two, she says that he was there when the shooting occurred."

"That's interesting," Estelle mused.

"What is?"

She leaned over the table and tapped one of the folders. "There was no reason for Dennis Wilton to be friends with Rudy Davila. In fact, I'm willing to bet a week's pay that he wasn't, until his eighth-grade year. And if Dennis Wilton wasn't in that same history class when Davila tried the pill trick, he would have been near by. He would have heard all the gory details from any number of kids before the morning was out. He latches onto a kid who's teetering on the very edge. A self-destructive, violent kid who has nothing going for himself. Giving him that little extra push was easy. Wilton might even have pulled the trigger himself, figuring he'd get away with it."

"You're talking about a manipulative, scheming monster, Estelle," I said.

"History is full of them," she said. "Only I'd call him a psychotic opportunist."

I grimaced. "I'm no shrink, but I don't know if I buy it. None of it explains the business with Ryan House."

"Maybe, maybe not. It might have been easy to strike up a friendship with Ryan House during their senior year. In a small school, there are endless opportunities. Also, remember that House had just broken up with his girlfriend of three years."

I frowned. "You're saying that Wilton might have been planning something all along?"

"No, sir. I don't think so. At first, they might even have liked each other. Who knows? But it's dirt common for one kid to talk another into doing things that he normally wouldn't have considered. Maybe the date with Maria Ibarra was a bet, I don't know. Maybe it was genuine curiosity on their parts. We're tending to paint Ryan House lily white in all this, but maybe that's not the way it went down. But when things went wrong, Dennis Wilton reacted in a predictable fashion, from what this evidence tells us."

"He was afraid Ryan House would start talking, so he killed him."

"Yes, sir. That's what I think happened. And I think it was impulsive, when he saw that Ryan wasn't going to go along."

I picked up a pencil and toyed with it for a minute. "It would have been thoughtful of Vanessa Davila if she had spoken up earlier about seeing Wilton coming out of her brother's bedroom window."

"I suspect she was grateful to him," Estelle said, and I looked up sharply.

"Grateful?"

"Yes, sir. I suspect that her relationship with her brother was a carbon copy of what she went through with her father before he left home."

"We don't know that."

"No," Estelle said and took a deep breath. "But I can guess. The signs are there."

"And the rage this time? She steals a gun and sets out to ravenge a friend? Maria?"

Estelle nodded. "It'll take a while to put a profile together, but I'll bet the election that you'll find the two were inseparable, Maria and Vanessa. For once, Vanessa had a pal whose life was more miserable than her own."

"Kindred spirits," I said. "Misery loves company." I smiled. "And I won't bet."

"I'd like to have three pieces of evidence before we make a move, sir."

"The gun?"

She nodded. "If we can substantiate Vanessa's story by finding the origin of the rifle that killed her brother, that's one step. After four years, the rest of that story is just her word against Dennis Wilton's."

"And?"

"I want the grille guard from Wilton's truck. That would tie him to the attempt on Crocker's life. I think he feels that Crocker might have seen something, anything."

"And you think Wilton saw Crocker walking along an empty street and took his chance."

Estelle frowned. "He's an opportunist, sir. I have no trouble imagining that Ryan House was beginning to panic after the girl's death Thursday night. Some time Friday afternoon, the Wilton kid sees Crocker walking, but it's daylight. He can't do anything. Later, when the two boys are together and maybe trying to decide what to do, maybe talking about Crocker and trying to guess what he saw and what he told police, they see him again, walking along Bustos Avenue."

"And this time it's dark," I said.

"I can imagine what Ryan House's reaction to the hit-and-run was," Estelle said. "Maybe it was the last straw as far as he was concerned. Wilton might have thought first about calming him down, so he raided his parents' medicine cabinet when they went home to take the bent grille guard off. That was logical. And then the next step was to get out of town, and the football game was a perfect cover. Maybe it was on the drive out of Posadas that he put the rest together."

"And third?"

"I want at least a couple of points match on that thumbprint that I took from the seatbelt buckle. Ron Bucky is going to call the minute he has something."

I shook my head. "Don't wait, Estelle." I stood up. "If you're right, we don't want to run any risk. When you talked to Wilton in the hospital last night, was there anything that led you to believe that he might suspect what we know?"

"No, sir. I got the impression that he felt entirely comfortable with his performance."

"His performance," I said and grimaced. "And neither he nor his parents think there's anything unusual about the truck being impounded?"

"I'm sure that they imagine it's because of the blood tests and litigation, sir."

"They're scared stiff, and young Wilton could care less, I'm sure," I said. "Did Martin Holman talk with them?"

"Yes, sir."

"Then we're covered. Talking with Martin Holman is enough to give any felon confidence."

"Sir," Estelle chided gently, "that's not true."

"You don't sound much like a politician," I chuckled, but the humor didn't last. "We want to move fast with this son of a bitch. Based on a deposition from Vanessa, and with the gun's record, that should be enough for a warrant. And if we get lucky and find the grille guard, that's another piece."

"I'm willing to make another bet," Estelle murmured.

"What's that?"

"The grille guard is in the Wilton's garage somewhere."

"You don't think he'd be smart enough to get rid of it?"

"Oh, he's smart enough, sir. But he's also confident."

I grunted in disgust. "This kid is eighteen?"

"Yes, sir. His birthday was in September."

I nodded with satisfaction. "Good. Then the bastard won't just pull two years in reform school. We can put him away for life."

"He'll probably earn his law degree in prison," Estelle said, and I muttered a curse.

"You didn't used to be so cynical," I said. "You've been around me too long."

37

The serial number of the .22 rifle was thoroughly documented on Chief Eduardo Martinez's reports. The rifle itself was no doubt still rusting somewhere in the back room of the village department. I was sure that the Bureau of Alcohol, Tobacco and Firearms had the same information somewhere in the bowels of their enormous database, together with information about the gun's original purchase. But they weren't going to talk to us on a Saturday night. And if Wilton had purchased the gun from an individual, the paper trail would be even more remote.

"Let's just ask the son of a bitch," I said, and Estelle's left eyebrow went up a notch. I glanced at my watch. "It's as good a time as any. We'll see what we can find out, and then I'll buy you and Francis a late dinner. How about that?"

She agreed, although not with the enthusiasm that a dinner at the Don Juan de Oñate should have prompted.

As we pulled out onto Bustos Avenue, she keyed the mike. "Posadas, this is 310."

Dispatcher Gayle Sedillos responded, and Estelle said, "Posadas, we'll be at 390 Grant for a few minutes. Three-oh-eight needs to stay central."

"Ten-four, 310. Three-oh-eight, did you copy?"

Sergeant Bob Torrez sounded like he was eating a sandwich when he acknowledged. In his typical fashion, he didn't ask what we were doing, or why.

"Three-ten, P.D. copies. I'm ten-eight."

Estelle glanced across at me at the sound of Tom Pasquale's voice. I reached out and took the mike from Estelle. "P.D., meet with 308."

"Ten-four," Pasquale said, and I could hear the eagerness in his voice drop a couple of notches. Bob Torrez had probably choked on his sandwich.

"That's just what we need—Tom Pasquale crashing the only other car the P.D. owns into the Wilton's living room," I said.

We turned south on Fifth Street, drove two blocks, and jogged west on Grant, into one of the oldest neighborhoods in Posadas. The homes were adobe, all on large, irregular lots with an irrigation ditch running along the property lines. If all the junk that had sprung up during the 1950s mining boom were to vanish, this was one of the neighborhoods that would be left.

The Wiltons' home was attractive, a big rambling place not unlike my own, with ancient elms surrounding the buildings. Behind the attached garage was a small barn, its shed roof recently repaired with bright corrugated metal.

Estelle eased 310 into the driveway.

"Are you doing all right?" she asked.

"I'm doing fine," I said, and pointed at the porch light that had just flicked on. "They're home."

Dustin Wilton greeted us at the door with a guarded smile, but his face was pale, the worry lines etching his broad forehead. He held out a hand and shook with a firm grip.

"Sheriff, how are you?"

"Fine, thanks. You know Detective Reyes-Guzman?"

He nodded. "We talked at the hospital earlier."

Wilton was a big man, well over six feet and burly. Long hours of wrestling heavy equipment for the state highway department in the hot New Mexico sun had built muscles like rope and aged the skin of his face and hands to leather.

"We just wanted to stop by and bring some good news," I said. "It's not much, but it's something. How's Dennis doing?"

"Sleeping," Wilton said. "It's been pretty rough for him."

I nodded. "May we come in for just a minute?"

He nodded and held the door for us. The saltillo tile of the entryway was polished to a high sheen, and I stopped just inside the door.

"Let me get my wife," he said.

"Well, no need," I started to say, but he shook his head.

"She'll want to hear anything you have to say."

"Fine." We waited for a moment, and I stepped forward so I could see into the living room. A mounted elk head hung above the fireplace. Before I had a chance to inventory anything else, Dustin appeared with his wife in tow. DeeDee was thirty pounds overweight and wore lavender stretch pants two sizes too small. Her top half was inside a sweatshirt with NOTRE DAME blazoned across the chest. Fortunately the material had plenty of stretch.

Dustin, DeeDee, and Dennis, I thought. Eighteen years before, the proud parents had probably entertained all kinds of cute thoughts.

"Ma'am," I said by way of greeting. I thrust my hands into my pockets, trying to look as casual as possible. "The results of the blood test on your son are in, and I just wanted to tell you folks in person that it was clean in every respect."

I saw relief on their faces and DeeDee Wilton said, "He told us that he hadn't been drinking."

"Then he told you the truth, ma'am. The boys were just plain tired after the excitement of the game. It looks like he just dosed off. Just for a second, but that's all it takes."

Dustin Wilton shook his head. "I'll tell you what I think happened," he said, and his voice rose a notch or two. "I think some son-of-a-bitch drunk probably swerved into their lane and run 'em right off the road."

"That's something we're pursuing," I said easily, knowing that it was pointless to argue. If that pipe dream made them feel better, they could cling to it all they liked.

"We needed to ask Dennis a couple of things, just to clear up the last of the paperwork, but if he's asleep, it's not important enough to bother him."

"What do you need to know?"

"Well, one of the deputies mentioned that the truck didn't have a grille guard, but that the bolts and brackets for one were there. He hadn't found the guard at the scene, and wondered if it had been removed from the vehicle before the time of the crash."

Dustin Wilton's brow knit together and he looked at me as if I were senile. "Now that's a hell of a thing to be concerned about," he snapped.

"The officers try to be thorough," I said mildly.

"If the guard wasn't on the truck," Wilton said, "then I'm sure it's out in the shed. Every time Dennis sees the least little stone nick, he's got to sand and paint that thing again. He might as well have gotten it chrome plated. It would have saved him a lot of time." He looked sorrowful. "That truck was his pride and joy, Sheriff. His pride and joy."

"Could we take a look?"

"Hell, yes. We can go right out through the kitchen."

We did that, with Dustin Wilton never breaking stride to stop and wonder just why the hell we wanted to see a grille guard, or what difference it made whether it was on the truck or not. DeeDee stayed inside the house. Such was the magic of ignorance, I thought.

The barn was home to Dustin Wilton's major hobby. Parked in the center of the floor was an ancient truck that was so pretty it took my breath away.

"Look at that," I said in genuine admiration.

"Nineteen eighteen double T Ford," Wilton said, and stroked one gracefully curved front fender. "We've got some final work to do on the oak racks in the back, and then she's done." He patted the metalwork. "Show-quality restoration, frame up."

"Impressive," I said.

"And I don't see any grill guarde...No wait, here it is. He's getting set to work on it," Wilton said, as if the truck from which the guard was taken wasn't a shapeless mess.

The guard was under one of the workbenches, and Wilton bent awkwardly to retrieve it. He grunted and grabbed the edge of the bench to support himself.

"Goddamn back," he said, and yanked the grille guard free.

"Did you hurt yourself?" I asked.

Wilton shrugged it off. "Twisted it last week doing something stupid."

"Isn't age wonderful," I said, reaching out to accept one end of the heavy guard. The right side was badly bent.

"Someone probably smacked him in the parking lot at school," Wilton said. He lifted the guard so I could see it, then slid it back under the bench.

"Probably so," I said, glancing at Estelle. She smiled.

"So," Wilton said, stroking the fender of the old truck again. "That's that. What else was it you needed to know?"

"What year did you say this was?" I asked.

"Nineteen eighteen."

I looked inside the cab. "Wood and metal. No plastic," I said and turned to grin at Wilton.

"Not a scrap."

"Beautiful," I said. "How's she drive?"

Wilton patted the fender and grinned slyly. "Well, let me put it this way. There have been a lot of improvements in the past seventy-eight years. A lot of improvements. I'll tell you one thing...if you set out down the road in this, you'd better keep your mind on your business. She don't have no cruise control." He laughed.

And no air bags and no seatbelts, I wanted to say. Instead, I asked, "Does your son work with you on this?"

"Oh, yes," Wilton said. "In fact, I made him a promise. He graduates from college, this sweetheart is his."

"That ought to do the trick," I said. "This is a rough time for him. Something like this is good to keep his mind occupied."

Wilton nodded. "In fact," I added, "I hope you don't take offense at an old man sticking his nose in other people's business, but I've got four kids of my own...and some of them went through some tough times, too. For the next day or so, you might want to spend as much time as you can with the boy."

"Well, sure."

"I mean even if it involves taking off of work. He's going to be feeling pretty alone right about now."

"I know what you mean."

"So, take him fishing, take him hunting...something like that. You hunt? The two of you?"

Wilton tried to put the manly bluff to it, but I could see it hurt him. "Oh, we used to. A few years back. But these kids get into high school, and I don't know. Their world is sure different from mine. Different from what mine was, I mean."

I nodded sympathetically. "Might do him a world of good for just the two of you to pack off in this sweetheart for a week deer-hunting up north. Something like that."

"Well," he said, "you know how it goes."

"I don't mean to be nosy," I said, "but I noticed the elk over the fireplace inside, and figured that you two probably got out a lot."

Wilton scoffed. "Hell, I won that at the club in a raffle." He grinned sheepishly. "I haven't hunted in twenty years. And the boy never took to it. I bought him a rifle once, for his twelfth birthday, as a matter of fact. Brand spanking new. Almost a hundred and fifty bucks over at George Payton's. You know what he did with it?"

I shook my head.

"He loans it to a friend of his who's going hunting up in Wyoming. The damn fool kid *lost* it. Can you imagine that?"

"Kids," I said, and glanced at Estelle. She looked like she didn't understand English.

I thrust out my hand as if I had all the time in the world. "Mr. Wilton, thanks for your time. We really appreciate it. And like I said, keep a close watch on the boy for a while. These things can be rough."

He nodded and followed us out of the barn. We didn't go back in the house, but walked around to the front yard under the glare of a sodium vapor light. DeeDee Wilton didn't come outside, and I didn't see Dennis's face peering through a curtain.

I settled back in the seat of 310 and closed my eyes.

"Well done, sir," Estelle said, and I opened my eyes and turned to see her smile.

"George Payton's," I said and pointed down the road.

Estelle pulled the car into gear. "What do you suppose Mr. Wilton takes for his sore back?" she asked.

"I was thinking the same thing," I said.

38

George Payton and I were the same age and damn near the same weight. There the similarity ended. While my blood pressure was finding new and creative ways to bust pipes, George's personal demons were diabetes mixed with equal parts glaucoma and gout.

I'd known George for twenty-four years. We'd stood in front of his shop on summer afternoons, soaking in the sun, chatting about this and that. And we'd gone for coffee hundreds of times, ducking our heads against the winter chill. We'd both had large families, and now we were both living alone, probably both trying not to think too hard about next week. I'd never been in his house, and he'd never been in mine.

Over the years, George Payton had assisted the sheriff's department in a number of ways...and what he didn't know about firearms wasn't worth knowing.

I'd always suspected that George didn't need the income from his small gun and tackle shop just off Pershing. There was nowhere to fish within fifty miles—not that distance ever deterred the avid fisherman—and his firearm sales had to be equally slow.

He made exquisite muzzle-loading rifles by hand, maybe one a year. That was his first love.

Now that he was alone, George Payton lived in a small apartment behind his shop. He greeted Estelle and me with a frown and a mumble and waved us inside. His firearm sales records were in large, black-bound ledgers in a bookcase in his office, kept in addition to the yellow federal forms that the ATF demanded.

"Who are you after tonight?" he asked, and he squinted through his bottle-bottom glasses at me. "And you look like shit, as always."

"Thanks, George. We need to find the serial number of a .22 rifle purchased from you in 1992. Either in late August or early September."

"Well, that's easy enough, as long as you know who bought it."

"We do. At least we know who says he bought it."

"Well, have at it," Payton said. He ran a hand along the volumes, pulled 1992 off the shelf, and laid it on the table. Estelle opened the cover and leafed through the pages, scanning down the left margin. With Payton's business, the scan didn't take long.

"September 8," she said and silently read across the columns of name, address, make, model, and caliber. I held out the copy of Chief Martinez's report and she read the serial number. I watched the numbers click off, in perfect order.

"Bingo," I said.

George Payton stood quietly by, his myopic eyes sleepy and uninterested. He didn't ask again who we were after, and he didn't invite us to stay for dessert. We were probably interrupting his favorite television show.

We left the shop with the ledger and a copy of the ATF form that Dustin Wilton had filled out four years before.

"The kid lied to his father about the rifle...Either that or the father is making up stories to protect his son," I said to Estelle when we were back in the car.

"The only trouble is," she replied, "he could have given the gun to Rudy Davila, or sold it to him. There's nothing illegal about that. It's Vanessa Davila's word against his. And if Vanessa testifies that she saw Dennis Wilton climb out of her brother's window after the shots, then that doesn't help much either. He could deny that he was ever there, or he could say that he was there and was trying to talk Rudy out of it. He could say it was an accident and that after it happened, he just panicked."

"He could say lots of things," I agreed. "And if he didn't actually pull the trigger, then the most he's guilty of is assisting suicide. That's just a fourth-degree felony in this state."

"He's clever," Estelle said.

"Tell me something," I said and twisted sideways in the seat. "There's something about Vanessa Davila that makes you want to believe her story, hook, line, and sinker. What is it?"

"It's just that there's too much rage there," she said. "If Dennis Wilton had nothing to do with her brother's death, I don't think Vanessa is bright enough to make up a story like that. And there wouldn't have been any reason to. Not after four years." She thumped the heels of her hands on the steering wheel. "I think she sees something in all this that we don't see, sir."

"She sees Dennis Wilton in school every day, for one thing."

"I wonder what he'll do," Estelle said.

"Who?"

"Wilton. You know, if we're right, he's sailing along on a cloud of self-confidence a mile thick. It's been four years since the Davila case was closed, with a no-questions-asked ruling. And he's gotten his share of sympathy from the wreck last night. This is about the time he's feeling invincible."

I watched Estelle's face as she guided the patrol car back into the parking lot of the sheriff's office. She pulled 310 into the slot, pushed the gear lever into park, and turned toward me.

"In order to collect any evidence about the sedative, we're going to have to show our hand, sir. We don't know where the drug came from, but if it was close at hand, my first guess is the Wiltons' medicine cabinet. There's the possibility that Ryan House got it himself. We don't know. As soon as we start digging into that, there are going to be some very unhappy people. More so than there are right now."

"You want Wilton now?"

She nodded slowly. "We've got Vanessa Davila's story. We've got someone caught in a lie about a rifle...either Wilton or his father. We've got a lie about a seatbelt. We have the bent grille guard. We have Wesley Crocker's statement that the vehicle that struck him was a pickup truck, and that he saw it earlier in the day with two occupants, and that he can identify it."

"Pieces, pieces, pieces," I said. "I don't want this kid on hit-and-run, or failure to report a death, or assisting a suicide. If he popped Ryan House's seatbelt buckle with the intent of sending him through the windshield, then he's guilty of murder."

"Yes, sir. We can't prove the seatbelt yet, but we've got plenty of ammunition to set up a powerful bluff. We have enough evidence to talk Judge Hobart and the DA into an arrest warrant. That will give us some time. We can see how Wilton reacts."

"He's arrogant enough that it should come as a pretty powerful surprise," I said with satisfaction.

"And we need the time," Estelle said. "If it was Dennis Wilton who gave old Manny Orosco a spiked bottle of wine, it may take us a day or two to track down the liquor sales."

I looked at her with astonishment. "You think he might have done that, too?"

"It wouldn't surprise me a bit."

"What would be the point?" And I knew the answer at the same time the question left my lips.

"If Dennis Wilton never intended for Maria to come home alive that night, it makes a lot of sense. Drunk as Orosco was most of the time, he still might have been able to identify a face."

"But Wilton couldn't have been certain that the bottle would have killed the old man."

"No. But at the very least, it would have made him so drunk he wouldn't have remembered a thing. And that's all part of the kick. Wilton takes his entertainment where he can."

"You're not painting a very pretty picture, Estelle."

"No, sir. And none of it is what Maria Ibarra hoped to find when she came here."

39

At 9:07 that night, Thomas Pasquale parked his patrol unit on the west end of Grant Avenue where it T'd into Sixth Street, a hundred yards away from the Wilton residence. I hoped that would be far enough away to keep him out of trouble.

Deputy Tom Mears parked at the east end of Grant. With those two officers as bookends, Posadas Police Chief Eduardo Martinez, Sheriff Martin Holman, Sergeant Robert Torrez, Estelle Reyes-Guzman, and I arrived in front of the Wilton residence without fanfare or notice.

The chief had voiced neither misgivings nor surprise when we filled him in. Ever cautious, he rode with Bob Torrez on this particular call, leaving Tom Pasquale in the dark at the end of the street. I got the impression that the sooner the mess was cleaned up and he could sit back down in front of his television set, the happier he would be.

Martin Holman had spent the afternoon searching through high school student notebooks with Glen Archer and later in the afternoon had visited with Ryan House's parents again. According to the sheriff, they told the same story over and over again…the boy always wore his seatbelt. *Always.*

Holman looked at the Wiltons' house as we pulled to a stop. He shook his head in disbelief. "You just never know, do you," he said. Torrez parked behind us and I waved him over as I got out of the car. Holman looked at the shotgun that the sergeant carried and then at me. "Do you really think—" he started to say, then bit it off.

"I don't think we're going to have any problems, but you might want to cover the back," I said to Torrez. "Chief, if you'd stay here and take care of the radio, I'd be obliged."

Martinez ducked his head, not in the least offended at having his turf turned upside down. "Gayle Sedillos is on dispatch tonight, so you won't have any trouble," I added, and Martinez nodded. He held the mike in his right hand, and I could see a tremor—whether from age or anxiety, I didn't know.

We made our way up the front walk, and somewhere a couple of houses down a dog started barking. After a couple of half-hearted yaps, he gave up.

With the front door at arm's length, I counted to ten while I scanned the neighborhood and listened, holding my breath. I pushed the doorbell. Inside I could hear voices, but couldn't tell if it was the television. No one answered the bell, and I pushed again. This time, faintly, I could hear the chimes inside.

We heard the deadbolt snick back and then the door opened. Dustin Wilton's eyebrows shot up when he saw the three of us. He looked past us to the two patrol cars.

"What's going on?" he asked. He looked at Holman. "Sheriff, I haven't seen you around in a while. You campaigning?" He glanced at his watch.

"Mr. Wilton," I said, "we need to talk with your son."

"He's asleep." He said it as if he expected my reply to be, "Oh, gosh, I'm sorry. We'll come back."

"Then you'll need to wake him up, sir," I said. Wilton frowned and I added, "May we come in?" I gestured toward the interior with the antenna of my handheld radio.

Dustin Wilton didn't move, and his bulk effectively blocked the doorway. "Tell me what this is about," he said.

"Mr. Wilton, we need to talk with your son about the death of Ryan House last night. And about the death of Maria Ibarra the night before."

"My son had nothing to do with that," Wilton said, with the kind of instant denial that came with the turf of being a parent.

"We need to talk with him, sir," Estelle Reyes-Guzman said, but Wilton ignored her.

"Dustin, don't make this harder than it has to be," Sheriff Holman said. He stepped forward and pulled open the screen storm door. "You know that we wouldn't be here if we had the choice." The sheriff sounded confident and in control...and surprised the hell out of me.

Wilton backed up a step and made a hopeless gesture with his hands. "Shit, come in, then. You'd think things weren't hard enough."

He turned and shouted toward the living room, "Dee, get Denny out here."

DeeDee Wilton appeared and looked at us intently. "What is it?"

"More red tape," Wilton said. "These guys have a burr up their ass and can't wait until tomorrow. They need to ask Denny some more questions."

"He's asleep," DeeDee said.

"Yeah, yeah. They heard that already. Go wake him up."

DeeDee Wilton was gone for only a moment, and when she returned, she said, "He's up. He's just getting dressed."

For thirty seconds or so, we waited in the foyer, both parents casting expectant glances down the hall, both wanting to see their one and only appear toussle-headed, sleepy-eyed, and innocent from his room. The wait was long enough that I thought more than once about Sergeant Torrez, standing out in the dark behind the house, shotgun cradled in his arms.

It was the first time since the truck crash that I'd seen Dennis Wilton. I remembered his calm face from Friday morning in Glen Archer's office. He walked down the hallway toward us, dressed in sneakers, jeans, a white T-shirt, and a Posadas Jaguars jacket. I sensed Estelle Reyes-Guzman shifting position at my right, but I didn't take my eyes off the youngster.

He was a young, lightweight version of his father, with a handsome square face, patrician nose, and ice-blue eyes that regarded us with wary interest.

"Son, these people want to ask you some more questions," Dustin Wilton said. Dennis stopped two paces away and put his hands in his jacket pockets.

"What about?" he said. His voice was soft and husky.

"Dennis," I said, before Sheriff Holman decided to jump into things, "did you sell your .22 rifle to Rudy Davila four years ago, or did you just give it to him?"

Silence hung heavy in the foyer for about the count of ten. During that time, Dennis Wilton blinked twice. A muscle in his right cheek twitched.

"What the hell..." Dustin Wilton said, finally finding his voice. "What are you talking about?" He took a step toward his son, a natural, protective reaction. I held up a hand.

"No, no," I snapped and the father stopped in his tracks. "Son, answer the question."

"I loaned it to him."

"Are you talking about that rifle—" his father started to say, and then he turned to look at me. "Is this what we were talking about earlier this evening? When you brought up all that horseshit about hunting?" I nodded. Wilton turned back to his son. "You told me that you loaned it to Scottie for a hunting trip. And that he lost it."

"I loaned it to Rudy Davila," the boy said.

"Wasn't he the kid who...who shot himself?" Wilton said in disbelief.

"With your son's rifle," I said.

"Son, is this true?" Dennis Wilton nodded silently. "You loaned him your rifle and he committed suicide with it?" Again Dennis nodded. "And you didn't say anything?"

Dennis Wilton shrugged and looked off toward the living room.

"Holy Christ," Wilton murmured. His wife stood by his side, one hand hooked through his elbow.

"Dennis," I said, "we have a witness who says you were in Rudy Davila's bedroom when he shot himself...with your rifle."

This time, the silence lasted less than a heartbeat, not even long enough for Dennis Wilton's parents to suck in a breath of agonized astonishment.

Dennis Wilton turned as if to say something, but instead dove into the living room, crossed it in two leaps, and crashed through the doorway at the other end.

"Son!" Wilton shouted, and even as he lunged after the boy, I fumbled for a finger that would do as it was told and keyed the radio.

"Bob, he's going out the west side." I pushed past Martin Holman and charged out the front door. At the same time that my boots hit the brown, dry Bermuda grass of the Wiltons' front lawn, I heard Bob Torrez shout, followed by a loud crash of banging metal.

Dennis Wilton knew exactly where he was going…the rest of us didn't have a clue. And as I breathlessly barged across the front lawn toward the street, hoping to catch a glimpse of the fleeing youth, I realized why Estelle had shifted uneasily when we were inside. The kid had come out to talk to us fully equipped—running shoes, jeans, jacket.

Bob Torrez's huge form appeared on the other side of the neighbor's fence. "He went down that way," he shouted and pointed to the west, taking off at a rapid jog, shotgun at high port.

"P.D., heads up," I barked into the radio. "He's headed down your way." I groaned with frustration. The only one in Dennis Wilton's path was Thomas Pasquale. I wasn't sure if the two barks I heard over the handheld were a quick acknowledgment or my imagination. Chief Martinez was looking west, befuddled.

None too gently, I moved him to one side and dropped into the idling 310, yanking the gear lever into what I hoped was drive. The heavy car's tires spat stones and gravel and in the headlights down the street I could see the blue village patrol car.

The driver's door was open and the dome light was on. Patrolman Thomas Pasquale wasn't in it.

40

I leaned against the patrol car and cursed loud and long. It was all I knew to do. I looked across at Pasquale's unit and saw his handheld radio lying on the front seat, useless.

Every dog in the neighborhood had taken up the call, barking their fool heads off in frustration at not being part of the chase.

"Torrez, this is Gastner," I said into my radio. "Pasquale is after him on foot. I don't see any sign of them."

"Ten-four," Torrez said. "Mears, circle around back by Garland. I think they went that way. See if you can cut him off."

Standing in the dark, I tried to put myself in Dennis Wilton's shoes, but it was a waste of energy. None of us could predict where he'd go. The instinct was to run, and that's what he was doing. If he could put enough nighttime between himself and his pursuers, he'd gain a nine-hour head start. It was that long until dawn, and he'd spent the day resting.

I struggled back into 310 and opened the windows so I could hear. Pulling the car into gear, I rolled south on Sixth Street, eyes peering into every shadow. The street rose sharply as it crested over one of the irrigation ditches. On the south side of the ditch, Garland Avenue ran east to west. I paused, listening.

Directly ahead of me were a half dozen houses, and then Henry Gallegos's farm, a small island of overgrazed pastures, barns, and long-dead machinery. Beyond that was the right-of-way for State Highway 17 and then, just another few hundred yards south, the interstate.

I had started to turn the steering wheel left, planning to drive along the ditch, heading east toward the school, when I heard the gunshot. It was a single report, flat and muted, off to the south. With racing pulse, I cranked the wheel hard to the right and accelerated toward Gallegos's farm.

The road narrowed to one lane of dirt as I reached his cattleguard. Henry Gallegos and his brood lived in one of the oldest adobe houses in Posadas—it had been built a dozen years before New Mexico became a state...and it had been built by a Gallegos.

A porch light was on, and I saw Henry standing in front of his door, looking off to the south. I slowed and leaned forward, hugging the steering wheel. Two figures came around from behind one of the low, flat-roofed barns. I snapped on the car's spotlight, keeping the beam low.

Thomas Pasquale was limping slightly, his right pant leg from midthigh down soaked in blood. Dennis Wilton walked beside him, head down. His hands were cuffed behind his back, and Pasquale kept one hand on the kid's elbow.

I stopped the car when they were still fifty feet away and got out. My right hand drifted down toward my revolver, but it was just the remains of an old instinct. Earlier, I hadn't been able to manage a damn coffeepot, and sure as hell would have fumbled the Magnum off into the darkness.

"Officer Pasquale, are you all right?" I called.

He nodded, but he kept blinking and squeezing his eyes tightly shut. I turned off the spotlight and then intercepted them a dozen feet in front of the patrol car. I took Wilton by the other elbow. The kid didn't need to know it was as much to steady myself as anything.

"Mr. Wilton," I said, "it's good to see you again." I watched with satisfaction as Officer Pasquale put Dennis Wilton in the backseat of 310, secure behind the security grille. He did it smoothly and efficiently, even remembering to protect the kid's head from smacking the sharp edge of the patrol car's roof. That's more than I would have found the heart to do.

"What happened to the leg?" I asked as Pasquale straightened up. I could see that his face was pale and his lower lip was quivering.

"I managed to tackle him just behind that building," Pasquale said. "In the struggle, he got my weapon away from me somehow. It went off and grazed me across the thigh. He's a fast little son of a bitch, sir."

I bent down and peered at the rip. There was no spurt of arterial blood, and I straightened up with a grunt. "First we stitch the eye, then we stitch this. You're costing us a lot of money, son." He smiled weakly, and I patted him on the shoulder. "Good work. Let's get back."

He started to walk around the car but I called him back. "You drive, Officer. Even shot up, you're in better shape than I am."

As I got into the car, I waved a hand at Henry Gallegos. He'd been joined on his front porch by his wife and a handful of their children. That wave was about all the energy I had left except to point at the radio. "You want to call in and tell the others that you've got him?"

"Yes, sir," Pasquale said.

***

I took considerable satisfaction out of hearing Judge Les Hobart deny bail for Dennis Wilton. That satisfaction drained away when I turned and saw the expression on the faces of his parents.

It was the same expression of loss, I suppose, that Sheriff Martin Holman had seen just a few short hours before when he'd broken the news to Ryan House's parents that they'd lost a son.

At 10:18 that Saturday night, Estelle Reyes-Guzman drove me home. There were reams of paperwork to be done and still a dozen bits of evidence to pursue and sift. But I'd made a promise and managed to keep most of it.

Estelle opened the door for me. That was a first. I took off my hat slowly, as if it were glued to my scalp.

"Long day," I said. In the back of the house we heard a thump, and then Wesley Crocker appeared, supporting himself with his crutch and wearing the bathrobe I'd tossed on his bed.

"Wesley, how are you doing?" I said, and shuffled down the hall toward him.

"Just fine, good sir. Just fine. You look on the tired side."

"I am tired, Wesley. Really tired. And you need to call your sister."

He frowned, and I nodded, pointing toward the kitchen. "You call her, or I will. And I'd much prefer that you did it. I'm too tired to dial."

"Well, I wasn't—"

I cut him off. "I'm going into the hospital, for how long, only her husband knows." I nodded toward Estelle. "There won't be anyone here to make sure you don't do something foolish. So that's your only choice. Call her and tell her that one of our deputies is taking you to the Las Cruces airport first thing in the morning. She can expect to see your smiling face by noon."

"Well, I just don't know what I'd say to her," Crocker said. He was so flustered he was blushing.

"You'll think of something," I replied, and beckoned to Estelle. She walked down the hall, puzzled, and I put my arm around her, giving her a hug. I grinned at Crocker. "For starters, when you get her on the phone, you might thank her. And then just go."

I turned to look at Estelle Reyes-Guzman. "Will you be kind enough to drop me off at Posadas General and then tell your hubby that I'm waiting for him?"

She nodded, and I added, "Doesn't seem to be much point in waiting for Monday. Let's get a jump on things."

I extended my hand to Wes Crocker. "Take care of yourself. Ride back this way sometime." I grinned. "Make sure the front door latches when you leave tomorrow morning. Of course, if the lawyers need more than just a signed deposition from you, we may be seeing more of you than you'd like."

I didn't give him time to argue. Estelle made a quick call, and when she hung up we left the house, with Wesley Crocker still propped up on his crutch in the middle of my living room.

The drive to Posadas General Hospital was silent most of the way. By the time we reached North Pershing, I broke the silence and said, "You have a lot of work to do."

"Yes, sir."

"You can handle it."

She looked over at me. "Thanks, sir. I'll be by in the morning, though. After you're settled. There are some things I'd like to go over with you."

The car came to a halt, parked appropriately in one of the "doctors only" spots.

"Estelle," I said, and I rested my hand gently on her arm. "Save your time and energy. You don't need my help. Just go for it." I grinned at her. "Thanks again."

Before she had time to answer, I slipped out of the car, damn near stumbled on the rough pavement, and then trudged up the sidewalk toward the entrance of the hospital.

To receive a free catalog of other Poisoned Pen Press titles, please contact us in one of the following ways:

Phone: 1-800-421-3976
Facsimile: 1-480-949-1707
Email: info@poisonedpenpress.com
Website: www.poisonedpenpress.com

Poisoned Pen Press
6962 E. First Ave. Ste 103
Scottsdale, AZ 85251